I0831506

Neon Kiss

Also by Grant Tracey

Five Hard Bites

A Fourth Face

Cheap Amusements

Toronto, 1965: Cheap Amusements' Beat

Final Stanzas

Lovers & Strangers

Parallel Lines and the Hockey Universe

Playing Mac: A Novella in Two Acts, and Other Stories

Neon Kiss

Grant Tracey

A Hayden Fuller Mystery

Published by Twelve Winters, a literary project.

P. O. Box 414 • Sherman, Illinois 62684-0414 • twelvewinters.com

Neon Kiss was first published by Twelve Winters in 2021 as part of the collection *Five Hard Bites*. This Collector's Edition is its first time in print as an individual work.

Cover and interior page design by TWP Design.

ISBN
979-8-9891086-2-6

Printed in the United States of America

For Effy

Contents

Introduction xi

Neon Kiss 3

A Hayden Fuller Timeline 217

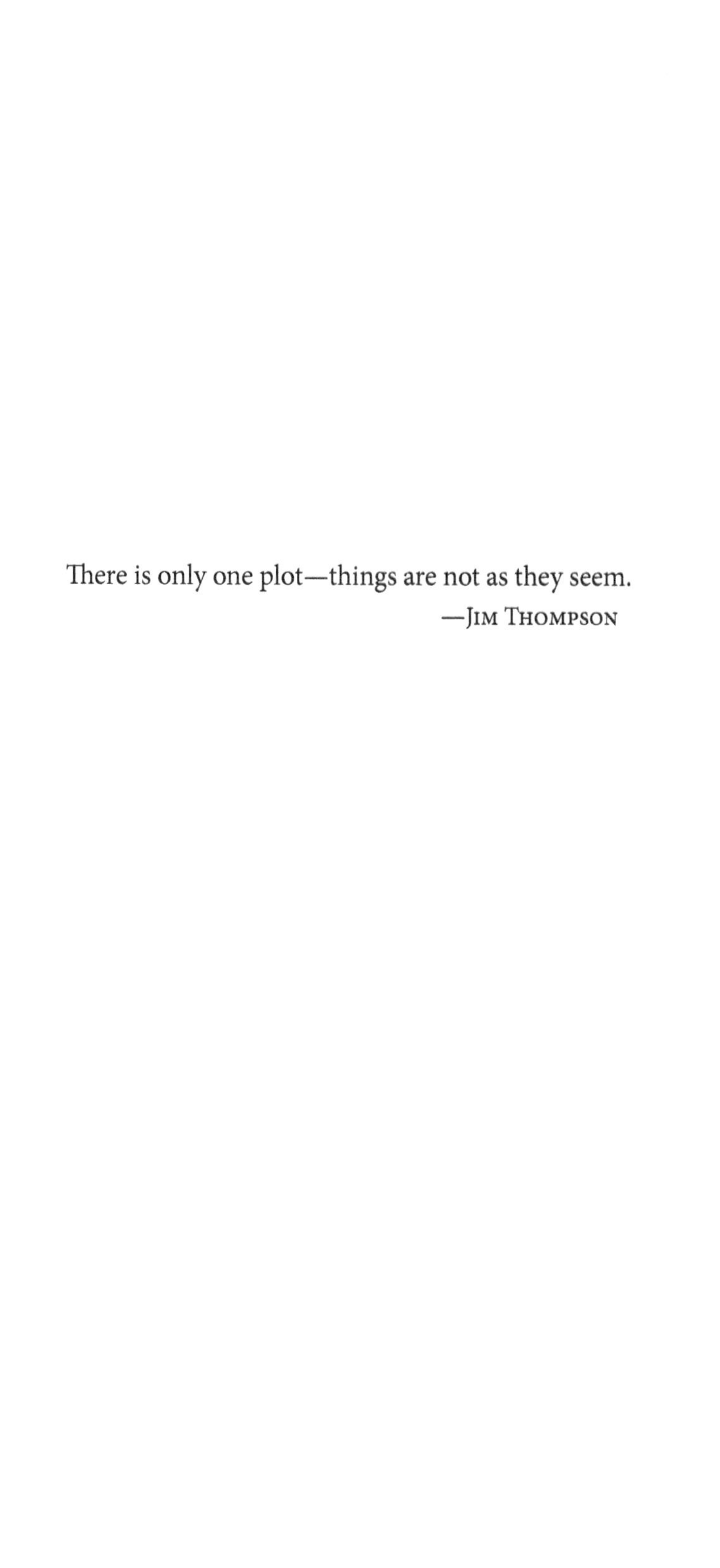

There is only one plot—things are not as they seem.

—Jim Thompson

Introduction

Crime Noir and the Poetics of Uncertainty

Pulp writer Jim Thompson once said, "There is only one plot—things are not as they seem."

I love this quote because it gets to the heart of crime noir. Crime stories demand that readers are always at the ready, suspicious of every encounter. People lie and the smallest of clues can reveal a crucial aspect in the psychology of a character, as an outer-surface prop or a gesture can let us inside to the why: a cluttered desk, an ill-designed room, two cigarettes in an ashtray (each with differing shades of lipstick), or a book that sits haphazardly on a shelf. All of these details can imply a shadow self behind the masks characters wear.

All three of my previous novels and a fourth, the forthcoming *A Shoeshine Kill*, spin on lies that characters tell.

Ever notice how when people tell stories about themselves they are either a victim, a bystander outraged by an injustice, or a good person trying to make a situation better? They are never the "bad guy" causing someone else pain.

But everyone has it in them to hurt other people. I've acted in over forty community playhouse productions, and I never judge the characters I play, but all of them were flawed, and all of them had inflicted pain on others, directly or indirectly. That doesn't make any of those characters necessarily bad or unrelatable, but it does make them interesting.

—

CRIME FICTION RELIES on attitude, of seeing the darkness within all hearts. We readers accept a certain fictional contract: we're always on our guard; everyone is a suspect; everyone has something to hide and everyone is prone to half-truths and lying to protect themselves or others. What clue will reveal the hidden truth?

In *The Big Sleep* Vivian Regan tells Philip Marlowe he doesn't "put on much of a front," and he replies, "You can't make much money at this trade, if you're honest. If you have a front, you're making money—or expect to." In crime novels, every scene, every person the detective interviews has a front, and there's money to be made in how those fronts are perceived.

The hero has to keep his distance. How does the detective do this? Repartee, one-liners, a sense of humor, judgmental descriptions of characters' appearances, and the numbing effects of alcohol.

Thus, crime novels place the reader in perpetual uncertainty. Cognitively, readers are in a much different space than they are when reading a literary work of an Alice Munro who tells large-canvas stories with alternating perspectives, timelines, and texts within texts. We believe, *trust*, in her narrative voice. In crime stories, we often believe in or side with our hero, but we don't believe in the multiplicity of narratives, the competing voices, that spring up around him. The night, to play with a famous quote by Raymond Chandler, is never just the night, it's always something more than.

CHANDLER ONCE JOKED that he wasn't good at writing three-person scenes so his debut novel begins with three two-person scenes. But despite that shortcoming, Chandler establishes character/voice/attitude that is at the heart of the American detective ethos:

> It was about eleven o'clock in the morning, mid October, with the sun not shining and a look of hard wet rain in the clearness of the foothills. I was wearing my powder-blue shirt, tie and display handkerchief, black brogues, black wool socks with dark blue clocks on them. I was neat, clean, shaved and sober, and I didn't care who knew it. I was everything the well-dressed detective ought to be. I was calling on four million dollars.

This opening establishes Marlowe's wry attitude, his self-deprecating humor (the display handkerchief cracks me up), and a subtle reveal (he has a drinking problem, his escape from the Pyrrhic, the cost of every quest he undertakes). Moreover, the threat of a "hard" rain underscores the violence, the "mean streets" down which this man must go. Finally, his quip about "four million dollars" establishes, via contrast, Marlowe as a hard-working, honest man, navigating his spaces in a world of privilege, entitlement, and excess.

Later, in chapter three, when Marlowe meets Vivian for the first time, Chandler further explores this theme of excess and his lead character's distance from such a world:

> This room was too big, the ceiling was too high, the doors were too tall, and the white carpet that went from wall to wall looked like a fresh fall of snow at Lake Arrowhead. There were full-length mirrors and crystal doodads all over the place. The ivory furniture had chromium on it, and the enormous ivory drapes lay tumbled on the white carpet a yard from the windows. The white made the ivory look dirty and the ivory made the white look bled out. The windows stared towards the darkening foothills. It was going to rain soon. There was pressure in the air already.

My favorite moment here: "the enormous ivory drapes lay tumbled on the white carpet a yard from the windows." Talk about excess. This detail, along with the too-high ceiling and too-high doors, shows that Vivian lacks precision and control. No wonder there's pressure in the air. Her life contains *too muchness*. And the judgment behind "dirty" and "bled out" is all you need to know about Marlowe's protective armor, his distancing himself from the world he must travel in. This is setting as attitude. This is a character who is never completely comfortable in the world he navigates.

By contrast, in the European detective story/procedurals of Georges Simenon, his Inspector Jules Maigret has a keen eye for detail that reveals the hidden psychology of the characters he's pursuing, but the world for him is a much friendlier place.

In *Maigret Sets a Trap* (translated by Daphne Woodward) Simenon establishes the possibility of Marcel Moncin's guilt with a detail that appears, possibly, just tossed away: "She had opened the glass-paneled door of a drawing room done up in a modern style which was unexpected in this old house, but which had nothing aggressive about it; Maigret told himself he wouldn't mind living in a setting like this. Only the paintings on the walls displeased him, he couldn't make head or tail of them." The last sentence is the punch line, the clue. The paintings are a mess because they mirror the disordered mind of a serial killer.

Moreover, unlike the distance in Marlowe's voice, Simenon humanizes Maigret as a man who connects with the world and its simple comforts: "Maigret told himself he wouldn't mind living in a setting like this." Marlowe would never feel this way about any setting he walks through, except perhaps his lonely apartment and the chessboard in front of him. Maigret is very secure, moving about the arrondissements of Paris. The world is non-threatening. Throughout the Maigret novels Simenon presents his Chief Inspector as enjoying the quotidian: drinking a beer, standing by a warm fire, going to the cinema, Saturday nights, with his wife, and walking with his wife in the evenings and surreptitiously sticking out his tongue to catch falling snowflakes.

AS MUCH AS THE FRENCH loved the Maigret novels, they also championed American crime stories and film noir. They were among the first to really lean into the genre/style and see value in the work for deconstructing and challenging the myth of the American Dream.

Now, just for the record I'm Canadian, and Hayden Fuller, like me, born in Toronto, is also Canadian. So what's with this American Dream stuff? I deliberately made Fuller a Jew because I wanted to present a whiteness in the 1960s that has both a foot in the mainstream and one foot outside of it (I can't tell you how many times I've had to call out someone in Iowa for saying, "I jewed the guy down." *Seriously?*). Fuller's status mirrors my own. My parents were the children of immigrants from Eastern Europe. They believed in the Canadian dream, of fitting in, of becoming invisible. My parents changed our surname from Traicheff to Tracey to not sound so "foreign," or dare I say "commie." Moreover, in pursuit of the Canadian dream they adored American films, and looked to movie stars as models of behavior. Many of the women on my mother's side had rhinoplasties to have ski-jump noses. And I was constantly questioned by my classmates as to my identity. All through grade school and later junior high they asked, "Where you from?" "I'm from Toronto," I'd say. "I was born here. St. Michael's Hospital." "Yeah, but where are you *from*?"

I didn't look Anglo.

My mom's eyes narrowed when I told her about these encounters and she'd snap, "Tell them you're Canadian!"

So, in setting my stories in the 60s and early 70s, and making my hero a white male who feels caught in a liminal space, I was returning to my childhood and a time of personal, ethnic identity confusion in a Toronto that was predominantly English, Scottish, and Irish.

The model that my family followed was not the notion of Canada as a cultural mosaic, different parts of a quilted fabric making a country; instead, their vision was more an American one of a melting pot, which we wanted to blend into.

I wasn't taught to respect my Macedonian ancestry.

My experience was of an American-Dream type, living in Canada.

Fuller, however, is a proud Jew, and I'm proud of him. He's what I wish I could have been, back then.

DURING THE OCCUPATION of France American films were banned by the Nazis. By 1946, following the liberation, the French would suddenly view in curated groupings the collected works of so many great directors working in America, and what a canvas of darkness. By Alfred Hitchcock, *Foreign Correspondent* (1940), *Rebecca* (1940), *Suspicion* (1941), *Shadow of a Doubt* (1942), *Lifeboat* (1944), *Spellbound* (1945) and *Notorious* (1946); by Howard Hawks, *To Have and Have Not* (1945) and *The Big Sleep* (1946); by Fritz Lang, *Hangmen Also Die!* (1943), *Woman in the Window* (1944) and *Scarlet Street* (1945); by Henry Hathaway, *The House on 92nd Street* (1945) and *The Dark Corner* (1946); by Billy Wilder, *Double Indemnity* (1944) and *The Lost Weekend* (1945).

Through this sheer volume of chiaroscuro, the French recognized patterns among the films and discovered authors (the films' directors) where none had been seen before. They asked, what had happened to the Hollywood formula of happy endings? Here were films that reflected a French mindset, post-occupation, films that showcased family dysfunction, marital murder, institutional corruption, existential alienation, financial greed, and sadistic violence.

Paint it black, baby.

The French valued writers like Chandler, James M. Cain, David Goodis, Dashiell Hammett, and the legendary Jim Thompson. Directors Claude Chabrol, Jean-Luc Godard, Jean-Pierre Melville, and Francois Truffaut all cited Roman policiers and crime noir as influences on their early French New Wave films. Truffaut's *Shoot the Piano Player* (1960) and *The Soft Skin* (1964); Godard's *Breathless* (1959) and *Bande a Part* (1964); and Melville's *Bob le Flambeur* (1956), *Le Doulos* (1962) are indebted to American noir. The French admired and championed American crime authors long before the American Library put out special editions validating their work.

I CAN REMEMBER how undervalued crime noir was in the academy. In creative writing workshops of the 1980s, I was discouraged from writing crime dramas. I could only do so after putting up three "serious works of literary fiction." One of my professors went so far as to say, "We're going to strive for something more than *that* here," when I admitted to admiring the TV noir of Rod Serling and *The Twilight Zone.*

But by 2008 the landscape shifted as speculative fiction started making inroads into creative writing classes and hybridized generic stories appeared in high-end literary journals, stories that mixed literary emphases with genre scaffolding (science fiction, fantasy, crime).

The French were way ahead of the curve in seeing artistic merit in crime fiction. And it's no surprise that Frenchman Patrick Modiano won a Nobel Prize for Literature a few years back for his stunning mix of existential literary styling mixed with a variety of genres: crime, mystery, surrealism, and historical fiction.

Just as the the French appreciated the artistic seriousness in tone, mood and subject matter to American noir films and crime novels, I've come to admire the genre's ability to tackle taboo subjects like incest, child abuse, domestic abuse, exploitation, police corruption, institutional corruption, and sexual assault.

Some of Thompson's novels have unreliable narrators, corrupt law enforcement, who act in self-interest and whose minds are one mangled corkscrew mess (see *The Killer Inside Me* or *Pop. 1280*). Mickey Spillane's Mike Hammer bestsellers are full of a high-octane verve, a hatred for "commies," and a two-fisted hero who enjoys being judge, jury and executioner. Sadism rains down. But Hammer, a Marine who saw action in the South Pacific, is clearly a figure who suffers from PTSD, a condition rarely explored in novels at the time. And Ross MacDonald's Lew Archer series often explored dysfunction inside extended or mixed family relationships (especially plots consisting of second or third marriages and troubles between stepbrothers and -sisters and stepparents and stepchildren).

These and other stories are full of twisted power dynamics, and this is why the journey that detectives go on is a Pyrrhic one: they discover dark truths: personal, familial, and societal, that kill them a little, figuratively, on their way.

IN MY NOVELS AND STORIES I seek to leave some loose ends to suggest that not only is the cycle of crime ongoing but the detective is never fully victorious. *Cheap Amusements* ends with a dark secret that the detective has to keep or else risk his life to reveal; *A Fourth Face* has a notorious killer free and loose in Europe. And with *Neon Kiss*, well, let's just say the reason behind the evil is never fully explained because it is in and of itself full of an irrational chaos that is beyond reason.

This is one of the elements that I find most haunting and inviting about crime noir. They are libidinous stories that exist outside the Enlightenment, a period that inspired writers to create flawed characters who are treated by their authors with respect and dignity, characters who can't be defined around a single truth. But in noir, as in the case of Max Cady in John D. MacDonald's *Cape Fear* (originally titled *The Executioners*) or Harry Powell in Davis Grubb's *Night of the Hunter* there are antagonists who are "all bad." Antagonists in crime stories aren't always presented with equanimity and balance. Instead there are those evil Iago types lurking in our world who enjoy hurting people for the sake of hurting people.

I've always believed that people are inherently good, that we care about each other, that we want to connect, to empathize, to understand. I'm not a believer in what some Old Testament church goers believe: all of us are depraved sinners deeply in need of salvation. However, what do we do with a nightmare in the sky story? FBI File: 1955, Flight 629 out of Denver, a bomb planted in the luggage compartment kills 44 people mid-air (39 passengers, 5 crew members). John Gilbert Graham is arrested, appears remorseless, and is found guilty. He succeeded in killing his mother (who traumatized him throughout his childhood). He didn't succeed in collecting on her life-insurance policy. After the guilty verdict he wound up breathing in cyanide gas. But that doesn't really bring closure, does it? Capital punishment, for me, never does. There are still loose ends. I can kind of understand, but not condone, how someone could kill a parent who they perceived as abusive, but why kill 43 others? I can't wrap my head around that—

Cruelties in crime noir often go unexplained: why a woman scalds a mother's child to death, why a cop breaks a teenager's jaw with his pistol, why a gangster buries a witness alive in a freezer.

Crime noir has such a hold over our collective imagination because many of us live with trauma. In my own life I was a victim of childhood abuse (both physical and emotional). It still haunts me. I will never fully understand it. To this day, because of all the fights and drama around my birth family's supper table, I still can't sit comfortably around a table. Church potlucks? Forget about it. Even family dinners with the one Karen and I brought into this world were often situated around the television watching sports while we ate because of my anxieties.

Although I view myself as a somewhat open, upbeat person, seeking the good in others, the inexplicability of my past finds itself in the crime novels I write. Many of my stories focus on the abuses of power, of underaged youths exploited by those who have the means and sickness to do so. "Shot, Reverse Shot"* ends with a disturbing finale, Hayden reflecting on the meaning behind a shadowy image inside the glass handle of a walking cane!

IN CASE YOU HAVEN'T NOTICED, my stories are indebted to the pyrotechnics of Mickey Spillane and his emphasis on the thriller over the whodunit mystery. Like his works, I want to solve a mystery but more importantly I want each story to end with a jolt, a "hey wow" climax that leaves the reader gasping for air. Who can forget the last gut-punching lines to his *I, the Jury* ("'It was Easy,' I said") or *Vengeance Is Mine* ("Juno was a man!"). From Max Allan Collins, a Spillane fan and executor of his final works, I've lifted the idea of the double twist: the one that the reader can figure out, followed by a second moment of sheer surprise or betrayal. His Quarry novels often involve this turn. I hope you enjoy the double-twist to *Neon Kiss*.

And be looking for it in next year's *A Shoeshine Kill*.

Hayden Fuller's larger plot trajectory in the first three novels of the series involves his coming to terms with his having been sexually abused. I wrote the first novel without knowing that this was the super objective or spine to his identity theme. But in the second novel the character just spoke to me and out came this story (no doubt hiding in my own psyche). And as I look back over the first novel, I suddenly saw why Hayden has the reactions and makes the decisions that he does.

* "Shot, Reverse Shot" is collected in *Five Hard Bites*.

—

HAYDEN WAS A VICTIM of abuse, but it's important to me that he maintains a moral equilibrium, that he always tries to do the right things and works to protect his client. As much as I love Dashiell Hammett and *The Maltese Falcon*, I'm not a Sam Spade fan. Yes the dialogue is wonderfully hardboiled, the action spare and terse and two-fisted, but Spade's anti-hero status (is he just pretending or is he kind of in with the bad guys?) I find unappealing. Moreover, the fact that he's sleeping with his partner's wife just doesn't sit well with me. I prefer the tarnished-knight quality of Philip Marlowe who maintains his professional distance, is loyal to a fault, and takes a knightly vow of chastity while working on a case. Unlike Spade and Hammer he doesn't cat around. But that's not to say he's perfect. In *Farewell, My Lovely*, Marlowe feeds an alcoholic drinks to get information from her. He feels terrible about it, but he does it.

Hayden is aware of the psychological triangle that those who are abused have been placed within (abuser/victim/bystander). And therapists have indicated that prior victims can become future abusers or bystanders to others' suffering. Hayden slips into these modes, now and then. In "The Final Portrait," a story that appeared in *Twelve Winters Journal*,* Fuller leans into and possibly even enjoys killing someone in that yarn's final words. In *A Shoeshine Kill*, he takes justice, indirectly, into his own hands, slipping into a kind of Mike Hammer Old Testament hero. These are moments where Fuller breaks from his knightly vows and falls into darkness. However, for the most part he is a decent man, a liberal who cares about righting injustices.

But, on occasion, the downtrodden beat of the Pyrrhic journey forces him to behave badly.

Heroes should be flawed and constantly have their moral compass tested.

* Available at twelvewinters.com/tracey-the-final-portrait.

—

WILLIAM P. MCGIVERN'S *The Big Heat* presents such a flawed hero. Set in the early 1950s, it challenges the post-war American Dream of prosperity, of owning your own home, raising a family, and having enough money for appliances, vacations, and possibly league bowling on Thursday nights. Dave Bannion, is a hard-working cop who enjoys marital bliss and reading bedtime stories to his daughter. He does his job, but he finds it tiring, and is not fully present in the investigation of a high-ranking police official, Tom Duncan (Tom Deery in the novel), who killed himself.

Director Fritz Lang takes this awesome potboiler and through some dynamic editing choices complicates the narrative, creating black veils of death at all the story's sadistic edges and plot turns.

The film's darkest turn occurs after Bannion's wife Katie is killed by a car bomb meant for him. Her present absence is a nasty subversion of the American Dream. After resigning from the police force Detective Bannion stands in his hollowed-out home (all of the furniture and accents have been removed) and from a slightly high angle, subjective point of shot, he takes in the emptiness, the loss of what used to be present: Katie preparing steaks in the kitchen and their joyous sharing of sips of beer and sexual bantering. The now empty spaces embody a metaphor for the hollowness within his soul and Bannion's emotional state of despair. The title of the film, and its trace meanings of an atomic blast, are now present in the emotional ash, the fallout of a destroyed family.

Katie's death spins the narrative, as Bannion is no longer doing a job but seeks to punish all those responsible. When pressure is put on him by the higher-ups in the police precinct to back off, he turns in his badge and, like a westerner, clutches his gun and deepens his resolve to commit murderous vengeance. He becomes alienated and cynically retreats from his Catholicism and his trust in people: he sees everyone as a bunch of "scared rabbits."

But here's where director Lang transcends what's possible in crime noir. He challenges our concepts of masculinity. Often a woman's death (what the comic book industry, following the brutal murder of Green Arrow's wife, calls "the woman in the refrigerator" trope) spins the hero onto a fast highway for justified violence. Moreover, crime noir at times pits a morally ambiguous hero against a femme fatale, a deadly woman who lures men into a life-threatening world. In the classic *Out of the Past* (1947) Robert Mitchum's Jeff Bailey is ruled by his libido and the sexual energy of Kathie (Jane Greer). He knows that she's trouble and might bring about his death, but he can't help himself: "Baby I don't care," he says, leaning fully into the film's fatalism. But in *The Big Heat* there really isn't a classic femme fatale.

Instead we have a l'homme fatale, the fatal man.

Bannion is indirectly responsible for the deaths of four women.

First there's Lucy Chapman, a "B-girl" at the Retreat (a local bar) whose story he fails to take seriously. He tells Bertha Duncan about meeting with Lucy, and Lang ends the scene with a closeup of a stern-faced Bertha (Jeanette Nolan) looking out a window. Superimpose a teletype stating that a woman has been tortured, murdered and thrown from a moving vehicle. Bertha's look is connected with Lucy's death. Why did this death happen? Bannion talked to Bertha. Lang then cuts to an ME telling Bannion that before she died Lucy was burned repeatedly with a cigarette. Disgusted, Bannion responds by butting his cigarette and saying he saw "every one of" the burn marks. Through Glenn Ford's gesture and the director's use of props Lang strongly suggests that Bannion is responsible for those burns. He had an invisible hand in Lucy's torture—

Katie's murder is a direct result of Bannion's toxic masculinity. After Katie receives an obscene phone call from Mike Lagana's gang, Sgt. Bannion rushes over to the mobster's home and "tracks dirt into it." In a a showdown with Lagana, Bannion punches out his bodyguard and tells the kingpin, "You know, you couldn't plant enough flowers around here to kill the smell." The insults and direct challenge to Lagana forces his hand and Katie winds up the unintended victim of a car bomb.

Later, Bannion discovers that Bertha has her husband's confession, a list of all of those on the take, Lagana's payroll. She winds up blackmailing the kingpin, receiving monthly kickbacks for her silence. The only way the "the big heat will fall," revealing those on the take, is courtesy of her death. Bannion almost strangles Bertha in her home, but he's a man of principle and can't bring himself to do it. But how principled is he, really? He tells good-bad girl Debby Marsh (Debby Ward in McGivern's novel) of how close he came to fulfilling his secret dark wishes. Suddenly, he learns that police protection has been pulled from the apartment his daughter is staying in, and he tosses Debby an extra gun, says, "Here, keep this for company" and rushes to his daughter's side.

What do you think happens next?

Debby fulfills Bannion's wishes, becoming an extension of his shadow self. She takes the gun he gave her for "protection" and visits Bertha and guns her down. It's a great scene, both women trussed up in mink coats, and Debby claiming after the kill, "I never felt better in my life." She tosses the revolver on the floor and Lang does an amazing lap dissolve, linking an image of the gun on the carpet with that of Dave Bannion standing with his back to the camera outside Vince Stone's plush apartment, connecting Bannion and his gun and Debby's actions directly to Bertha's murder.

Shortly after killing Bertha, Debby is mortally wounded by Vince.

Four women, four deaths, all inextricably linked to the actions of Dave Bannion.

These are the kind of nuances that make crime novels and their film noir companions complicated and worthy of appreciation. They explore pathologies, social stigmas, and troubled representations of gender construction that question the very foundations of the American Dream. What Jim Thompson had to say about plotting a novel can apply to pulp art. The best stories in the genre are those texts that appear deceptively straightforward, but upon closer analyses, reveal complex contradictions in our shared representations and ideologies.

Lang's film ends with a stunning Pyrrhic moment. Bannion, through the actions of Debby, is now brought back from the black ocean of hatred and vengeance to the shore of humanity. He returns to the police force, receives a phone call, a hit and run to investigate, and he tells Hugo to "keep the coffee hot." As Bannion re-enters society and his place in fighting the cycle of crime, Lang boldly displays in his mise-en-scene a Red Cross poster that screams, "Give Blood Now."

A fitting epitaph for the women in this film and for crime noir in general, and why we read these dark stories where nothing truly is what it seems.

Grant Tracey
October 2023

Neon Kiss

Pre-Game

I don't know why I'd thought he'd be there.
When had he not let me down before?

Two Green seats several rows up from the Habs bench. Vacant.

Stana Younger sat in the row behind, a new set of hoop earrings glinting in the glare from the ice. Her shoulders were thrown forward, experiencing every rush, every hit, every pass, shot and save as if she were on the ice herself. It's what I admire about her. Commitment.

It was great to see her.

But those two other seats.

I quickly flexed my fingers inside my gloves and skated half-circles by our goalie, Charlie Hodge.

"We got this, Hodgy," I said.

His eyes focused past me, lost in the meditative realm of projected successes: a save, the clock winding down, a clear and breakout from our end, and the puck sliding over the checkered line across the way.

The crowd at the Gardens was wobbly rocks whumping around inside a hubcap.

I glanced over my shoulder, water dropping from my chin, tight coins. Near the end Blues, set into a wall like a private WWII bunker, were my former bosses, Leafs owners Steven Smith and Cal Bullard. Both of them were facing trials for illegal gambling and embezzlement. Things were even worse for Smith, who was up on charges of extortion and racketeering. How could they still show themselves in this grand old barn that once housed the likes of Syl Apps, Max Bentley, and Teeder Kennedy? Bunting draped from their bunker, red and white, with a cluster of inlaid poppies asking us to remember sacrifices made.

It was November 11th. Remembrance Day. My father had a cousin who died at Vimy.

The eleventh day, on the eleventh hour of November, the Great War ended. There are Canadians buried in fields all over Europe, Belgium mostly.

I took in a deep breath.

Flexed fingers once more.

The whump-whumping was a rhythmic wash of loud, louder, loudest, and then silence, followed by a slow winding rush of loud, louder, loudest all over again. I wiped the corners of my mouth and smiled in the direction of Jean Béliveau. Far post, he pointed.

I nodded.

Before the game the 48th Highlanders played "The Maple Leaf Forever." Bagpipes never sounded so damn good.

It was great to be back in the place I once called home.

From his bunker, Bullard hunched, readying for the faceoff, absently reaching into his large bag of potato chips, pulling out chips that looked like an ear or two. Sharp flecks dripped from his chin and speckled the inlaid poppies with grease stains. Christ.

Smith, a blur of white phosphorous, his skin parchment thin, slouched back, belching into a skinny hand. He'd been in the hospital last month for bleeding ulcers. Looked like he'd lost forty pounds.

I guess I should have sent him a get-well card.

Their trial was set for January, 1966. And Perry Mason isn't a real cat so these guys are fucked.

I parked in front of our far post, cutting the ice in half, giving the Leafs less room.

Fifty-two seconds to go.

After my last case, involving N'oublie jamais, Red 45, and a plot to poison the water filtration system in Montreal, Anne Chevalier and the RCMP implored NHL President Clarence S (as in Soupy or Shithead, you decide) Campbell to reinstate me, with the Habs. And he did. *Bless his heart.* In the South, such a phrase, bless his heart, can be ironically inflected.

I'm intending the inflection.

Bless his heart.

Anyway, this was our ninth game of the season. Our record: 4-2-2: my stats: three goals, four assists, three fights on the season. Potted my third tally of the year, the go-ahead goal, midway through the second, high stick side on Bower, just under the bar.

Also, assisted on the first goal: Cournoyer on the power play. And, earned five minutes for fighting to start the third. A Gordie Howe hat trick.

I don't know why we call it (a goal, an assist, a fight) that. Howe only has two in his career and the last one was in 1954 for Chrissakes, but the guy's like a regular registered trademark: "The Gordie Howe hat trick."

I'm surprised he doesn't have his own line of hockey sticks.

Béliveau was waved out of the circle for cheating, leaning in. He skated a loose-lined lariat around the linesman and then dimly smiled at me. "It's all yours."

The Leaf net at the other end was empty.

Coach Hugh "Two-Fisted" Farrell had a foot up on their bench, shouting something about streetcars and desire.

Some things never change.

I shook my head, and then set myself behind the dot. Boos rattled, waffling over the whump-whump of cheers. I gave Pully my lopsided leer. He didn't say anything. I had five stitches in my chin from our fight and a bitter taste of tin in my mouth. My stick hit the ice, then his stick, then the puck.

But I didn't go for the puck. I went for Pulford and his stick, tying him up, knowing the refs wouldn't call it, keeping him from drawing the puck back, and J. C. Tremblay picked up the biscuit on the dot, backhanded it behind our net, and Jacques Lapierre cleared the zone.

Horton quickly retrieved it at center and rushed up ice, dumping it back in. Pully crashed the boards behind our net, gathering in the puck, but I wedged my stick between his legs, up against his left skate so he couldn't move. I locked my hand on his sweater. There was no way he'd fall and draw a tripping call, and our Captain Le Gros Bill scraped up the leftovers, saucered a pass to Tremblay, who alley-ooped one to Claude Provost who lumbered over the blue line to center, and rifled a shot into the middle of the Leaf net. 3-1.

I shrugged and smiled at the crowd as the whump-whumping flattened into waffling notes, and then a warbling waterfall.

Two vacant seats.

Stana stood, applauding, the purse on her wrist the size of a large milk crate. She wore a brown pantsuit and a sandy pillbox hat.

The Leaf fans around her were giving her the business, thumbs down, mouthing off, and she mouthed off right back at them. I waved in her direction and then their thumbs were thumbing me down.

Programs waltzed and curved my way, sharp-edged Frisbees.

They weren't asking for autographs.

Béliveau tap-tapped my shin guards. "Heady play, mon ami." He ruffled my buzz cut. "I always told you, you'd like playing for Montreal."

Damn straight.

Béliveau was my roommate and the nicest cat I've ever suited up with. "Merci," I said.

Bullard crumpled his bag of chips into a large rock and threw it at the ice.

I think it bounced off the head of an usher, two aisles down.

Class.

As I left the ice, the timekeeper tapped me on the shoulder and said McClelland Stuart, the voice of the Leafs on radio, had selected me one of the game's three stars. I hung around in the tunnel, fans jeering, shouting frog lover, pea soup, and I just breathed and breathed and looked off in the direction of my father's empty seat.

My shoulder pads felt heavy. My left leg shook. Why was I scared of a curtain call?

Ladies and Gentlemen the third star: Hayden Fuller.

Okay, yes, it was my first game back at the Gardens, and I guess I wasn't expecting a parade or some damn thing, but I wanted to be respected, and the fans were actually cheering me, many of them. Sure, there were some boos, but there was a greater mix of appreciation, and it filled me with thankfulness, and I smiled, pointing an index finger, acknowledging the crowd, our past connection. Nine years I was a Leaf, 458 consecutive games, 107 goals, two Cups, before those assholes, those arrested adolescent playboys Bullard and Smith bounced me to the AHL for "moral turpitude"—I had taken nude photos of a cheating wife, divorce case, for one of my teammates, Bobby Ehle.

At twenty-nine I retired. At thirty I was back.

But not with the blue and white, but with the bleu-blanc-rouge.

My dad's seat: empty.

Bullard crunched back in his bunker, eyes hard, hands across his chest, face dour. Smith slithered in his seat like a long white worm, his Lombardi glasses resting on top of his head as if he were some kind of famous general at the Plains of Abraham or some damn thing.

And then I did it.

I always was a smart-ass.

They had fucked me over. I was a Toronto kid, listened to the games on radio throughout childhood, stood in the standing room only section of the Greys as the Leafs won the Cup in 1951 on Bill Barilko's goal. They took that away from me.

Moral turpitude my ass. Their idea of fun was having naked women pose as human lamps in their office. I was there for such a display of morality. Great guys.

I skated in the direction of their bunker, and their bunting, and their bullshit, imagining it a kraut pillbox, and took a phantom grenade, pulled the pin with my teeth, and with a straight arm gesture lobbed it in their direction.

The crowd really liked that. Standing. Applauding.

They weren't booing anymore.

As you can imagine, the post-game Canadiens dressing room was raucous; Coach Blake gave me a strong slap on the back and said something in a combination of French and English about that's why we got you Third Star, to help us beat Toronto. He was excited. Usually he talks to me in English.

I shrugged sheepishly, the edge of my shoulder pads no longer itching my chest, my legs no longer shaking.

I like Coach Blake. No nonsense. Tough guy. But unlike Farrell and his streetcars, Blake wasn't into mind games. He doesn't go to the media and trash-talk us and prattle on about grit and fists. Short, quick passes, *always be moving*, that was his philosophy. Sure, he trashed the other team, but never his guys. Before this game, he said the Leafs weren't as strong as in the past, their run was done. Montreal was the team to beat. Cup winners last year, and planning on being Cup winners again. Hell, Chicago was better than Toronto, Blake said. Maybe even Detroit was better than Toronto.

Coach Farrell responded like a drill sergeant with a run of words the papers couldn't print. Loose translation: "We'll see who has the last laugh tonight."

Yeah, we did see, didn't we?

Dick Bledsoe of *The Star*, his King Lear Fool's hat a triangle wedge pushed down on his forehead, asked me about the grenade toss, his eyes dancing.

It was a spur of the moment thing, Dick. I shouldn't have done it, I got caught up in getting even with the fellas who let me go. It was wrong.

Shit it was Remembrance Day. And what about the honored dead, in hallowed Flanders Fields?

"It was great theater," Bledsoe corrected, his hands gesturing with enthusiasm. He hadn't seen such pyrotechnics since "Terrible" Ted Lindsay fired an imaginary machine gun at the fans back in the 1950s.

"I got nothing against the fans," I said.

"No. And they still like you." Bledsoe smiled, a warm genuine expression that invited you to join him in a beer. He figured the fans wished they'd thought of it, the grenade thing. "Believe me, Fuller, if the Gardens ushers were handing out hot pineapples instead of felt poppies tonight that bunker would be under rubble right now."

"Yeah." I rubbed at the dirty adhesive bandage pinching my chin. There were spots of blood on my sweater. Five stitches.

Then some other reporter asked how it felt beating my old team.

I love the fans of Toronto, love this city, I said. "I guess you can tell how I feel about management."

That got quite a few laughs.

"Hmm." The lanky reporter, with some kind of fraternity pin in the lapel of his blazer, tapped his heavy lower lip with a twisted finger.

I didn't recognize him as a regular beat writer; he was new, and wasn't I rubbing it in, with the grenade toss? I mean, real people, young Canadian men, died in Vimy, and Ypres, all through the dirty trenches of war in Europe. "Yes, I know. You're right."

"It was a grandstand play." He refused to let my indiscretion go. This cat, with his pinched lips, blue eyes, was old school, a United Empire Loyalist, a lover of decorum, blue laws, secret handshake society shit.

And he smelled of money. You really can smell money. It's there in the starch of freshly pressed clothes, and the high-priced cologne behind the ears.

This guy sported both.

"Strictly American Hockey League hijinks. Bush league." His fraternity pin glinted.

"Oh, come on, Franklin." Bledsoe was having none of Franklin W. Whitfield's remarks. I caught the name after squinting at his press pass, a lanyard around his neck. I took a second look. It really was Franklin W. Whitfield II. Who puts Roman numerals after their name? Christ.

He wore a crew-neck sweater vest over a razor-sharp dress shirt. *The Toronto Telegram*. His outfit. Surprise, surprise. With a name like Franklin W. Whitfield II he might even have some American plantation owners kicking about in his storied past.

"Those two crumbs should be in jail, and you know it." Hayden was expressing how we all feel, well, all of us who don't work at the *Tely*, Bledsoe said, his hands flashing about as if juggling three or four pins. "I mean, God bless the Queen, the Empire! Rule Britannia!"

None of the pins hit the floor, but the room filled with a crash of laughs.

And then the laughing stopped.

Sal Lambertino, my old pal, Toronto's top cop, who I hadn't seen much of since signing with Montreal, stood with a felt hat in his hands, eyes full of sadness, Sloan Wilson grays sagging his shoulders. Stana Younger, my first real love and a woman I still loved—we had only spent a couple of weekends together since my time in Montreal and the start of the season nearly three weeks ago—was full of an equal sadness, standing behind him, the freckles of her eyes invisible beneath the pillbox hat and locker room light.

And I knew.

Dad.

Dead.

First Period

The small house on Gradwell had three little trees in front of it, a lawn that was balding, and shutters on the windows that hung crookedly. Inside, it was dank and full of soiled food and decay.

The windows were open, letting in cold air, and an ME, with slicked-back hair and early 60s fashion (black pants, white shirt, skinny tie), stood over the tangled-up corpse, sheets bunching like errant snowballs around legs and arms, glassy eyes full of vague ceiling reflections. Dad had been dead for about three, four days, the ME figured, latex gloves on his hands, a syringe in his right. "Looks like drugs. An overdose." The ME placed the syringe in a plastic bag, sealed it.

"Can't you guys cover him up. At least—"

Stana gasped when she saw what I had seen on the living room couch: Dad naked, left foot touching the floor, lower extremities exposed, a rocket-sized erection knifing the air.

As a prepubescent eight-, nine-year-old, I had seen such erections. After mom died.

Sal, biting his upper lip, snapped his fingers, and they covered up Dad, the sheet tenting.

Stana seized my shoulders, hands a heavy, worn fishermen's net. And then she cried. "I'm so sorry, Hayden."

I had been trying to work out things about my father with my therapist. She told me I needed to talk to him about the past, about what he did and why, and I was no longer a victim because I could talk to her about it. That was a first step. My troubled relationship with my father was connected to the man I killed in my first real case, blew his head off. Now there was no time to work out a fucking thing.

Sorry, the ME said. Sam Ross was his name.

We shook hands. His latex fingers felt full of Silly Putty.

And then he spoke quickly about what I'd seen, about methane gas, and how because Dad had been here for a while, gas had escaped up his legs, engorging his penis.

"How long would you say he's been here?" Sal scratched at his uneven Hemingway beard.

"At least three days. Judging by—"

I sighed. "The size of—"

"Yeah." Ross looked away.

"My dad never did drugs."

Ross held up the bagged syringe. Needle marks, inside on his left arm. Fresh. "A deadly dose of heroin, most likely." He shrugged. "Probably uncut."

"Were there other marks there? On his arms? Any sign of a habitual user?" Sal asked.

"No." Ross rubbed the edges of his mouth. "Probably a first-time experiment."

"Experiment?" Stana shook her head violently, her teeth denting her lower lip. "Hayden's father was in his sixties. Experiment? He wasn't the kind of guy to wear Nehru jackets and hang out at head shops."

"She's right. He was a chain-smoker, a beer drinker." I smiled dimly. All around the living room couch were empties of Molson Canadian. I pushed back my porkpie hat.

On the coffee table was also a copy of *Playboy*, Hemingway's *The Old Man and the Sea*, and Morley Callaghan's *More Joy in Heaven*. When did Dad start reading? He never read. Except the sports page and Mickey Spillane's *I, the Jury*.

Dad wouldn't touch drugs. That shit's poison, he'd say, blowing a river of cigarette smoke into a far corner of the room. Poison.

Ross shrugged at the evidence, the room. There were no signs of struggle, nothing stolen, no cupboards left open. Nothing.

"He has forty dollars in his wallet," said a blue-eyed cop, hanging over Sal's shoulder. "TV's still here. The radio."

"The washer and dryer—"

"No one takes a washer and dryer, Hayden." Sal corrected.

"I know. I'm just saying, I'm being ironic." I shrugged. "He was murdered."

The house may not have been rousted for goods, but it was a fucking mess. Dishes in the sink weren't done, piled high, covered with hardened bits of canned meat, broken triangles of grilled-cheese sandwiches, and three bottles of Coke and an Orange Crush. Dad didn't drink soda pop. Ever.

His choice of poison was Rothmans. The tiled floor in the kitchen needed to be washed, grungy scuff marks smudged the walls, and a filmy layer of gray streaked the inside of the windows. Ashtrays were full of cigarettes.

"Who found him?" Sal asked.

Someone from Silverwood's. A Bob Waterman. Dad was a milkman for them, making deliveries in the McGowan Road area of Scarborough, and when he didn't show for work Saturday, Monday, or Tuesday, Bob dropped by, smelled decay, and came in.

I wrote the cat's name down in my yellow notebook.

It was now almost Wednesday, November 12th.

Sal, holding his gray fedora, sighed. "No other marks? On his arms?"

Nothing. Just the fatal dose.

Three burly fellas slid Dad slowly into a black body bag.

"He was murdered," I said. "Dad was left handed. The needle marks, if he shot himself up, should be on the inside of his right arm."

Ross looked over at Sal. "A lefty—?"

We all nodded.

Sal clamped his hat back on his head. "Start dusting for fingerprints, fellas. This is a crime scene."

"A lefty. The killer didn't know that—" I said.

"Neither did I, apparently," said Ross.

FORTY-FIVE MINUTES LATER, Stana and I were walking down Gradwell Street toward a Becker's on the corner, its green sign glowing. I could use a donut. Maybe three.

Dad wouldn't be buried in three days. There would be an autopsy. Saturday funeral. Maybe.

There were shallow puddles on the sidewalk. It had rained a lot the last few days, and I walked on through them, recalling being a kid, my boots on the wrong feet, stomping about in the splashes of fun. At four, I never could figure out how to tie shoe laces, so I loved wearing boots. One time, Dad got so mad at me for not tying my shoes right—I always made two separate loops before joining the laces and that just never could work out—so he walloped me again and again, saying I had to get it right before kindergarten started. *For fuck sakes, get it right, dummy.*

"What are you going to do?"

"Find who killed him."

"You don't owe him anything." Her pillbox hat dipped to the left, the freckles in her eyes dancing. "Nothing."

"He's my father. Doesn't matter what I thought about him—"

"Or what he did to you—"

"He's my father. Good or bad—" *There were some good times: flying kites on lazy afternoons; walking along the sand of Balmy Beach; listening to the Leafs and McClelland Stuart on radio.* "I *do* owe him."

"It sounds good in theory, Hayden, but what about the Montreal Canadiens?" She stopped and turned my face toward hers, kissed my nose. "You got a good thing going. You owe them, the Habs, for giving you a second chance." Her lower lip quivered. "You owe the NHL the best you can give the game."

And I played great tonight. A goal, an assist.

"A fight too." She lifted the tip of my porkpie.

"That was stupid," I admitted.

"It was."

"Pulford called me a traitor for playing for the Habs. I couldn't let that go."

"You couldn't let that go? What are you ten years old? With your history of concussions—" A thin line skated between her eyebrows. "How's your chin?"

"It burns a little."

She peeled back the bandage. "It looks infected."

"It's nothing—"

"Maybe tomorrow. See a doctor."

I smiled my lopsided grin and pulled her toward me, kissing her.

She kissed back.

"You want me to stay with you tonight?"

Part of me did. I still owned my home in Willowdale on Houston Crescent. *Another part of me sought loneliness, isolation.* "No. Thanks. I just need to reflect, to—but stay with me for a little while."

"Sure." She smiled, and then reaffixed the bandage and kissed my chin. "I love you." She laughed inwardly. "I don't say it enough, but I do."

"Yeah."

I love her too. I think. Dr. Jeanette Cohen, my therapist, however, told me to be careful and not rush things. Victims of abuse live their lives inside a triangle: the abuser (my dad), the victim (me), and the bystanders (my rabbi, my school teachers who couldn't read the signals, who didn't acknowledge how much I hurt, how my shyness and solemn retreat from the world was a signal of trouble, of painful trauma; they all should have known better, they should have *been listening*).

And as a victim of abuse gets older, Dr. Cohen said, they manifest all three sides of the original trauma in their later relationships with others. *Face it, Hayden, at times, as a detective, you become the abuser, bullying clients, manipulating others to get what you want.* I guess, in my first case when I blew the head off of a rapist, I was exacting revenge, abusing him for abusing others. "But he wanted me to do it," I said in her office on a particularly dreary afternoon, the rain spitting pencil streaks. *You did it because you wanted to. You wanted to exert the same power over someone that your father exerted over you.*

Maybe so.

How am I a victim? Now? How am I?

Perhaps in going back to Stana, perhaps you feel this is what you deserve. She hurt you. Maybe you want to be hurt again? And all those donuts you eat—

Okay, okay.

You certainly are a bystander in your relationship with her, refusing to acknowledge her betrayal, to address it.

We've addressed it.

How?

We have. Trust me.

"I really think you need to think about all this, Hayden," Stana now said. I had been out of the league for a year. Montreal was a good fit for me. "I've never seen you happier."

I nodded.

The Habs played Detroit on Friday. That was less than three days away. I promised Mr. Pollock, our GM, that I'd be there for that game. He gave me a temporary leave from the team, to sort things out, but I needed the team, I told him, the safety, the clear rules that the game of hockey provides. Hockey makes sense. My father's murder? "Please don't make me sit," I told Pollock. He smiled with his eyes. A man never forgets the day his father died, never, Pollock said.

"So, you have three days to solve a murder?" Stana now said.

"Something like that." I shrugged.

"What if you don't solve it?"

"I'll be back with the Habs."

"Will you?"

I didn't answer. My PI license didn't expire until the end of December. I hadn't thought of re-upping until now. Shit, I had work to do. "Yes. Yes. My commitment's to Montreal."

She glanced down at her hands, flipped up on her thighs.

I lifted Stana's chin. Dr. Cohen said that me and Stana had a lot to work through, and because my love for her made me feel good and her good, then that love *was good*, and I shouldn't feel ashamed all the time; however, because of her past betrayals involving Lisa Steinmetz and Spinner Terrien, and my vulnerable condition, I might not be ready for a fully healthy, sexual relationship. I laughed when she said that as the pencil streaks continued to fall outside. *When have I ever been sexually healthy?* I can't make women come. Sometimes, but it's rare. *A lot of men have that problem, she said, not just men who have been abused.*

Yeah, well, I never feel that I completely give of myself when making love. There's always a part of me holding back.

That's the victim in you. Feeling unworthy. I know of all these levels, Hayden. I live them every day. I saw my siblings, my uncle, my parents, killed at Auschwitz. I survived. There isn't a day that goes by where I don't feel like a bystander, someone who should have done more.

Should have? You couldn't do more, Doc. Surviving was what you did. You should be proud.

Please don't call me Doc. But your empathy for others is a good first step in healing yourself.

I admire you, Dr. Cohen.

Let's not get maudlin.

Uh-huh, I said.

And we laughed. She doesn't laugh a whole lot, but she did that day.

It was a sad kind of laughter that made you want to cry.

And I think we both cried, truth be told.

I squeezed Stana's hand and told her she and Sal and Doc Cohen were my only friends. It's weird to call your therapist a friend, but, yeah, she's in the club. All those years playing hockey and my three closest friends aren't hockey players.

I had taken Stana to a couple of sessions with me, to discuss us, and my fears of sex, of really being present, there, for the other person. Why was I so afraid to just love and be loved? *Not every moment of intimacy was a test, like the final 52 seconds of a 2–1 hockey game. God, I was good tonight.*

Anyway, we walked into Becker's. The lights hurt my eyes, and I didn't say a word about it to Stana because she'd just give me shit over that damn fight with Pulford in the third period. What was I thinking? I felt a little dizzy, nauseous, and figured nothing a donut or two couldn't fix. I found a couple of cream-filled chocolate frosted ones from Margaret's, and a box of fresh bandages. Stana bought a deck of Parliaments.

I wish I had worn sunglasses.

The cashier had dark eyes and a brown beard that didn't quite match his black hair.

"You didn't get harassed by a fucker with a beanie cap, did you?" He huffed as he spoke. His lower teeth, crooked. He wore a white butcher's coat over a dress shirt and black-knit tie. The cuff on the left sleeve was pulled back.

"Huh?"

"Outside. Crazy guy. Beanie cap, goggles, green coat, long. Pushing pamphlets for some kind of church down the street."

"No, didn't see him."

"Called the cops on him four times this past week." He bit his upper lip. "He's disturbing my business."

His anger was palpable. There was a backstory here.

I asked him if he knew my father, Ira Fuller. Molson Canadian, Rothmans, looks a lot like me but thirty years older.

"Oh, yeah. Ira. A regular. My name's Gus by the way. Gus Carhart. Ira. Yeah, comes in every night around six for the paper. *The Star.* A pack of smokes and a six pack. Rothmans. Yeah, that's his brand. Rothmans. Good old Ira."

"Yeah, well, good old Ira's good old dead. He was murdered."

Gus gasped and looked down at his fingers. They were dirty, and along his right index finger were black, greasy marks of a butcher's pencil. There were marks also dotting his left wrist. "What happened?"

"He was killed in his home. Drug overdose. But he didn't give it to himself. Wrong arm."

"Huh?"

"He's a lefty. Needle marks were on the left arm. Wrong arm. He was killed."

"Who'd want to kill Ira?"

I didn't say anything, but boy did I want to.

"Did you see him come in here with someone strange or—" Stana cut in.

"No. The only strange cat I've had to deal with is that beanie-cap guy, talking about giving up all your possessions for the kingdom of heaven. A regular nut." He shrugged again. "I'm trying to run a business and he's talking to my customers about giving that business to a church."

"Yeah."

"Down the street they are. Anyway, who gives up everything for the kingdom of heaven?"

"Some people do," Stana said.

"Sure, sure. This is a democracy. To each his own. Love your neighbor and all that, but Christ, not in front of my store."

I nodded.

He apologized, mumbled something about so sorry for your loss, and I asked him again if he was sure he hadn't seen Ira with anybody recently.

Ira. Ira Fuller. I have his middle name. Hayden Ira Fuller. It was mom's idea.

"Did he buy any soda pop? Coke, Orange Crush."

"Yeah. Six or seven bottles the past week."

"The past week you say?"

"Yeah."

I turned to Stana. "Dad didn't drink pop."

She nodded.

"Never saw Ira with anyone?" Stana asked Gus.

"No, always by himself." He looked up and then locked eyes with Stana, like he had something to share, just with her. "The last time he was in, though, he bought something kind of odd."

"Uh-huh?"

A box of Tampax, he whispered.

STANA AND I SHARED A SMOKE (I don't know what was the matter with me, I never smoke), walked along the edge of a park to a dirt path above the Scarborough Bluffs, and looked over Lake Ontario, and up, up, the stars, sharp points, the water a black disc with painted spots a deeper black. "Maybe, now's not the time," she said, "but I want to stay with you tonight."

We don't have to sleep together, she assured me, but I'll give these next three days over to you to help you. Before you head to Detroit.

Over to you. It sounded biblical.

"Maybe tomorrow," I said. But tonight, I want to be alone.

She nodded. Her eyes filled with black paint.

I smoked a second cigarette, my head spun cotton candy, the lake a dark mass of uncertainties.

THERE WAS YELLOW TAPE EVERYWHERE and the smell hadn't changed, even with two windows left open. The house had stilled. I was surprised that the clock on a low coffee table was ticking. I had expected it to be stopped too, like my dad. It was next to a row of beer bottles and an empty of Orange Crush and read 2:17. I couldn't sleep.

The police had left the scene and I had climbed through the kitchen window.

I had to be here. I said it was to find a clue, but I suspect I was here as a son, looking for what a father leaves behind. For a son.

I strolled through the kitchen. A ceramic sink was chipped, the marks resembling small leeches. A cupboard door was partially ajar. Behind the door was a dumbwaiter with small pulleys, wheels, and ropes that I used to play in, pretending I was an astronaut, the basement below Mars.

I pushed back my porkpie and picked up a bottle of Rémy-Martin that was parked by the sink. I don't drink, but in honor of my father, I poured two fingers, knocked it back.

It burned going down.

Goddamn it. *There were things I wanted to say to the son of a bitch that I can't now. So many things.*

I found a half-empty Tampax box under the sink in the bathroom.

No other signs of a woman: no perfume, no air fresheners, no intimates, no pink toothbrushes. Nothing.

But in the bedroom: a large portrait of a blond, blue-eyed Jesus, haloed with enough radioactive afterglow to burn out your retinas. Shit, Jesus wasn't blond; he was swarthy like me, and Dad was a Jew, I'm a Jew, so I don't know what's with the goy Jesus at the foot of the bed.

This had to belong to the woman with the Tampax box. So, she also belonged in his bedroom? Who is she?

And the box was half empty, and if the tampons were bought just a few days ago that meant the woman wasn't planning on coming back right away, if at all.

I plunked myself down in the living room, in Dad's slick leather chair with its worn-down arms and the heady smell of cigarette ashes and beer sweat.

I could still see him there, knifing the air, eyes darkened glass.

The phone rang. I wasn't sure I should answer it.

Béliveau.

"How did you get this number?"

"Information. Where else would you be but at your father's?"

"My relationship with him was troubled, Jean."

"We don't need to—"

"You're not prying. It's—how the fellas?"

The team had just arrived in Montreal, and he was calling from the train station. He wanted to know how I was and assured me that if I needed more time to take the time, the team will get by.

"Jean, Jean, I need you guys, man. I'll be there in Detroit." We had a home and home, Friday, Saturday against them. It was a four-hour drive from T.O. "I'll be there."

"Okay, mon ami. You played great tonight."

"Thanks." I sighed. "The reporters been asking questions about me, my absence?"

"They don't know yet. We covered for you."

"Sure. Thanks for calling, Jean. How's Coach Blake about this whole thing?"

"He's not happy, but he understands. Me and Provie set him straight."

"Great. It means a lot to me." I'm totally committed to the Habs, I said. This was the happiest I'd ever been as a player.

"I know. I wasn't calling to check up on your loyalties, Hays, I was just worried about you."

"I know. I'm doing as well as can be expected."

Am I? Smoking cigarettes. Drinking Rémy-Martin? Breathing in stale tobacco ash and wishing I could have one last conversation with my father. Am I, really?

"Sure. Call if you need anything."

After he hung up I collapsed down in the chair, breathing in the darkness and the dirt, and wondering why Dad didn't take better care of himself, this place, and what's with the blonde Jesus, and then I saw it: the switch plate across from me, there was a sliver of clean wall, bleach white, above and around all sides of the plate's rim. It was an odd detail, but quirky enough to be important.

I snapped my fingers.

Dad had removed the switch plate recently and when he replaced it he over tightened the plate in place sinking it into the plaster, allowing some of the previously hidden wall to show.

But did he just replace the light switch? Or—

I grabbed a screwdriver from the silverware drawer (that's where he always kept that shit) and unscrewed the plate from the wall, pulled out the switch with its three wires, and wedged behind was an envelope.

I opened it.

Why did Dad hide this? Was this some kind of keepsake? Blackmail? Did he know he was going to die?

It was a photograph of a young woman, fifteen or thereabouts, with caramel-colored skin, high accented cheekbones, ragged black bangs, and green eyes. There was a space between her two front teeth and her face was vaguely amused at having her picture taken. It was as if my father wanted me to find it, knew I would.

But why? *To find her?*

On the outside of the envelope was written *11/14/65, Midnight Mass?* A Friday night mass. Where? What mass? What church? And why the fucking question mark? *Midnight mass?*

Moreover, who is the girl?

I really wanted to listen to some jazz right about now: Jimmy Smith, Kenny Burrell, Art Blakey. But Dad was more of a Johnny Cash, Marty Robbins, Hank Williams kind of guy.

I sank into the chair, removed my hat. Closed my eyes. The girl, the mass. This was the goddamn clue I needed, but what did it mean?

UNDER THE COFFEE TABLE, red with yellow trim and smelling of smoldering cigarettes and rubber cement, was a scrapbook. The pages were crammed with stories of yours truly: my first write-up in *The Star*, after making the Leafs, summer of 1957; an article from *Maclean's* on how I'm a new kind of forward, the defenseman as winger; pictures of me potting my overtime winning goal, game three against Chicago, 1962; a chatty piece on how I like steak and noodles with parmesan and olive oil before every game, and chocolate-chip cookies and milk after; a photo of me and the fellas, gathered around the Stanley Cup on a card table, center ice, 1963; my dismissal, 1964, from the league and Dad's heavily scrawled lines: bullshit, bullshit, bullshit. Bright, angry ink.

I didn't know he kept a scrapbook. I didn't know that he followed my career that closely.

Or cared.

The cigarette-rubber cement smell quickly diffused into a kind of perfume, sandalwood, and as the smell took over the room, scrapbook pages blurred into broken chips of ink and slivers of pulp latticed my fingers.

Auburn hair. Freckles. Stana's face. A bemused smile. "Sleep well?"

She wore a short red jacket, red hat, white gloves, and black slacks. Jackie Kennedy had nothing on her. Nothing.

Me, in my crumpled slacks and blue blazer, felt like I had been folded up into a suitcase. My arms, knees, the back of my shoulders ached.

"I thought I'd find you here." She tossed me my gun, snug in its side holster. She had retrieved it from my home on Houston Crescent. "I also thought you might want this." My license didn't expire for six more weeks.

The clock said 6:37.

I shook my head, ran a tongue across the front of my teeth, my mouth feeling as if a towel were in it. I looked at my hands. There was no goddamn scrapbook.

All that was under the coffee table were old copies of *TV Guide*, *Playboy*, and other men's magazines, featuring nudists playing volleyball and then having romantic interludes all over the beach. Of course, they did it on over-sized towels the size of swimming pool tarpaulins.

"Some legacy, huh?"

"Huh?"

"Never mind." I rubbed the edges of my lips. "Shit. I dreamed Dad kept a scrapbook. Of me. Instead, look what I find." I tossed the frolicking beachcombers on the coffee table.

Some of the pages stuck, pressing the magazine in the air as if it had hind legs. Stana picked it up, quickly fanned pages, and glanced at the volleyball players twisted about like taffy. "That looks really uncomfortable."

I waited for her to close the magazine and then reached into my back pocket and handed her the photo I found. I wondered if she recognized the girl. Was she listed as missing or anything?

"She's Indian. Métis maybe. The green eyes?"

"Yeah—"

Stana nodded. Looks like a runaway. We should have Sal check with CAS, but the face looked familiar. She stared at it again, eyes squinting. "Ellen Reynolds." She pushed back her red hat. Snapped her fingers. "Yes. Saskatchewan girl." She tapped her lower lip. "Regina. No, wait. That's where they took her."

"Who?"

"The police. Took her from her Mom. She has no father. Put her with a white woman."

"The police just—"

"A knock at the door—yes." Stana shook her head, face set in a tight grimace.

Ellen Reynolds *was* Métis. After living with a white family for several years she ran away from them. But she didn't head home. She knew better. The CAS would only take her back to them so she ran to the big city of T.O. and just disappeared, swallowed up in bath houses and shoe-shine parlors. The dark side of the streets. Fourteen then, fifteen now. "Probably a victim of abuse. White parents wanting to 'beat the red devil' out of her. That's what gets them to run. Often."

"Uh-huh."

Stana had wanted to write an article on the failure of residential schools in Canada, but the editors at the *Telegram* nixed the idea. "Some say Ellen became a child prostitute. Here." Stana nervously pulled at the fingers of one of her gloves. "At least that's the rumor, innuendo, dirty hearsay, who knows her real story." Her white parents had been trying to find Ellen for fourteen, eighteen months. "I'm sure that's the girl in the photo." She shrugged. "It wasn't my story, but I remember editing some copy for another columnist."

"Sure."

Trying to find herself in the city. Maybe she found Jesus. Or was just into kitsch.

"Oh, they probably beat Jesus into her. Literally," I said.

"Why's your dad have her photograph?"

"I don't know."

I wagged my thumb in the direction of the bedroom. "Check out the wallpaper."

Stana walked quickly down the hall, pushed open the door, and said nothing. For a while. "Really? A blond Jesus."

She returned smothering a laugh.

"Yeah. A gasser. I think she was here. Ellen."

"I think you're right."

I told her about the Tampax box I found, the bottles full of half-drank flat pop, the library books. *She was living here.* "I think he was protecting her."

"Or fucking her—"

"Stana—" Ellen's photograph wasn't a nudie. It was just a picture. Evidence. Of some kind. "There was a date too on the envelope the photo came in. 11/14/65. Midnight mass?"

"What's with the question mark?"

I laughed. "You got me. Either the time of the mass is in question or whether or not the mass itself qualifies as a mass."

"The time *better be* in question. Is there such a thing as a midnight mass in November?" She tapped her lower lip and quickly shook her head. The Catholics do midnight masses on Christmas Eve, she said. Not on November fourteenth.

"Yeah, two days from now."

"What's going to happen at midnight?"

"I don't know." I shrugged. "Dad was an ethnic Jew, not a religious one, and he sure the hell wouldn't go to mass." *Well, maybe, if the deal got him laid.*

"But he wrote it down?"

"It's his handwriting. Yeah."

She paced, pulling off the other glove. "A portrait of Jesus?"

My shoes needed a shine. And one of the laces was frayed. "Yeah. Overlooking the bed."

"I guess it's okay to fuck if Jesus is watching over you—"

"A goy Jesus." I shrugged again. "I don't get it. He has blond hair and is backlit by a halo the size of a hula hoop."

"Do you think?" She looked away. "Don't get mad, but let's not give up on the sex angle. Maybe your dad was keeping her, the Reynolds girl, abusing her, and she killed him?"

"What? No."

"Why not?" She crossed her arms and returned to working the fingers on the other glove. "We know what he did to *you*."

She couldn't look at me. "How did your dad feel about the Métis?"

"My dad was a lot of things but a bigot wasn't one of them. He hated Nazis."

She nodded.

I was now the one pacing behind the couch, reaching into my shirt pocket and pulling out two sticks of Juicy Fruit. Christ, my breath was awful. I handed Stana one. "I think he was trying to help her."

"When did he ever help you?"

"People change."

There was a long pause. The clock on the coffee table stuttered and ticked. "I guess so." Her eyes were wet. "But this case is really about you, your relationship with him."

"We're not talking about me." A knife's edge slid over my words.

"This whole case is about you."

"It's about finding my father's killer—"

"It's about you—"

I said nothing, breathing in, out. *Breathe. In. Breathe. Out.* The clock stuttered and ticked again. "Maybe it was *his chance* at redemption." I smiled my lopsided leer and she knew the double meaning to my words, that I was talking about us, my last case, and how Stana made amends for the wrongs of the prior one. "You believe in redemption, right?"

"Yeah." She still couldn't look at me. "Yeah. I guess so." She played with the edge of her hat. It looked like a giant steering wheel in her hands.

"We've got to find this girl." Maybe she knew what was going down with this so-called mass and hid and got away. Maybe she was responsible, indirectly, for what went down with my dad. Whatever the case, what did she know that cost my father his life?

"The mass?"

"Maybe. I'm just thinking out loud."

Stana figured we should check back at Becker's, the pizza place next door, and see if anyone had any leads about the girl and Dad. Show the photo. I didn't have that last night.

I stretched my neck. Shit it was stiff. I adjusted the side holster to my belt. "Yeah." My lower lip trembled and pain returned to my eyes. "Good idea." Suddenly my mouth was full of tears. *Everything was making me cry. I wasn't sure I was really fit to be doing this. Avenging the father shit. Leave that to mopes like Hamlet.* "I wish the scrapbook were real."

STANA LIT A PARLIAMENT as we approached Becker's, dead leaves crinkling under our steps, and exhaled sharply. There was a guy standing out front in a long green jacket. On his head was a beanie cap with a propeller, across his eyes, aviator glasses from the First World War. He was the kind of cat if you smiled at him he'd start talking to you, so I didn't smile.

That didn't stop him from talking.

Under the glasses: his eyes appeared dipped in honey.

"Do you believe in giving up everything for heaven's pearl?" His breath, despite the ragged clothes, was Listerine fresh. On his long-tattered jacket were bumper-sticker placards and buttons of various US presidential hopefuls, creating a walking billboard of "I Like Ike" and "Ban the bomb" sentiments. My favorite: a large red button, the size of a plate, with a line drawing of Emma Goldman that said: "If I can't Dance, I don't Want to be in Your Revolution."

This cat was some kind of religious hipster.

"I believe in getting another donut," I said. "Maybe a coffee. Black."

I can be such a smart-ass.

He was not waylaid by my words. Instead, he staggered my steps by humming a tune, plaintive, that startled me with its raw sadness. The song wasn't pretty, but its minor key held Stana and I in its sway and carried us to some quiet place of dissonance. The gaps between the notes were long, as the song's sadness crawled into our skins with its desperate desire to scream. It didn't feel holy, holy, holy the way a hymn should or a poem by Allen Ginsberg. Instead, something was slant about it.

Then he stepped sideways, slightly blocking my way to the store, arms raised scarecrow style.

He was no longer humming.

"The pearl is the way."

Poor Gus. I could see why he'd been calling the cops on this cat. He was hurting biz.

The fella un-scarecrowed his arms, dropping them to his pockets, and hauled pamphlets with the image of a bright sun glowing against the steeple of a church, The People's Way to Christ. I wasn't sure if that was the name of the church or the pamphlet's clarion call, a manifesto on how to live one's life in accordance with letting go.

He smiled. His teeth were straight and a thin mustache dotted his upper lip. The amber lenses to his goggles sealed his eyes tight to his face, making him look like a man walking in a desert sun, and the pockets of his green coat were ballooning with even more pamphlets, folded over like thin newspapers. Thousands of them.

His eyes, I couldn't tell because of the amber lenses, appeared brown. His nose, a bit pulpy.

And then he started talking as if nothing could stop him, as if his very words would change our lives, now, today.

There's this story, see, of this man, and he wanted a pearl, it was for sale, at a market, and the man, a rich man, offered a fair price for the pearl, but the merchant said no, that's not enough. So, the man doubled the offer. No. No sale.

Stana huffed on her cigarette and gave me a look suggesting that she was getting fucking cold. Her gloves were wafer thin.

So, this fella, he goes home, see, and he tosses and turns all night and he can't sleep. He wants that pearl, you know?

"Yeah. We call that addiction," I said.

"Or being horny."

Stana's a smart-ass too.

He smiled awkwardly, pushed back his beanie cap, the propeller slightly turning. "I don't like the man in there. Horny. I don't like a lot of people. People who make fun of other people. Listen in and mock—"

Where was this coming from?

He paused, aware that he had gone away for a few seconds, and smiled awkwardly. "Where was I?"

"Fella going home, tossing and turning. Pearls," Stana said.

"Right." *So, the guy, get this, sells everything, his home, his possessions, all of it, to get the pearl—*

"I'm not giving up my jazz records—"

The pearl is the kingdom. The merchant is Jesus or God. In Matthew *19—*

"It's actually Matthew 13: 45–46." Stana smiled. "I was a Catholic girl. Holy Communion and all that."

"That's right, that's right. I don't know how I got them mixed up. Matthew 13:45–46. Very good. Now, Matthew 19, however, has the best advice, 'Sell what you have and give to the poor and you'll have your treasure in heaven'—"

Two shots, underwater firecrackers, pock-pocked the early morning light. I pushed the guy and his pamphlets aside, told him to take cover, and unholstered my .38. Crouched, and waited for the shooter to hit the street.

Seconds.

The sound of a bus on a distant street.

The smell of coffee.

Nothing else.

"There's a back door," the guy with the beanie said. "A back door."

"Fuck. Jesus Christ."

I apologized to him for taking the Lord's name in vain and he took that as a sure indication that I needed a pamphlet. The People's Way to Christ. The outfit was located on McGowan.

"Thanks."

What else do you say to someone who's that earnest?

I ran along cyclone fencing, down the alleyway, kicking up curled dead leaves, heard a rush and pound of footsteps, a rattle of bumped-up against trash can lids, but saw no one. I ran and ran and ran. He must have climbed behind Becker's and cut through someone's yard.

There were a lot of yards. Seven I could see.

I threw my hands on my hips and breathed.

The back door to the store was still open.

I was afraid of what I'd find.

Stana was already shadowed over the corpse, calling the police.

Sure enough, it was our friend from last night. Gus. Two bullet holes in the back of his head. Brain matter, bone, and remnants of an ear splashed across his lower shelving and the cash register.

Sal Lambertino was on his way.

I asked Stana for a cigarette and we waited.

Our friend had left with Heaven's pearls.

Sal thought the entry wound and accompanying blood splatter indicated a heavy gun like a .45 at close range. "Bullets probably cut. Dum-dum style. Makes a mess."

I nodded.

The morning light, even for 7:30 a.m., felt like the liminal space of dusty twilight, between night and day, gray with little black scratches in the edges of sky like worn-down car tires.

"Dum-dum bullets, huh? Can I quote you on that," shouted Franklin W. Whitfield II, his blue blazer crinkled at the bottom and a scratch from a razor marking his upper lip. His aquiline nose was straight and his blue eyes intense bits of cobalt. He pushed his way through the crowd, pen poised like a microphone. There was a thumbnail of shaving cream in his left ear.

"What are you doing here, Deuces?" Sal said.

There were two other *Toronto Telegram* reporters on the

scene. No newspaper had three there. *What was he doing here?* Trying to make a name for himself, to be something more than just Deuces.

Deuces. That cracked me up.

"The name's Whitfield the Second, not Deuces, Chief. Police radio. Got one in my car." His father, he boasted, could afford it.

Deuces and his father. I bet they have skeet shooting in his backyard before tea at three. They're pushy people; they don't wait till four.

Yesterday, while we were at the Bluffs, Stana filled me in on Franklin's backstory: he wasn't a star columnist, but what the biz called a stringer, one of those extra staffers the *Telegram* carries so they could fill in wherever the press needed them, and Franklin, apparently this morning, aggressively pursued this story, wanting them to need them, to notice him. "Out on another case, Fuller?" He smiled cryptically. "No Red 45 on this one, I hope. People eating each other. Right out of *EC Comics*." He laughed. "Aren't you supposed to be back in Montreal?"

Before I could say a thing, Sal was between us, his shoulders leaning forward, a vein under his left eye throbbing slightly. "His father was just killed. Give him a break." Sal's voice was barbwire.

"Yeah give Hays a break," said a burly guy in a big wool jacket and garden gloves with holes in the thumbs. A twisted baseball cap perched to the left of his heavy head and flour dotted the bill like a cluster of constellations.

I thought I saw Orion.

Definitely, Taurus the bull.

"Thanks, pal." I shook his hand.

"Tony De Luca. I run the pizza joint. Next door."

"Hayden Fuller, hockey player."

"I know who you are. 107 goals as a Leaf." His head dipped, almost preparing to have himself knighted for his hockey knowledge. "You played great last night, you bum. Why the Leafs let you go?"

"Because they're assholes." Stana's shoulders lifted slightly, crowding her face.

"Oh, I like her." He pointed at Stana. "They are assholes. Hope Smith and Bullard wind up in the big house." He had no idea, listening to the game on radio last night what I'd done on the ice during the three-star festivities to cause such a commotion. Radio play-by-play man McClelland Stuart didn't describe my lobbed hand grenade in the most lucid light. Instead, he referred to the toss as obscene dumb-show pyrotechnics.

"*Dumb-show*, he said that?"

"Yeah." De Luca nodded and spit into the street. "He did." He shrugged. "I think he should just stick to 'he shoots, he scores.'"

Stuart's legendary call.

"Dumb-show was about right," Franklin offered, his hands dancing spider webs. "I thought it was obscene and about what I'd expect from a guy who should still be in the American Hockey League."

It had been a hard couple of days. Dad dead. I still needed to make burial arrangements. And now this crack—

I shoved Deuces.

Franklin staggered and balanced himself against a trash can. A slight smile crossed his mouth. "You see that, Lambertino."

"Yeah. Wind's picking up. Watch your step."

"Don't push your luck, Fuller. I'm not a bunch of lame French terrorists."

I adjusted my porkpie, pulling it down tighter across my forehead and grabbed a cigarette from Stana's deck, lit it, and sharply exhaled.

The so-called terrorist thing was my last case, the one that got me reinstated into the NHL. "They weren't terrorists. They were just thieves posing as terrorists. A dumb-show, if you will."

"Funny," he sneered.

A spot of dried shaving cream was on one of the lapels. "They wanted to ruin Expo," he reminded me. "They were terrorists."

That was the copy presented in the fine pages of the *Telegram*: "Libre Quebec Anarchists" in size 36 font. I wondered if Franklin had ghost written some of that shit.

"You got your bearings, Deuces?" Sal asked. "The wind just died down so you should be okay. Hold tight to the trash can if you need to."

Sal was in rare form.

Anyway, Toronto's Top Cop summarized the initial findings: looks like robbery; $77 taken from the cash register; dum-dum bullets, so whoever did the shooting was probably angry; initial dusting indicates the likelihood of two perps, one gun; found a bloody shoe print, size nine, at the foot of the cash register; all the beef jerky was gone.

"Beef jerky?"

"Who eats that much beef jerky?" Tony twisted his ball cap back in place.

"Yeah. Dead over $77 and beef jerky," Sal said.

"Sounds like kids." Franklin wrote hurriedly. "*Beef jerky*? You think it has anything to do with the Fuller killing? That happened just a block away."

"No comment."

"That means yes."

"No comment means no comment, Deuces."

"Don't call me Deuces."

"How about shithead? You like that better?"

Sal was no Shakespeare, but he sure knew how to turn a phrase. American Hockey League, he mumbled.

"Look, there was over $40 in my dad's wallet that was still there when they found the body. He wasn't robbed, motherfucker."

"Okay, okay."

He took more notes.

The beef jerky angle sure was an odd quirky detail and I got to wondering if it were but a false lead, something to distract the cops from a genuine hit that took place. Gus may have been targeted but for what? He seemed like an okay fella. Was he connected to my father? The missing girl? I took another drag. Exhaled.

"When the fuck did you start smoking?" Sal's eyes were gray ashes.

"Yesterday." I pushed back my porkpie.

Franklin turned to Sal and pointed in my direction. "Is his license still valid?"

"Can't believe you're playing for the Habs." De Luca sighed at the unreality of it all, the instability of a hockey life. You were always one of my favorite players, he said. "Shit, you look just like your dad."

"Yeah." *I get that a lot. I hate hearing it. I was now looking at my shoes. Still needed that shine and a new set of laces.*

"You didn't answer my question, Sal."

"What's that, Deuces?"

"About his license."

I still have my office on Yonge and Bloor, and Sal informed Deuces that my credentials were valid up through the end of December.

"I somehow think it's tied into the Fuller kill." He returned to writing more notes. They looked like the wheels of trucks.

Additional bystanders crowded around, staring solemnly at police tape. They wore mufflers, heavy coats, gloves, and expressions of disbelief. Gus was well-liked.

"What about this guy with the goggles and pamphlets?" Franklin asked. "I been hearing talk about some guy with goggles and pamphlets. A real nutter."

"What about him?" Sal was growing impatient, his right eyebrow arching like the back of a cat on a midnight fence. No one would ever call Sal Mr. Sociable.

"Suspicious character. He'd been chased off a few times—I

hear."

"Harmless, Franklin. Harmless."

"Your Dad, every Tuesday ordered a pizza. Pepperoni and black olives. And not those canned olives you get at Dominion's. Kalamata. Well, the last two Tuesdays it was half and half. Half pepperoni and Kalamata olives and half pineapple and green olives." And, Tony said—

I didn't hear what he went on to say, my hands shoved deep in pockets, mind wandering to a tenth birthday, and Dad tossing pizza slices off the edges of my face, the sticky cheese burning, because I forgot to put his damn twelve-pack of Molson's in the fridge. Nobody wants warm beer at a birthday party. *Christ, don't you know anything?*

Stana bobby-pinned her hat in place with a left hand. Yellow police tape stretched across the store's plate glass on the accompanying wind. "Gus didn't think this guy was so harmless—"

"I told you," Deuces said. "Follow up on this guy, Lambertino. He might be the key to it all."

"Goggles? Beanie cap?" De Luca asked.

I nodded. "Yeah."

"Always wears a long green jacket stuffed with pamphlets for The People's Way to Christ?"

"That's him."

"Hangs around my storefront, too, days, wanting free slices of pizza. I often gave him one so he'd go away and quit pushing his pamphlets."

Sal smiled. "We had to run him off a couple of times last week." He shook his head. "Earnest but not very bright."

"I'm not so sure about that, Sal. The way he quoted scripture and created a possible diversion. What if he was the lookout to the killing or something?"

"Lookout? The only thing you need to look out for with him is that he gets his Bible verses right," Sal said. "He thought the Beatitudes were in *Acts*. They're in Matthew."

Stana laughed, recalling our Matthew 13 versus 19 discussions, then she tapped her lower lip once. "What's this about pizza?" She moved toward Tony, pulling him aside.

"Half and half."

"As in, for two different people—" Her eyes narrowed.

"I guess so."

"You ever see him with anyone." She flashed the photograph of Ellen. "This girl?"

"No."

"Who's she?" Deuces crowding between them, pen filling his notebook with wobbly circles, trucks in the margins. They really were trucks and umbrellas and circles with dots in their centers. "Indian chick, huh?"

"Yeah. An Indian chick." Stana's words dripped with freezing rain.

"Routine police matter," Sal said.

"Never seen her." Tony removed his cap and went on about what a regular riot my father was, always making with the jokes. "Hell, after Hayden got sent to the minors, your father quit rooting for the Leafs. Said they were a bunch of bums."

"I didn't know that—"

"And when you signed with Montreal he became a Habs fan. Every Tuesday he came to the pizza parlor wearing a Habs toque."

I didn't see it in his home on Gradwell. "A Habs toque?"

"Yeah. Oh, there's the truck, pulling up back. Got to go."

The truck was one of those big green boxy things often packed with furniture.

Tony shook hands again and re-iterated how much he missed my tight, checking, defensive game. Hell, your dad was really looking forward to seeing you on Tuesday. That's all he could talk about. "How you were going to kick some Leafs ass." He smiled, waved at the truck driver, telling him he'd be released from the police soon. "And don't get me started on what he thought of Smith and Bullard, the club owners, a couple of assholes. Excuse my language. That's what he said. A couple of king-size assholes."

That sounds like my dad. He had a way with words.

I thanked De Luca again, and then he was talking to some guy with a clipboard and a handcart loaded down with crates of canned sauces and packaged cheeses.

"What next?" Franklin rubbed his hands, the pen behind his ear, like a kid playing at being a reporter. "Track down this beanie-cap guy?"

"Beat it," the three of us yelled, and he did.

The wind picked up, the police tape stretched tighter.

Sal rubbed at the edges of his Hemingway beard, the left side of his face a little ragged. I wondered if he'd just woken up when he got this call about Gus.

"What can you tell us about this church?" Stana readjusted her hat with an additional bobby pin.

"Not much." The building was just a few blocks down, next to a giant Army Surplus store. In the 1930s, the church was a dance hall known as the Neon Park Ballroom. "Held all sorts of soirees, dance marathons, mainly." He smiled. "It was always lit in oranges and greens, reds and blues, and was known as a great place to make out because of the lighting. It was some kind of dream world."

"A neon kiss, huh?"

"I guess so."

"And then by the 1950s it was passé, an empty Emporium. It re-opened in the early 1960s as a church."

He shrugged. Seemed they had a whole compound behind the church, little cottages or log cabins, of twelve or thirteen families, loyal to the church's principles. "People who gave up all to become part of the family."

A cult? Goggles was offbeat, to say the least, his humming edgy, haunting, a sort of plaintive hymn in a minor key that made the hairs on my arms bend back. His singing wasn't at all faithful, almost profane, as if he were one of the damned.

Stana showed Sal the photo of Ellen so that he could take a closer look.

"Where did you get this?"

I told him about the switch plate.

He bent at the waist, laughing. There was a heist case he was involved in years ago that hinged on putting together pieces of a cut-up photograph, a treasure chest if you will. One key piece of that map Sal found inside a floor lamp, hidden under a light bulb.

"That's pretty cool."

"I thought so." It was his first breakthrough as a detective. His first big success. He put all the missing photographs together. Found the treasure buried by the Gardiner Expressway. "You think this girl is connected to your dad's killing?"

"Some way. Yeah. At least that's what we want to know."

And then I told him about the life-size portrait of a blond Jesus. And the books. And soda pop.

"She was with him, we think," Stana said. "And she got out or got taken."

"Kidnapping, huh?"

"Maybe."

"I hope she got out," Sal said. Métis girl. He remembered the story. Ran away from her white mother. "Now there was a piece of work." Sal had talked to foster Mom on the phone. "Thought the girl had gone to the devil. If she said that once she said it a thousand times, 'Gone to the devil.' Couldn't see her own goddamn sins."

"Amen to that," Stana said.

Brother Durgana repeatedly called us brother and sister, even though I'm a Jew and Stana was raised Catholic, and I have no idea and I wasn't about to ask, figuring I might be in for a two-hundred-page sequel to the Sermon on the Mount, as to just what kind of denomination The People's Way to Christ really were. But Brother Durgana didn't seem to mind our lack of attention to such matters. He was giving us a guided tour of the church's interior, regardless. The offices had sixteen-foot-high ceilings and the main sanctuary looked like the inside of a prohibition speakeasy: red brick walls, heavy cedar wood beams, and hexagonal lamps attached here and there.

Close by each of the lamps were mounted cameras, closed-circuit security. The cameras were gray, the size of cigar boxes, and pivoted slightly when we moved. I wasn't sure why the church needed so much security, but I counted at least twelve or thirteen of them in the rooms we passed through.

But the oddest detail: instead of stained-glass windows, or any windows, The People's Way to Christ was full of neon kitsch: blue watery cherubims and red, wet angels and yellow ascension light above and dark blue burning pentagrams below. A red-haired Christ held aloft his heart on one of the walls, smiling, as a green Thomas poked a finger in his side. Across the way, a yellow Jesus was talking to a bunch of orange and green children, sitting within waving fields of grass. Orange. Grass.

There were no windows, no natural light.

Just neon light. And it glowed brightly.

And cameras. And they pivoted, stiffly.

Durgana, hair curly black and wet, full of holy oil, incense, and the smell of fried eggs.

I was getting hungry. I might even eat some peameal bacon.

Besides fried eggs, the sanctuary smelled of mold and fresh flowers.

Kneeling in the sanctuary before an empty cross, an ornate lectern, and a large curtain scrawled with obscure Latin: "Amissum quod nescitur non amittitur," were thirteen or so men and women, bent over, hands gently slapped against the floor. Ten others were standing about, quietly carrying a cross above their heads, moving in half-circles, forward and backward. Save for our whispers, there wasn't a sound. And nobody was looking at anyone, just quietly centering, eyes opened or closed, thoughts inward. Even from our distance of half a football field away, it was clear that beneath their uniformed clothing they weren't wearing underthings. I saw shadows of pubic hair, curves of breasts, dangles of johnsons. The church's followers were gussied up in low-rent hospital gowns.

They even had the requisite loose strings in back that barely kept a gown in place.

Brother Durgana caught my look. "We believe in order to get closer to God, one must free oneself, be in a natural state of grace to feel the presence of God everywhere."

I nodded.

Durgana was wearing a three-piece suit.

And had feasted on fried eggs.

His followers were fasting. No food until noon. It was 10:15.

I guess it was good to be the king.

"I assure you," he whispered, his voice barely audible. "We don't dress this way all the time. Just during three hours of devotions, meditations, in the morning."

I wanted coffee. And a donut. "And you walk around like that too? In transparent robes? For devotions?"

He smiled, his teeth a little too large for his mouth. His eyes black. "Yes. The body is a temple. I'm not ashamed of my body."

"Sure."

I was. Ashamed. I always had been. Hockey gave me some feeling of power over my body's imperfections, its failures to protect me, its moments of betrayal when I didn't want it to respond the ways it did. With my father.

"How many followers are there?" Stana asked as he ushered us out of the quiet room into a lobby covered with brutal neon depictions of biblical trauma: the red severed head of John the Baptist held aloft; the fall of a blue Sodom and Gomorrah; green unbelievers and infidels drowning in the dark red of Noah's flood; a yellow David standing over a green Goliath, a blue foot on his head; a black green and blue plague of locusts, faces covered with boils.

Again, there were no windows. Just red brick, the faint smell of mold, and a sweet, flowery fragrance.

Two cameras, positioned in opposite corners of the room, tracked me.

I waved at one of them. "I can get you tickets to the game in Detroit, Friday night. Interested?"

The camera shifted left and stilled.

"If you don't mind me asking, Brother Durgana, how do you pay for all this?"

Stana was always direct.

The neon art alone, although no Roy Lichtenstein, wasn't cheap.

And the architecture, the sixteen-foot-high ceilings. This place was at one-time a huge fucking music hall. The Neon Park Ballroom. "That's what is was called back then—"

"Well, we're now a church." He blessed himself or maybe he was flashing me signals from third base, asking me to lay down a bunt.

I had a headache right now and I dry swallowed some aspirins.

Stana gave me a worried look.

"Pulford," I mumbled.

Brother Durgana held up a sharp hand like a flag. "We have fifteen committed families, totaling thirty-three members. And we have roughly 70–85 folks who attend regularly who have yet to transition—"

He played with his left ear, in the crease by the lobe. I wondered if he had a bug bite, but it was November.

"Transition?" Stana was tapping her lower lip as she took notes.

"To total commitment. Matthew 19:26. 'With God, all things are possible.'" But in order to seize upon the possibilities one must give up everything.

"And the Latin? On the curtain? 'The Loss that is not known is no loss at all.'"

"Yes." He smiled at Stana, his upper lip quivering slightly. "Very good."

"I'm a retired Catholic."

"Retired?"

She sheepishly shrugged. "Yeah. Retired." Stana considered herself a spiritual person, a believer; she just didn't believe in all of the church dictates (anti-abortion, anti-divorce) or in a Pope decoding God's word for her. "I don't need a man telling me how to think."

Durgana raised a skeptical eyebrow.

The Latin phrase was their mantra, their manifesto. One has to have lived a certain life to surrender from that life, surrender from pleasure. "In there is real power. To accept simplicity."

"The pearl. Heaven, huh?" I smiled, the pain behind my eyes lessening.

"Yes."

I told him about the guy with the goggles, the green coat, beanie, and all the buttons, including "I Like Ike" and Emma Goldman's positive spin on dance and revolution. The latter were sentiments I can get behind.

"Brother Thompson—"

"Where is Brother Thompson?"

"Working the Yonge and St. Clair area today."

Stana pulled out Ellen's photograph from her milk-crate of a purse. "Ellen Reynolds. Recognize her. A follower?"

He tilted his head slightly right and studied the photograph as if an important quiz were to follow. He raised a different skeptical eyebrow, like he was holding back from saying something he might regret.

From the neon sanctuary, a rumbling chant filled the spaces between us. It began in dissonance and then built into a breathy hum, the chant not so much filled with words but notes, a song, like the one Brother Thompson was humming when we first came upon him. And as quickly as the rush of sounds made sense they became dissonant once again.

"What's that?" I asked. "That song?"

A lament, Brother Durgana said, massaging at his ear once again, in honor of our Latin mantra, a sad regret of a way of life that's no more, and the uncertainties about the new adventure to begin. In order to begin anew, one must acknowledge with some honesty the sadness of what is lost: lust, gluttony, envy. With his mantra on lamentations, I drifted to tyke hockey, first game, seven goals, and Coach giving me a pair of tickets to a Leafs game. Dad and I went, and it was on me, me, and it felt good to have that kind of control. This was just before Mom died. We drank Cokes, ate popcorn, and Dad didn't yell at me, not once. The Leafs won the game 3–1, Apps a goal and an assist, and afterwards we held hands walking out of Maple Leaf Gardens. Dad smelled of Old Spice and Rothmans. It was probably the best moment of my childhood.

The seven deadly sins, Durgana said, the wants that are like obesity to our bodies, unhealthy appetites that we crave but know we must reject in order to exist in a true state of oneness.

"And this oneness—what is that exactly?"

"Peace. Contentment. It is an experience that gives you stillness, a feeling of wonder and joy free of the stimulant derived from drugs and sex."

It was a natural, spiritual stimulant. Meditation contains the sparkle of life. With prolonged meditation, he had even found sex null and void. "Oh, I still think about sex, Brother Fuller, Sister Younger, but I don't crave it. Need it. I've moved beyond it."

"And that's a good thing?" Stana wasn't buying it.

His black eyes glowed with some kind of half-life of truth I couldn't quite get a handle on. "It makes life simpler. I have a much simpler life."

He smiled. It was a good look, a face on an election billboard. But there was something about that smile, that he could take it away as quickly as he granted it. "You've both been in love. With each other. How's that worked out for you?"

How did he know that?

Stana and I said nothing, looking at each other, and then the walls and neon boils and orange grass filled my thoughts.

"Life is so much simpler without the trappings of romantic love."

Simpler? Brooks Brothers suits? Diamonds on his fingers? And attaining oneness. That seems simple enough. "This oneness? Some kind of nirvana?" I asked.

"Well, that's a little too mystical for us—"

I bit my upper lip, hard, to keep from bending over at the waist and cracking up.

Stana couldn't help herself. She *was* bent over, laughing through fingers, cracking up. "I'm sorry. It just seems so—so—"

"Absurd?"

"Yes. Frankly." She shrugged. "Jesus was divine but he was also a man. I'm sure he had sex."

"I see why you left the Catholic church." He tented his fingers together. "Biblically speaking, there's no proof that Christ had sex—"

"Can we at least agree he masturbated?"

What would the Pope say to that?

By contrast, Brother Durgana said nothing, lips tightening. His skeptical eyebrows were now incredulous.

"Midnight mass. 11/14/65? Mean anything to you?" Stana leaned forward slightly, angry freckles returning to her eyes.

"Midnight mass. We're not Catholic. Mass?" He tented his fingers, three, four, five times, rubbed at his ear. "Friday, huh?" It's not even Christmas, he said. There are no other midnight masses that he knew of.

I told him about the envelope I had found in dad's wall: the photograph of Ellen Reynolds and the brief note. "Did you know Ellen? Ellen Reynolds?"

I pointed at the photograph that Stana was now holding.

He played at his ear once again, smiled limply. "I must have slept on the wrong side of the pillow last night." He gently tugged at his ear once more.

"Sure."

"Wasn't she a prostitute or something? Got mixed up in some bath houses or sleazy shoe-shine parlors on Charles Street?"

"That's one story." Stana's eyes were full of flames. "She's the kind of girl Christ would have sought out, spoken to, worked with."

"Point taken." He smiled. "We get those types here, too, but—"

Those types?

He didn't recognize the girl in the photograph. Or his own lack of Christian charity.

The bloody head of John the Baptist appeared to be peaking over my shoulder so I shifted a few feet to my left. Now I had the deadly plagues enveloping me, my face full of boils. "She was never one of your disciples?"

"*Followers.* No. She wasn't." He held the photo closely. Just looking at her eyes, he said, he could see it. The lack of contentment, the inability to find personal solace. "She is guided by pleasure."

"How can you tell that just by her eyes?" A line formed between Stana's eyebrows, and her shoulders narrowed in on herself. "Come on."

"I read faces. You two are skeptical." He pointed at me, traced the curve of an ear. "You are troubled. Something in your past haunts you and you seek answers. But first you must forgive yourself."

I said nothing.

"You—" He looked at Stana. "Carry guilt and anger in your shoulders. There's much injustice in the world you want to fix, but first you must fix your relationship with him. Guilt is in your eyes."

Stana now said nothing.

The girl might have arrived one time, weeks ago, sat in the back, but no, not a regular, and he knew nothing of her personal life.

Only what he saw in her eyes.

The chant-sing hum buzzed around us with a discordant beat that felt slightly behind the 3/4 rhythm. Or maybe it was ahead of the beat. Either way, no one was on the same musical page.

"What's Mr. Thompson's connection—how long's he been here, how—?"

"Two months." He held up both hands, rubbed them together. "He took to our practices right away. He's an excellent singer. And a respected member of our congregation."

Thompson had no earthly possessions to give; he was homeless before arriving, so he pays his way by sweeping floors and dusting the sanctuary and laundering the spiritual robes.

Spiritual robes. Threadbare sheets.

"When he returns I want to talk to him," I said.

"We can arrange that."

"Do."

Stana gave him the number at *The Toronto Telegram.*

"You've never seen this girl?"

"No." He shrugged absently.

"Her looks are striking—you'd remember—"

"We've had Cree, Ojibway tribe members drop by—drop in—and decide we're not for them. She might have dropped by—I don't—" He shrugged again.

"My father ever visit here?"

"What?" He laughed. "No. Your father strikes me as a man who saw his life as too practical for simplicity."

What did he mean by that? His words were full of riddles. It felt like a crack. "You knew my father? He was here?"

"I can read auras. I don't need to be in the presence of someone to know them. Through you, I know him." Auras, he said, were like books. If Steinbeck's *Grapes of Wrath* was influenced by the poetry of Walt Whitman, then while reading Steinbeck you were also "reading" Whitman. In reading my aura he could read my father's.

"Auras huh?" I pointed at all the boils and the neon surrounding us, a circle of menace. "Cute pictures."

John the Baptist's severed head was still staring me down.

And David wasn't wearing sandals. I think one of the laces on his blue sneakers was untied. PF Flyers. Seriously. PF fucking Flyers, his footwear of choice.

"A vengeful God. Vengeance is mine?"

"Darkness allows for the utterance of a simpler life." He smiled again. "Life is dialectics. There is no Jew without the anti-Semite. There can be no good without the accompanying evil. We must know the darkness to know the light."

"Sure." That's a lot of knowing. I smiled. "Do you know where I can get a donut?"

AFTER AN EARLY LUNCH of a hot open-faced beef sandwich at one of the diners along McGowan, Stana lit a cigarette and said she was going to check into Durgana's background. How does he run his operation? Who's backing him?

"His followers give generously just to hear him speak."

"Uh-huh," she said.

That cracked me up. "And see what you can find out from the folks that live in those little cottages in back of the church." *Quonset Huts to Christ.*

"On it. Already on it." She wrote down some notes on the back of a napkin.

We saw nine or ten of those huts made of some kind of fiberglass, sort of igloo-cubed Quonset huts. Small, cozy, rimmed in a circle so that they all could keep their eyes on each other. Perched high on two of the streetlights overlooking the compound were mounted cameras. They followed us as we moved about.

"Sure." She picked a strand of tobacco off her lower lip. "They'll be reticent, but I'll come up with an angle."

"Future follower—" I offered.

"*Followers.* I'm going to pretend you're my husband."

"I like that."

"Me too."

We both looked at our plates, listening for sounds round us.

A short-order cook barked back the waitress's orders, ham and rye on dark, hold mustard, as silverware clattered against hard plates, and hamburgers spit on an open grill. The diner was a mass of black countertops, chrome, and coffee-colored walls. The smell of grease and look of 1950s–style waitresses, curvy women with short sassy hair and bright lipstick, floated around us. "The sandwich was a good choice." I didn't know what else to say. *I wanted her, Stana. I want you.* Hot open-faced sandwiches were the diner's specialty since 1933.

"Not now." She patted my hand and blushed slightly.

"I said *that* out loud?"

"Yes."

"Sorry." Christ. All that talk of nirvana and Durgana's notions of simplicity were putting other ideas in my head. And all the damn concussions from hockey. I have no internal censor sometimes.

"Don't worry, I'm not moving *beyond* sex." She played with a huge hoop earring.

I laughed.

"What did you make of the no-window look? There were none in the sanctuary."

"Or lobby," I said.

"Creepy."

"I think they want to keep the distractions of the outside world outside, to attain oneness within."

"Or to keep us outsiders from seeing what the brothers and sisters are up to."

"Yeah." *Like a midnight mass in two days?*

"I'm not giving up on this 11/14 angle either. I'm going to ask the folks in ice cubes about it." She patted my hand and took a short drag. "This afternoon."

The shoes of one of the waitresses squawked across the freshly waxed tile, breaking the romantic kismet between us. And the short-order cook in back was now singing Sinatra.

"I mean," she said, "the place used to have windows but now they're bricked up. The red bricks in the former windows were a brighter color than the red bricks of the original walls."

"You'd make a good detective."

The short-order cook wanted to play among the stars.

After the interviews with the ice-cube people, Stana planned to follow Brother Durgana. Tail job.

"That's dangerous."

"I'll be careful."

"Take my .45." I had extra heat in the glove box of my Ford Galaxie.

"I don't have a permit." She played with the other earring and shook her head, bemused. "I don't trust the guy. A total phony. He was wearing a Brooks Brothers suit." She exhaled sharply off her cigarette and blew a wisp of auburn out of her eyes.

"I noticed."

"Did you also notice the pentagram in one of the neon tableaux?"

"Yes."

More dishes clattered and one of the waitresses laughed at the sexual overtures of a customer who said she should be on television or on a billboard or on the couch in his living room, wearing nothing but his necktie.

Whatever.

"I bet Brother Durgana's got a swimming pool, a circular bed, and throws swinging parties."

That sounded more like Bullard and Smith, the yacht-club set that owned the Leafs. Christ, Bullard used to pour potato chips over naked women, his idea of foreplay fun. And Smith had got his kicks filming people through a two-way mirror at Maple Leaf Gardens parties: lap dances and blow jobs. Playboy set. Gambling. Stuff he'd be up on trial for in less than sixty days. Brother Durgana was much more subdued than those cats, or so it seemed.

From the phone book, Stana had already retrieved Durgana's address, a home on Walmer Road.

Those were old modest houses, I told her, turn of the century, near Sibelius Park, with short postage-stamp lawns and wooden fences. I knew the area. Had a cousin who lived there. "Just be careful."

"I will."

"You got a good book to read?"

She didn't say anything, her fork tapping by the side of the plate. "For a phony, he sure is charismatic."

"Yeah. It's like he looks into you and sees things you don't want revealed."

"Yeah."

And he takes his time before speaking, waiting on the right words. He's like on a time delay, she said, wanting to be precise. "Never shoots from the hip. Very controlled."

"Yeah."

My plan for the afternoon was to go to Silverwood's on Danforth, the company Dad was a milkman for, and check his call sheets and see if he had any upset customers or conflicts that might erupt in violence and murder. It was a long shot, but maybe it would get me another lead. We'd check back with each other later in the afternoon. My place on Houston Crescent. Six-ish. I planned to take a shower, nap, and change my clothes. My mouth still felt like it had a towel in it.

"Sure, sure. Your phone number's still active?"

"Yeah."

"Christ, Hayden. I—I—" Her eyes filled with tears. She did carry guilt in her shoulders and eyes, like Durgana said, guilt over her past, and how I nearly died at the hands of Babe Migano's men, and how Brian "Spinner" Terrien and Lisa Steinmetz did die from their hands. "I didn't want you to get hurt. I didn't think they'd kill them, I just didn't think." And the worst part wasn't the larger guilt of inadvertently being part of the setup, the knockoff, but the bloody aftermath, the guilt of knowing they were dead but not being able to do a damn thing about it.

We'd made a pact of secrecy to protect each other and the Stabulas girls.

A handful of us. Numb about a murder. Bodies buried in Vaughan, Ontario.

Seven months since the killings. It felt like a decade of guilt.

And now there was a gangster, Lenny Cassel, who I tangled with in my last case, roaming the world free with Terrien's face, courtesy of plastic surgery. What ills was he performing with the face and name of another man, a guy, who really, deep down, was decent, a solid hockey player, a man who cared for and loved Lisa? "I think about it all the time. It's something I carry with me too."

She crushed her cigarette in an ashtray, her shoulders trembling.

I think mine were trembling too.

I ARRIVED AT SILVERWOOD'S SHORTY BEFORE 1 P.M. and none of the route drivers or managers were back yet from delivering milk and butter. Try around 2:30, a receptionist told me so I filled my 63 Galaxie with gas and wandered to a local bowling alley, had a plate of eggs and peameal bacon, and bowled three games: 133, 169, and 211. I was too tired to sleep.

And after a 211, I was feeling pretty damn good about myself.

And a little guilty about the bacon.

For the final game, I was rolling a big 16-pound ball, tossing it like a twelve-pounder.

Around 3:00, I met with Dad's boss, Bob Waterman, in Silverwood's garage. Yellow-and-blue trucks were all around us, with logos of bright yellow suns backlighting a pretty, smiling Scandinavian ingénue. Racks of empty bottles and product that didn't sell were offloaded. Bob nearly broke my fingers when we shook hands. He was wiry but had wrists the size of Popeye arms.

Some guys just have to assert their presence through a manly handshake. He was one of those guys.

And he was loud. When he spoke, he leaned back on his heels, his feet jet ailerons, appearing to want to lift off.

"So, what can I do for you?" Bob was a regular company man with his blue Dickies and yellow polo shirt.

"Wanted to ask about my dad, Ira Fuller."

"Ira? A fucking funny guy. Hilarious. Color of the day." He smacked his thighs. "Color of the motherfucking day!"

"Huh?"

Apparently, Dad had these shticks that his fellow workers found totally charming like *color of the day*. "He'd see a beautiful broad, right, and he'd say, blue. Blue is the color of the day. Cause she was wearing a blue dress. For the rest of the day we'd all be saying *blue, color of the day*." He laughed. "He made you feel good. One time, there was this chick with big knockers, I mean they were out to here, wearing a red sweater. But red wasn't the color of the day. No, sir. It was, get this, scarlet. Scarlet. Color of the day. Clever. Witty."

"Uh-huh."

"Because her knockers were so big. Red didn't do her justice.

Scarlet did."

"I see."

"I don't need to tell you, it was a shock when I found him." With the back of a heavy wrist, he wiped away run-off from his nose. "Can't wait for it to snow. Knock out these goddamn allergies." He wiped again.

"Any day now." We had a foot already in Montreal. I carried a shovel in my trunk to avoid getting stuck in grocery store parking lots and half-plowed side streets.

"How can you play for the Habs? You're a Leaf." He punched my arm. Playfully. It hurt.

I shrugged. "How did my dad feel about me playing for the Habs?"

"He loved it. Always rubbing it in when the Habs won and we lost. Go, Habs, Go. He'd just throw it in, in the middle of normal conversations. Just drop it right in. Right there. Like, 'How's the weather, Ira?' 'Oh, it's a bitch. Colder than a witch's tit. Go, Habs, Go!' Shit like that. Funny. He just made you laugh. Him and his Habs toque."

My eyes were raw.

"Wore that damn thing everywhere." His teeth were yellow, hair dry straw.

More small milk trucks arrived, backing into the bays along the walls of the loading dock, placing empties on conveyor belts to be cleaned. Water rushed over the bottles, creating an ongoing white noise.

"It must have been rough, finding my dad like that."

The garage smelled of gasoline and the heavy heat of truck engines driven hard in late fall. The heat in the room was awfully dry. No wonder Bob's hair stood straight up like pixie sticks.

"I'm really sorry for your loss."

I'm not sure how I feel about my loss. Really.

Bob assured me that when he was checking up on my dad, he wasn't trying to be nosy, *checking up on him*, you know, nothing like that, it's just that Ira hadn't reported to work in three days and he was always one of the first guys here to begin his route, 4:30 every day, every morning. "I think he really loved being a milkman."

"Yeah."

"I mean, it's like you're family." People let you into their homes, you see women in their pajamas and nighties, men fighting with their wives, children making a mess in the living room. "It's real. Not like the *Donna Reed Show*."

"That's for sure." When I was waltzing through puberty, Dad often bragged about how some of the women flashed him, just lifted the tops of their long T-shirts so they wouldn't have to pay their bills that week.

Bob suggested we leave the loading dock and talk in his office where it was quieter. On the way, I finally got to the point. I mean hearing about my dad's working relationships was nice and all, but I had a murder to solve and avenge. Could I see Dad's call sheets and was he having any trouble with any customers?

"No. Everyone loved Ira." He lit a cigarette and stood behind his desk, pulling out drawers and handing me four different call sheets. Customers differed depending on day of the week. One McGowan address jumped right out at me like an Agitprop fist in a Soviet poster, The People's Way to Christ.

"Dad delivered to the church?"

No wonder "Brother" Durgana knew how Dad felt about simplicity. Durgana and his goddamn auras, the goddamn phony.

It was a pretty big order. Every Thursday. Dad was found dead on a Tuesday. He'd been dead for three or four days. Saw the People five days before.

"Any trouble with any of them? Anyone call in to complain?"

"At the church?"

"Sure."

"No. No problems."

I wasn't sure how color of the day would go over with that crowd.

"He delivers just to the church or also the families in the ice-cubed Quonset huts behind?"

"Just the church." He pushed at and pulled up his dry hair. It made his head look like a set of drinking straws. "From what I understand they all ate their meals there. In the building." He leaned back, his aileron feet nearly lifting off. "I mean it was a big call. Thirty-five folks or so. Lots of milk." His lips twisted into a thin line. "No buttermilk though. Too much fat." He held up a hand. "I'm just reporting what *they* said. I like buttermilk. Silverwood's buttermilk. *Top*. *Top* of the line."

The guy wasn't wearing blue-and-yellow clothing for nothing.

"Sure." I pushed back my porkpie, wiped the edges of my mouth. His office, unlike the high ceilings to The People's Way to Christ, was low-ceilinged, crowded. If you were over six feet, you walked stooped. File cabinets nudged together in a far wall, a desk organizer was full of invoices, two phones were on the desk, a third off the hook on a filing cabinet, and the near wall was white cork board filled with hooks and round-tagged keys to the various trucks, I assumed.

"Any other problems, with anyone on the route?"

He gently lingered a wrist under his nose. "People took to your dad. He was funny." He pulled on his cigarette, offered me one. I took it. "Well, wait, there was one call. Mary something or other."

I spotted an address on the call sheet directly across from the church, Mary Hale. "Hale?"

I lit up. Exhaled quickly.

"Yeah. That's it. Widow. Saw him give a ride to a girl one day."

The sun kissing his window cut three gold bars across his desk.

"When?" I picked a sliver of tobacco off my lower lip. Everyone I know smokes unfiltered.

"I don't know. A couple of weeks ago. We have a policy. No riders. But you know, good old Ira. Marches to his own drum."

I handed him the photograph. "Is this the girl?"

"How the hell would I know? I didn't give her a ride."

"Did Mary mention what the girl looked like?'

"No. Indian girl, huh? Cute. No, no, the old broad just complained and wondered if we could start carrying margarine." He shrugged. "You know as an alternative to butter? We're a goddamn dairy. We don't do margarine."

"Right. Did Mary say if the girl came out of the church before she got a ride?"

He took another sharp drag. "Real pain-in-the-ass broad. I didn't really follow up on her story, to be honest with you. So, I don't know about the church angle. And I didn't talk to your dad about it. Figured what the fuck, you know? Good old Ira."

"Yeah. Good old Ira."

We quietly smoked for a few seconds. "You know, he did have one flaw, your dad had kind of a big mouth."

"How so?"

Every month the executives would come in and meet with the milkmen, go over their routes, suggest ways to put more business on them, and one Easter they were designing a new kind of pudding, not our usual chocolate but brighter, a vanilla to go with the pastel colors of the holiday, vanilla with bits of sprinkles in it. Ira thought the thing wouldn't sell, it was too girly, no, faggy he said. Too faggy. Anyway, that pissed off the bosses. How the fuck will you ever get promoted if you keep insulting the bosses' ideas, the company's ideas. "Ira just couldn't think like management."

"Uh-huh." I took a drag.

"But the fellas all loved him. He was a regular riot."

Those were the very words Tony De Luca had used. My father, the Jewish Jackie Gleason.

"Check this out—" Bob pointed at the cork board nearest to us. Next to the keys and posted invoices, and lithograph pin-up nude of Diane Webber leaning back in a canvas chair, was a big chunk of posted newsprint hanging crookedly with names, dates, and numbers on it. "You know what that is?"

"No."

"A pool. Like a lottery. A death lottery. Your dad started it. What day would Steve Smith, owner of the Leafs, die? You know he's got bleeding ulcers? The poor fuck." He flashed a mock smile. "We all picked a death date. The closest wins." He wiped at his nose. "So far the pool's up to $112. A riot, I tell you."

"Yeah, real regular."

I DON'T THINK MARY HALE WANTED TO TALK TO ME, but she let me in when I promised her an autograph for her niece and nephew. The latter was a Canadiens fan.

Before I could even open my mouth further, she handed me paper and a Bic pen, the cap chewed down. I scrawled my name and put a #28 under it. "You sure you don't want any extras for holidays or special occasions?"

That didn't lighten the mood. Damn.

She had a pie-shaped face with a crumbled-up crust. Her eyes were tired with crimped crinkles at the corners.

Her house smelled of wet wool and cat litter. Lots of cats. Tortoiseshell mainly. One oddball, a purple cat, Persian she said, rubbed against her polyester slacks as she spoke to me hurriedly in the hall. She didn't offer me a seat or direct me anywhere. We just stood in the hall by three cat litter boxes.

With her efficiency, she should be running General Motors.

Even her patter was efficient. She spoke quickly, with a slight lisp. Yes, she saw the girl come out of the church. Never saw her before or since. Just that day. Wearing a leather jacket and those stockings that look like fencing?

"Cyclone fencing? Fishnet?"

"Yes." Hopped in Ira's milk truck. And he gave her a pint of chocolate milk. "She didn't pay for it. I'm sure of that. And I'm pretty sure he didn't pay for it either." She wagged a finger at me as if I were Ira. "Pilfering is not okay. Where would this country be if everybody pilfered?" The wagging was still going.

The next day, Mary balled Ira out for giving the girl a freebie on the company's dime and a free ride. That's what the TTC is for: buses, streetcars, subways.

"I see."

"I order every Thursday three per cent milk, buttermilk, and chocolate milk. He never gave me anything free." The cat at her legs was still nuzzling, probably hungry. "I like buttermilk pancakes."

"Me too," I said.

"I told Ira, it's unsafe to pick up hitchhikers." She wagged her finger again as if Dad were in this very room, as if he were looking over me like Hamlet's ghost.

"You look a lot like him." She paused, eyes roving over me, up and down, as if she were about to buy a piece of furniture from Leon's. "You sure do."

"I get that a lot." I showed her the photograph of Ellen Reynolds.

We were still standing, my autographs in her left hand.

"Yup. That's the girl." She glanced down at the Persian cat, scuffling her legs, leaving thin slices of hair on her slacks. "I read she ran away from a white Mom. No matter how much we try to do the right things for those people we just mess things up. We should just let them be."

"Or not assume that we know better how to raise their children—"

She nodded.

"You saw her get in his truck?"

"Yes."

I snapped my fingers. "And that was the only time you saw

her, the day she hopped in my dad's truck?"

Her lips moved as I spoke, trying to guess my next word. She had an index finger lifting up her chin, her other arm, with the autographs, pushed across her chest. "Yes."

"But she came *out* of the church?"

"Yes. I told you that. Weren't you listening?"

"Not happening to just stand in front of it but came out of the doors of the church?"

"Yes. Absolutely." She nodded firmly. "With fishnets."

I quickly signed some more autographs for her. "Always good to have them on hand, in case," I said. "Unexpected guests?" I shrugged.

She laughed this time.

That's the way with comedy. Don't give up on a good bit, re-think it, re-tool, re-contextualize, and try again.

"What do you think of margarine?" Her eyes squinted and she leaned closer, almost conspiring in her spirited marketing plans for the company. "I've been trying to get Silverwood's—"

"I prefer maple syrup on my pancakes," I said, smiling. "With blueberries."

"Well, that goes without saying, young man."

"It sure does," I said.

And we both laughed.

STANA WAS PARKED UNDER THE STREET LIGHTS of a donut shop. A box of donuts on the dashboard. She was hunkered down the front seat, a Maple Leafs ball cap shading her eyes.

I tapped on the car window. "Some disguise." I pointed at the cap.

She lowered the window and placed a book next to the box of donuts. *Last Exit to Brooklyn.*

I rubbed my hands together. It was cold.

Across the way, in the Army Surplus store, people were buying up fatigue jackets, commando toques, and black boots. It didn't seem right to me to wear the gear if you haven't served. I guess I'm a little old-fashioned.

"This fella doesn't understand women at all—" She pointed at the book on her dash.

"Then why read it?"

"To understand you." Her words were full of light comic touches, but we all know what Freud says about jokes.

No movement so far on the Durgana front. She called the *Telegram*. At one time he was a broker, worked the floor at the Dow Jones, became a financial adviser, and left the business at thirty-five, three years ago. Other than that, his record: clean.

"Any religious piety in his background?"

"None." She smiled. "So much for the circular bed." He's no playboy. Doesn't mess around. She had asked. The whole afternoon had been rather quiet. Church business, I guess. A woman with a metal cart full of vegetables squeezed through the front door. That's it. "Shit, there's a passage in this here book about giving birth that's just pure horseshit—"

"Anything else?" The inside of her car smelled of cigarettes and the ashtray was full.

The families, those that were available to speak, appeared strange and aloof. And they walked weird she said, little half-steps.

"Half-steps?" I wrote it down in my yellow notebook.

"And two or three of them hummed that same damn song we'd heard in the sanctuary as they now went about their work. If you can call it work. She wasn't sure what they did all day but read scripture, weave baskets, make garments in their spare time, and walk in half-steps. "And get this, no one has a television."

"That's fucking sick."

"But there are surveillance cameras in their living rooms."

"Christ."

"They don't read newspapers, and I didn't see any books.

None. Everyone dresses the same, same kind of canvas clothes. Tops, pants. Hair cut short. Women too." She lit a cigarette. Stared at it. "And nobody smokes."

I reached for a donut and got powdered sugar all over my face. Donuts like Mexican food always add to my fashion statement.

Did they know the girl, Ellen? Had they seen her?

No, nothing, she said. No light in the rooms either, Hayden. Coleman lanterns, candles. Incense. No lights. No radios—

"Coleman lanterns? Army surplus stuff."

"Huh?"

I pointed to the giant store next to the church, red brick, large rectangles of stained glass filled with Canadian flags and Union Jacks.

"Come to think of it, some of them had Sternos in their rooms." She tapped her upper lip. "And one girl was drinking water from an aluminum canteen."

"Check into it."

"I will." She shrugged and tapped a set of fingers along the car's dash. "You know what was creepy? I swear. I felt like the cameras moved as I moved."

"Hmm."

"What the fuck's that mean? I've just finally figured out your uh-huhs and now you're throwing hmm at me."

"Hmm means hmm." I laughed, hands in pants. "It means I'm pondering."

"Well, just don't get ponderous."

That cracked me up.

She looked in the direction of the store. Someone carried out a cumbersome backpack and an oar for a kayak. "They have heating. The insides of those ice-cubes were very hot."

"The simple life, huh?"

"Yeah, but the people I saw, their emotions. Complex." She couldn't get them to say anything about the mass in two days.

Some denied it outright, but others just looked away, as if they couldn't lie to her, but wouldn't commit to a truth either. "There's a mass and it's happening in two days. I'm sure of it."

And that was the extent of her covert ops.

They ran her off.

She took another drag, slowly exhaled.

"Who's they?" For some reason when I ask key questions, I have a habit of pushing back my porkpie for emphasis. Now I had powdered sugar all over the brim of my emphasis. Damn.

"Thompson. Durgana." She shook her head, laughed, grabbed my hat, and dusted it with a forearm. "I mean they were polite about it. Even quoted scripture, but they weren't happy."

And I wasn't happy either. The autopsy report meant Dad would be buried on Saturday, but I had a game that night so the levaya would have to be early that afternoon. Aunt Miriam, my Mom's sister, was handling the details for me and I promised to pay my respects, drop in a few times for shiva over the next few weeks, but I wasn't missing the game in Detroit this Friday or the one in Montreal, Saturday. No way.

She wondered about my priorities, saying little, telling me we all mourn in our own way.

I wasn't sure I wanted to do a eulogy and all, but she said I ought to think about it, a few words might be nice, but she understood. The rabbi would deliver the kaddish.

"Dad wasn't a practicing Jew," I said.

Once a Jew, always a Jew, she said.

I didn't say a word about once a son always a son.

I told Stana all about Miriam and my meetings at Silverwood's and Mary Hale's.

"The girl was there?"

"In fishnets, apparently. Miss Hale mentioned that twice. Fishnets."

"Wow. What does that mean?"

Ellen was a follower, The People's Way To Christ?

Two women came out of the surplus store carrying a tent, the box the size of a large dog house.

"The people there—" She blew wisps of auburn from her eyes. "Hard-scrabble."

"Yes."

She smiled. All of the folks she interviewed struck her as the transient type, the lost, the homeless. "They wouldn't talk about their pasts. I asked. Believe me, I asked." But she didn't think they came from money.

"Then where does the money come from to run such an operation?"

"The surplus store?"

"The surplus store," I said. "Of course. See who backs it."

She'd check with the *Telegram*, their fact-checking staff, and find who owns the lease to both buildings. She also had a lot of the surnames of the church's followers. Check their money trails.

I leaned across the window and kissed her nose.

"What's that for?"

"I don't know."

She opened the car door and pulled me toward her, giving me a kiss that made a dark wing turn inside my stomach. "Maybe later tonight? Your place?" She handed me my dusted-off porkpie. "Sixish?" She smiled, her cigarette dangling. "You'll be done with your nap?"

"Yeah."

"Be careful when you go up against Thompson and Durgana."

"Huh?"

"Thompson's coat. It's carrying more than just pamphlets."

"His coat." I snapped my fingers. "Army surplus. Military issue. So's his aviator goggles—"

"Will you let me finish?"

"Sorry."

When Thompson escorted her from the cubes, his coat bumped up against her hip and she felt the hard edge of a gun, .45 most likely. "Like I said, he's carrying more than just pamphlets in those pockets."

BROTHER DURGANA WASN'T TOO HAPPY to see me. No grin, no talk of oneness, no pithy scripture passages to ruminate over, nothing. He didn't even get up from behind his desk to shake my hand or share any of his food.

I couldn't help but think of Jesus and the fish and the feeding of the 5,000.

Not that I really wanted any of Brother D's food. It was all green, telephone lines of seaweed, and some kind of vegetable I didn't recognize that had holes in it, like you'd find on a bass fiddle.

"Lotus root. Very tasty. Improves brain power."

"Uh-huh," I said. All that so-called simplicity stuff sure wasn't on point in his office: famous paintings centered three of the walls, including a Renoir full of yellow green light and a girl looking away from the sun; from wood beams hung flowers in rust-colored ceramic pots; along the front of the desk clustered white plaster figurines, angels, kids on bicycles, ballerinas, dancers; and covering the floor was an expansive red and black Oriental rug. As was the case in the sanctuary, there were no windows. Only chalky, red brick.

"You lied to me, Durgana. Ellen Reynolds was here."

High above our head twirled a ceiling fan out of a 1940s-film noir.

I hoped he wasn't looking there, but at my blazer as it flashed open, giving him a momentary glimpse of my side-holstered .38.

I pushed down my porkpie and told him all that Mary Hale had spoken.

I left out the fishnets.

He wiped the edges of his mouth and smiled as if he were an ad man for Chrysler. We have a lot of transients, roamers, indigents, who fall into our building and discover our ways aren't their ways. She might have been a one-time guest. I told you she may have been here. We've had a lot of tribal people. His black eyes glimmered. "I see so many troubled, lost souls. I can check the visitor registers if you like."

I got a better idea, I said, check your surveillance tapes. "You got cameras everywhere. See if she's on those tapes." I pointed at the camera directly above me, waved. "I still got those tickets."

"I can't do that." He crossed his hands in front of him. "We only save the tape for a week—"

"Then let me see last week's tapes."

He whistled. It had a lot more bounce than the church's theme song. "Sorry. Privacy matters."

"Privacy matters." My tone was ironic.

I'm not sure he caught it.

"Only if you have a warrant—"

He caught it.

"Stana tells me a different story about your clients. They *all* appear to be former transients."

His ear was bothering him again, only this time it was the right one. He rubbed at the back of it, smiled shyly. "I assure you that is a mere appearance, part of the process of transition, not an ultimate reality. You see, a kind of confusion of the mind sets in, a vacuous expression that eventually fills with its new identities as the transition is completed."

"Bullshit."

"Excuse me?"

I placed my hands on my hips. "What's really going on?" *Were the people drugged? They were so listless, wandering without purpose.*

And the excess heat of the Quonset huts. Incubate their minds, keep them lethargic. Followers, indeed.

"We are a church. Nonprofit." His black eyes barely moved. "I can show you the paperwork."

"I'd rather see the surveillance tapes."

"I told you I may have crossed paths with her. The Reynolds girl. So many people visit our temple, asking for money to pay a water bill. Buy groceries—"

"Uh-huh."

"We have an emergency fund." He played with one of the figurines, a fisherman, getting him re-aligned, in step, with the angels. He didn't remember the Reynolds girl. That's all. "I was wrong." He shrugged.

"Your followers didn't remember her either, but Stana had a strong feeling they were lying. You see, you taught them well, some of the brothers and sisters can't lie at all, and it was their silences that told a different story. How long was Ellen here? Why did she leave? How is my father's murder connected to her and to you and this place? Enough bullshit!"

Brother Thompson, still wearing the long, akimbo green coat with all the buttons, including my main woman Emma, stumbled shoulders first into the room, the propeller in his beanie cap spinning randomly. His right hand gripped an upside-down broom like a cop's truncheon. His goggles were too tight against his face and eyes. The broom's handle was grimy and appeared to be covered with bed sores. "I heard loud voices?"

"Matthew 5:38–40, Brother Thompson. 'If anyone slaps you on the right cheek turn to them the other cheek also.'"

Thompson nodded, tap-tapping his broom handle on the floor, and then turned about in the opposite direction, showing me the other side of his face.

He was a pretty literal cat.

And then he started humming that dirge of longing and the walk of the soulless. The space between the notes was as unnerving as always.

I was feeling nasty, wanting answers, and I became abusive

like in Dr. Cohen's triangle. "She was here, and I'm going to find out what went down. My father was killed. That girl was with him before he died. And if you're involved, *Brother* Durgana, in my father's killing, you're going down," I pointed at the two of them.

Durgana played with his right ear.

Thompson was singing, again, and in mid-aria picked his nose. He didn't seem to mind that I noticed.

"My, my, such a temper. Fiery. Meditation would do wonders for your inner qi."

"My inner what, what the fuck is that?"

"The life force, and yours is spinning in all the wrong directions."

"Thanks. I'll buy a compass." I pushed back my porkpie. "Maybe from that surplus store next door." I turned to Thompson whose dirge-like notes continued to bleat bleat. "Is that where you got that coat?"

"We have an exclusive contract with them," Durgana explained calmly, fingers tenting twice. "We buy all our supplies there. Twenty-five percent discount."

"Uh-huh." I shook my head. "What about swords beaten down into ploughshares?" I figured the simple life would include a peaceful life, not one adorned with products of the war machine.

"I like army clothes," Thompson said absently, his singing and the propeller on his beanie now still.

"Sure. But if you enlist, learn to play taps, buddy. Please. If you sing for those cats they'll kick you out on a medical discharge."

That startled him. Suddenly, he swung the broom at my head and I ducked under it, grabbed the handle, turned right, and twisted him off the stick, toppling him into a book shelf of strange works of mysticism—Aleister Crowley's *The Book of Lies*, Francis Barrett's *The Magus*, Volume Two—and two gems of realistic, stylized photography: Weegee's *Naked City* and Robert Frank's *The Americans.*

Thompson sat on his elbows and stared.

One of the propellers on his beanie cap was bent like a frayed popsicle stick.

A book or two toppled off his shoulders.

"You read some pretty weird shit, Brother Durgana."

"There are many different truths."

"But just one god, huh?"

He didn't answer me right away. "Well, yes, of course."

"And no one else is privileged enough to read, huh? Stana said there were no books in your little ice cubes out back."

"They read, but they need to be guided in what they read."

"Where you the lookout for Gus's kill, Brother Thompson?"

He said nothing.

"Please, be gentle, Mr. Fuller—Brother Thompson is—"

"*Mr.*, now? I guess the brother bit wore thin. It had such a nice ring to it. *Brother Fuller.*"

"You're not nearly as funny as you think you are, Mr. Fuller."

"Really? Brother Ed Sullivan wanted me for his show just last week but he booked a bunch of Brother Russian bears instead."

"Please, Mr. Fuller. You're very droll and beginning to bore me."

"Brother Durgana, I insist. Call me Brother Fuller."

"You are a real pain in the ass—" He looked down at his hands resembling dolphins floating on their backs, the black glimmer glare of his eyes dissipating. "I apologize—my outburst was—unprofessional."

"Don't be so hard on yourself. I was being an ass." I smiled lopsidedly.

"I'm not the sensitive one. But Brother Thompson. Extremely." He leaned forward, one of the figurines toppling, whispered. "Don't push him too far. He breaks easily."

"Oh yeah he's real sensitive. Let me show you just how sensitive—"

I tugged on Thompson's lapels, pulling him up from the floor, then jacketed back the lapels over his shoulders, wrapping him in a Saran Wrap of cloth, making it impossible for him to use his arms, and removed the .45 from the left pocket of his coat. I popped the round from the chamber, slid out the clip, and tossed the works on Durgana's desk. It didn't land softly. Two figurines fell, one of them, an angel, broke apart at the knees.

I pointed at the fat, blocky gun. "Something else procured at your friendly neighborhood surplus store?"

Durgana said nothing.

"Why do you let a kid like this carry around that kind of heat? He's not big enough." I wiped the edges of my mouth. "Guns are dangerous." I pushed down my porkpie. "And if Brother Thompson's the sensitive type a .45 can sure take care of a lot of sensitivity in a hurry."

Brother Durgana looked at the .45 as if it were soiled fish. Three of the fingers on his left hand were covered in diamonds. He shoved the .45 into a drawer. Closed it.

"Thompson, you talked to me and Stana. For five, seven minutes. And then Gus was dead."

He was killed by a .45.

"I hear it was all about beef jerky. I assure you—" Durgana pointed at his plate. "None of us eat beef jerky. Or hotdogs." He smiled, a finger on his right hand rubbing at a diamond ring on his left. "And you really should eat fewer hotdogs, Mr. Fuller." The ways of the East. Berries, nuts, rice, and veggies. You'll live longer. Green. Could live to a hundred eating green. "Hotdogs? Dead at sixty-five."

"Dead at sixty-five," Thompson said, mouth full of tears. "I liked Gus." Thompson blubbered, hands covering his eyes. "He gave me milk. Bread too."

And then he let fall big spots of tears.

The leftovers, he said. The first will be last. Gus gave him the leftovers, the last, the stuff nobody wanted, stuff about to expire. More tears.

That got Brother Durgana off his Brooks Brothers ass. He comforted Brother Thompson and shot me surly looks.

"I wish he wasn't dead. He gave me bread." *The last shall be first.*

Thompson rocked, snot running down his mouth.

He cried and cried, his whole body shaking. Even the buttons on his green coat were vibrating.

Durgana held him and said something or other about a camel through the eye of a needle.

And then they sang. The same song, same pitch.

I felt like a total prick.

Their singing really wasn't half bad.

SHE WAS AFRAID TO LEAVE THE OFFICE.

It was 7:00 p.m., the city shrouded under a black asphalt sky. Her whole office was black: low lit, drawn dark curtains, darker shades on the lamp. Her professional ensemble matched the décor: black dress, tight black turtleneck, black-red lipstick.

"Someone's trying to kill me."

Her voice was low as if that someone might be in this very room.

Forty-five minutes ago, her phone call woke me from a power nap that had slipped into a deep sleep. I had gone back to my Houston Crescent home in North York, jiffyed up some spaghetti and marinara, showered, and fell asleep watching an Audie Murphy western from the couch. When I woke up, I showered again.

It was that kind of case.

Dr. Cohen called between the two showers. My second one was very, very short.

Dr. Cohen.

My therapist.

My friend.

I left Stana an apologetic note propped against a glass in the kitchen. "Gone to Doc's," the note said, with "love, Hayden," and a smiley face that looked like a forgotten Peanuts character. Next to the note, I left a Coffee Crisp, Stana's favorite.

Dr. Cohen reached into one of her lower desk drawers and tossed me a sheet of paper creased awkwardly in half, reminding me of those awful, unreadable teacher handouts that had stuttered and stuck across a ditto machine's drum. It smelled of duplicator fluid.

Damn. It was made on a ditto machine.

The artwork wouldn't give Andy Warhol a run for his money, but it was just as edgy: a blue, crude drawing of the Star of David, none of the triangular points matching in height or shape. It was off-balanced, a wobbly, drunken Star of David. Under the star was scrawled in an equally messy hand, as if the author were using his left instead of right, "We know what you said."

Oh, and the final touch? The star was splattered with brownish-red contours.

Fresh. Not ditto-copied.

"Blood?"

"I don't know." I smiled awkwardly. "You have any hydrogen peroxide?"

"I have a cabinet in the bathroom." She smiled politely and tugged at the cuffs of the turtleneck. The bathroom light flashed on, off, and Dr. Cohen screamed a subterranean howl.

I was by her side in seconds.

I turned on the light. The flash hurt my eyes.

But that was nothing compared to the hurt I felt when I saw what was in the room. Bloody Stars of David were wallpapered everywhere: on the bathroom mirror, the floor, the shower curtain, the ceiling, dozens of them. All duplicates, same quote, same crooked looking star.

But the blood patterns. All original. Different. Fresh.

"They've been in my office. Inside."

"Yeah. I know." It was an intimidation game, one of fear mongering. I grabbed her shoulders and hugged her. "Just stay with me. I'll keep you safe."

We stood like that for several minutes.

She didn't cry. She was tough.

From the cabinet, I grabbed the hydrogen peroxide and some Q-Tips. And several of the bloodied stars. Part of their intimidation was to hint at biblical-sized sacrifices, God said to Abraham kill me a son.

I spread the papers across her desk, uncapped the hydrogen peroxide. Dipped the Q-Tip in.

"What's that for?"

Blood contains an enzyme, catalase, which breaks hydrogen peroxide down into water and oxygen gas. If it's paint it won't bubble, but if it's blood, watch.

Two or three drops hit the reddish-brown stubble and bubbles popped and ran along the page.

And many other pages too.

"Shit," she said.

I lifted the sheet.

Where could you get that much blood at short notice? A blood bank; a recently executed corpse, from a host of zombielike followers at a McGowan Street cult.

What did We know what you said *mean?*

"I don't know." Her black bangs didn't move as she shook her head and sat down at her desk across from me. "I'm so sorry I called you, and I know you're dealing with your father's murder—but I didn't know who else to ask—"

"Forget about that. Friends ask friends for help."

She pulled her lips together. "They got into my fucking office."

I wondered if she'd said something in her past that she regretted.

"In Auschwitz?"

"No. Here, in this office with a client."

"I can't talk about my clients."

"Your life's in danger, Doc." I knew the rules. That whole doctor-client privilege thing was a myth. If lives were in danger, your life, your client's life, or if you knew about sexual abuse you had to report it. In this case I was sensing a lot of danger, alarm bells banging a death knell and Dr. No's island was about to go under.

Dr. Cohen didn't get the allusion. She reads *Scientific American.*

I leaned across the desk, placed my hands in hers. "Let me help you." Could any of this have anything to do with me? I too am her patient. Did we talk about something that made us targets for this hate group? It had to be a hate group, anti-Semites of some kind, or else why use the loaded symbolism of the Star of David? *And the blood. The death of first sons?* "When did this first note arrive?"

It was shoved under her office door when she returned from a late afternoon coffee break. They could be lurking now, waiting for me to leave, she said. That's why she kept calling my home, afraid to move.

"Why not call the po-lice?"

"After I called you, I did. I tried to call the police—" She picked up the receiver, held it out to me. "Dead."

I dropped it back in its cradle. They cut the line, outside. Professionals.

It could be Lenny Cassel haunting you, me, a murderer roaming the world with Brian Spinner Terrien's face. In my last case, Cassel killed a woman and fled Canada with the aid of plastic surgery as a new person, getting a new start. But Cassel knew that I knew that the real Terrien was no longer with us and maybe Cassel's Detroit mobster boys were taking matters in hand, making sure their boss would be protected from future exposure by a Toronto PI and Montreal Canadien hockey player.

I had also spoken, during several of our sessions, to Dr. Cohen about Terrien, my feelings of guilt over the secret I kept from his family in not revealing his death, the guilt I felt in knowing he was buried in a field in Vaughan, Ontario. I saw him die, beaten to death by Babe Migano and his men, one of Terrien's eyes hanging from its orbital bone, his last breath a blood bubble. Could it be related to that?

Terrien and Cassel.

Dr. Cohen didn't think so.

Seven months ago, when I told Dr. Cohen the story of my first case and the man I killed, blowing his brains all over the wall and across the face and hair of his daughter seated next to him, and the other man, Terrien, whose death I kept quiet about, she listened, nodded her head, and said that survivors often carry dark secrets with them to the grave. She carried several: the burdens of her patients, the burdens of her brutal past.

I know she survived Auschwitz. Saw her mother, father, sister and uncle die there. We all make compromises to survive abuse, she always says, but did she say something she shouldn't to survive in Auschwitz?

"I don't think they are Nazis." She smiled dimly, and I moved to the window, parted the curtains. On the street below, under a flickering street light were two men in long overcoats and fedoras, smoking cigarettes.

Hit men. "Then it has to be a client, Dr. Cohen. Someone's angry at you."

Before I closed the curtains one of the men looked up in the direction of the window. I couldn't make out his features, but his face was too long for his short, stubby body. "You can talk to me vaguely about your cases without mentioning names. Keep it general, but vaguely specific."

"I can talk. Violence is involved."

She smiled faintly, her eyes filling with a friendly light. "You know, since we have the hydrogen peroxide out, let's clean that damn cut. That adhesive tape on your chin has turned from white to off white to mud cakes."

I sat in a chair across from her and she gently removed the bandage. It pinched a little. She applied the topical antiseptic and it burned. "It's a little infected."

"So I hear."

She gently squeezed and gathered puss in a Kleenex. She applied a new bandage, new adhesive tape, her fingers almost soothing. I felt like a kid again. And I mean that in a good way. Seriously. I didn't have someone, like a mom, caring for me. Dad was often asleep on the couch, in a boozy freefall.

Dad's fingers were boxing gloves compared to Dr. Cohen's.

"Neither did my client. If it's the one I think it is."

"Huh?"

"Her mother died when she was three. Suicide," she said. Dr. Cohen looked down at her hands and let loose a deep sigh. "Those men were in my office. They have access to me."

"Was Ellen Reynolds one of your clients?"

I showed her the photograph.

"Ellen?" She recognized the name, not the girl. The same motherless client had spoken of an Ellen Reynolds and the church on McGowan she was a part of, a church the client found appealing and had, through Ellen, visited a few times. The client liked the church's philosophies because it was about letting go, finding inner peace, surrendering from a life of the seven deadly sins for a life of—

"The pearl of heaven?"

"Yes. And oneness. Those are the very words she used. Yes."

Ellen was one of the last people to see my father alive, he was taking her away from that church. Somehow she and Dr. Cohen's client were connected. "Did your client stay at that church?"

"Susan never told me that Ellen was—Métis, is it?"

"Yes." I rubbed the edges of my mouth. "Susan?"

"My client." Dr. Cohen didn't offer up the last name. Attended it several times, Susan did. Found it quaint, another word she used, quaint, and then she dropped out at the University of Toronto.

"Why?"

"She was pregnant. And wanted an abortion." Dr. Cohen discussed it over with her client through three sessions and because The Criminal Code of Canada views it as a crime to "procure a miscarriage," the client was seeking the help of a young medical student at the U of T, who performed such services for friends and desperate women.

"This doctor? Was he a friend of hers?"

"Yes. Part of her inner circle." She has a group of friends at the U of T; they call themselves the Defeatniks, beat-down hipsters of the nuclear age.

"The Defeatniks?"

"Yes."

"The law on abortion will change," I said. "Some day. Soon." I shrugged absently. "Her family was opposed, I assume?"

"They didn't know."

"And you suggested?"

"That she make her own choice."

"Those were your very words, that's what you said, 'make your own choice?'"

She saw where I was going with this. Someone connected to the client wanted the messenger dead. Maybe the family *did know* that the girl was pregnant, maybe a family member or one of the Defeatniks, or both, knew and wanted to *do something* about it.

"Yes, that's what I said." She picked up several sheets full of bloody Stars of David. "I'm a firm believer that we must be free to choose what we choose."

"I know." I kissed her on the forehead. She smelled of lilacs. "That's why I love you, Doc."

She leaned her head left, eyes smiling. "Don't—"

"I know, I know. 'Don't call me Doc.'"

She laughed.

"There's something else. I don't know what it means." She opened the center drawer to her desk, slid out folded-up blueprints to a floor plan. Ellen had given them to Susan for safekeeping. Susan passed them on to the doc. "'You can look into it,' she said."

I pushed back my porkpie. "Look into what?"

"I'm afraid my client was rather vague. It was her standard MO."

"Right."

I unfolded and smoothed out the floor plans. It was the McGowan Street church. I recognized the spacious sanctuary immediately, the fire exits, and the places were windows should be, now bricked up and covered over with neon kitsch. The basement to the plans was circled. Down there were laundry facilities, three or four separate showers, and something that looked like a bunch of condensers to a central-air system. "Why all the cloak and dagger? Why not just tell you?"

"She was into mind games."

"Another part of her MO?"

"Uh-huh."

That cracked me up.

"Why did Ellen take the plans?"

"My client didn't say."

"Swell." My palms were sore. "Speaking of cloak and dagger—" I smiled my lopsided grin. "I don't want to alarm you, but there's two men downstairs. Under a street light."

We crossed to the window together and she saw them, still smoking, their hats catching star points of yellow.

"Is there a back way out of here?"

She nodded.

"Susan have a last name?"

"I don't want to tell you, but maybe, for the client's safety, I should."

"Right now, Doc, I'm worried about your safety"

Susan had gone missing for over a week since dropping out of U of T.

"Do you know any of her friends, the Defeatniks?"

"No."

"Did she get the abortion?"

"I don't know. Haven't heard from her."

"Your case connects to my case—to Ellen—Ellen Reynolds, to my father, Ira Fuller, who wasn't a good man, but he was a man. His murder—"

"Susan Whitfield." She's the daughter of Mr. Franklin W. Whitfield, a munitions engineer, who made his fortune in WWII armaments. Family lives in Rosedale.

"Whitfield? Deuces' dad?"

"Huh?"

I filled her in, the stringer, the wannabe crime reporter.

Yes, the Whitfields, she said. Susan and her brother were close, two years apart. During their childhood they spent all their free time together, creating their own language that no one understood but them. Wrote a host of twisted fairytales where the Evil Queen wins and Cinderella's body is fed to the birds.

"Charming." I suggested we better find a back way out of here and head to my place where Dr. Cohen could hide out for the interim.

The door to her office kicked open, pulling from the wood, briefly hanging from the hinges, before falling.

One of the men had a long angular face, too long for his stubby body.

They were both holding machine guns.

And silence followed.

They weren't going to kill us.

Yet.

"Let's go tour the Bluffs," said the bigger of the two, his accent French.

I don't think they were about to offer us bus fare, motel accommodations, or a free continental breakfast with the tour.

Oh well.

Second Period

They weren't very talkative.

The bigger guy, red cowboy kerchiefs around his wrists, drove the car, the inside of his left wrist atop the steering wheel, twelve o'clock high. His right hand held a Gauloises cigarette, bobbing now and then like a baton. He wore a blue Cavanagh hat with a white band, Sinatra–style, Capitol Records, 1953.

The kerchiefs around his wrists hung down raggedly, broken bird wings. It was quite a look, somewhere between tough urban cowboy and folk-singing college kid. The fuzzy shadows filling his face like seconds of fabric meant he had probably started shaving last week. The poor bastard also had a cold. His eyes were red and his nose ran. I put him at twenty, maybe twenty-one, if that.

His partner, the stubby guy with a long face, didn't believe in deodorant. He gave off a gamey air, like that of a dog coming in after lollygagging in the grass in the rain. He gnawed on a chunk of beef jerky, its broken off shards reminding me of balsa wood.

Dad bought me a balsa wood airplane when I was a kid: thin wires, rubber band to spin the propeller, and red, plastic wheels. The plane's wings often broke on its third or fourth backyard flight. One time, Dad tossed me such a plane still in its packaging. "Don't get out of the car," he said, and entered a bar, the Highwayman, on Sherbourne Street. Three hours later he returned, having lost all of his paycheck on beer and darts.

His head collapsed against the steering wheel. On the way home, I prayed he kept the car between the lines.

This here now was a different kind of ride.

The stubby fella gnawed harder on his jerky. Every now and then he broke off a piece of balsa wood with enough flourish to resemble a toreador flashing a red cape.

At our feet, in the backseat, were twelve or thirteen beef jerky wrappers, eight or nine empty paper cups, and an assortment of pop bottles, including Orange Crush and Hires Root Beer. *Was Ellen Reynolds in this car? Ever?*

They probably killed Gus.

"Where you taking us?"

Dr. Cohen said absolutely nothing, her face a resolute mask, eyes ahead, faraway, lost in irretrievable memories most likely, hands politely positioned in her lap, the collar of her black wool coat up, shadowing her face.

"This isn't the movies, imperialist American horseshit," said the driver.

Definitely a college kid.

"We're not going to reveal secrets or reasons for our actions to help fill in the gaps to the story you're trying to decode."

"Right." Stubby smiled, his face full of beef jerky hash. "No Western storytelling here. That stuff's dead."

"Dead as a doornail," said the driver.

I wanted to tell him Rocky Sullivan said the exact same words in *Angels with Dirty Faces. Things are dead as a doornail around heah*. I couldn't stop laughing. "Dead as a doornail." James fucking Cagney.

"Shut up or you'll get it right here," said Stubby.

"You sure you guys aren't right out of the 1930s?"

"You guys killed Gus." Dr. Cohen's hands raised up from her lap and floated back down. She pointed at the wrappers filling the backseat floor.

"Like I said," the driver smiled. "This isn't the movies. No answers. No tying up of loose ends."

Streetlights danced over the hood of the car, ricocheting with comets of color. Loose ends. This case had several. *What did the note mean*, We know what you said? *What was said?*

"Too much, that's what was said." Stubby laughed and then the driver.

Big jokes all around.

"We're dismantling the universe," the driver said.

"What?"

"Shut-up. You talk too much," Stubby said to his partner.

"You worry too much. Don't worry. Those words mean nothing to them."

Dismantling.

The universe.

A gas station gleamed on the corner, its red-and-white sign a light buoy warming an empty street.

The stubby fella handed me college-lined paper and a Bic pen, the cap a broken golf tee. Write what I tell you to write, he said.

Streetlights fissured against the car's side mirrors.

A suicide note. That's what he wanted. Dr. Cohen and I had made a pact to end it together. We were going to jump off the Bluffs.

The plan, according to the driver, was to place the note on my father's kitchen table in Gradwell by a glass of warm milk and cookies.

"Like for Santa Claus," Stubby said.

"Yeah, like for Santa Claus," the driver echoed.

Big laughs. These guys should write for the Hemingway estate. They kept repeating themselves. Do that a few times and every utterance will take on a kind of helium-elevated gravitas.

They figured the cops being in and out of Dad's pad were bound to see the planted note and conclude that Dr. Cohen and I walked from there to the Bluffs and jumped. What these two PhDs of crime hadn't figured was in having me write the note now, instead of, say, at a table, the police would notice the rushed, uneven letters, the lopsided lines curving out of the page's inscribed lines, and deduce that the note had, in all probability, been composed in a hurry, in a moving vehicle.

"Okay, Hemingway, what do you want me to write, exactly?"

We rushed past a dull white and black-trimmed strip mall: a quickie Chinese Food restaurant; a flower shop; a Becker's; a donut joint; and a one-hour martinizing. My shirt sure needed to be pressed.

"I told you survival."

"Well, that's a little vague, Ernie."

"Just write."

"Sure thing, Ernest."

The driver chuckled. He had a better sense of humor than I initially gave him credit for. His eyes were gentle, full of apologies. "How about this, *Fitzgerald—*" He smiled. "Dr. Cohen couldn't take the guilty memories of Auschwitz." He swallowed, the broken-winged kerchiefs tapping the side of the steering wheel. "And you couldn't take the memory flashbacks of repeated abuses at the hands of your father. Just a kid: eight, nine, ten—"

Dr. Cohen shot me a look of sadness.

"Where did you get that information?"

If I had my gun he'd be dead. But they made me slam away the snub-nosed in a desk drawer at Dr. Cohen's before they shoved us into a 1957 Ford Fairlane, four-door, hardtop, orange and black, Quebec plates, white-wall tires, and rust slicing along the bottom of the passenger door.

"Our intel is pretty damn good," said Stubby face.

"We got it." The driver was unable to look at me in the rearview. His voice quieted. "We got it."

"How?"

"Other people. In this case." He leaned his wrist harder atop the steering wheel. "That's all you're getting from us. Death to Western mythology and narrative storytelling."

Fuck, Durgana may have been an English major, but these guys were star pupils from the Philosophy department, and Marxist-Leninists to boot.

"Dismantling the universe? What's that about?"

"Think of it as the McGuffin, baby," the driver said.

"Oh, so you are into Western storytelling."

"He has you there." Stubby said, smiling, shoulders pulled up as if on a giant hanger.

"Who are you?" Dr. Cohen's voice was steady, the spaces between the words even. "Why the posters in my office?"

"I'm an art major," the driver said.

"McGill?" Quebec plates. And I had remembered the combination of letters and numbers.

"I told you, you talk too much," Stubby said.

"Leave him alone, Hemingway," I said.

"Will you shut the fuck up with that. That joke's getting old."

"Sorry, Jake Barnes."

The driver was chuckling again. He rubbed away, with the back of a hand, nasal drip from his upper lip. "I like art. I just go for it."

"Dr. Cohen." Stubby's voice revved like a Porsche. "This, this drive, in this, this car, is not a therapy session, seeking some magical rubber ducky moment that will explain everything. 'I kill people because I didn't get enough cookies when I was a kid' kind of thing, come on—"

"No, you kill people because you just don't get enough—"

"Is that a sex joke, Doctor? Oh witty."

"I thought it was pretty good," said the driver.

So did I.

"Shut up."

I guess I said the last three words out loud.

"You killed Gus," Dr. Cohen restated her previous claim. This time the words were rabbit punches to the kidneys.

"Yes. He was part of the, uh, dismantling."

"Now who's saying too much?" said the driver.

Stubby shrugged. "They'll be dead soon." Stubby liked words, the sound of words, how they filled spaces, but he wasn't going to fill our time with answers. Sorry. He smiled. The color of his bridge had yellowed.

"Soup cans," said the driver. "I want to do Pop Art but not with soup cans like Warhol. Donuts and beef jerky. That would be cool."

"Marilyn eating donuts and beef jerky that would be even cooler," Stubby said.

"Oh, that's good. Marilyn." He nodded his head with amped-up approval.

How did killing Gus help them dismantle the universe? What universe? Who's? What did this all have to do with Brother Durgana and the church and his goddamn neon fixtures and rooms without windows? How about Bob Waterman and Silverwood's? Was there something there I missed? What was I getting too close to? What did Dr. Cohen say that somehow involved me? We know what you said. *Fuck. Maybe they feared what my upcoming meetings with the Defeatniks might reveal? What about Ellen Reynolds? If she were alive, maybe she'd tell me something they didn't want me to know. How was Susan Whitfield caught up in all this? And how did they know my backstory, the lurid moments with my father? Did my father tell somebody? Ellen?*

"Enough kibitzing. Start writing." Stubby spoke with his gun, a .45 that not so gently nudged my face. Christ, I wish I had my .38.

I couldn't see too well in the dark, but I scrawled something about my unrequited love for the doctor and how I couldn't go on anymore. The fellas at *As the World Turns* and *The Edge of Night* would eat this shit up. The doctor wouldn't give me a tumble so I was willing to jump into the abyss. Doc had her own issues, the horrors of Auschwitz. It was pretty soapy. I hoped the cops who found the note could read through the suds.

Streetlight caught the top of the ribbed bench seat and a small, faint perforated line of white appeared, dots of confetti. I dipped a finger in it.

I expected it to taste like cinnamon, but it didn't. It was vaguely metallic.

I signed the note. Dr. Cohen did too.

And then I thought of Bob Waterman and his allergies, the constant nasal drip, the red eyes. Allergies. Uh-huh.

Stubby seized his pen back from me as if it were Tiffany diamonds or some damn thing. He quickly read the piece I had up for the writers' workshop.

"Which of you is the junkie?" I leaned back, arms crossed. "There's coke on the bench seat. I guess you don't get no kicks from champagne, huh?" I looked at the driver, propped myself up, whispered in his ear. "My bet's on you, Cavanagh Hat. Your eyes, red. Even in the dim light of the streets I can see your nose running."

Was Waterman a cokehead too? Instead of just finding my father was he in on the kill?

"It's not coke." Cavanagh Hat laughed.

"So, this is all about drugs?" Dr. Cohen exhaled sharply. "Drugs? That's why we kill people?"

Is that the universe they sought, a drug-addled one? Dismantle this one for that?

Stubby hit me hard with the side of the gun. I skidded back into the seat, blood dotting my chin, wind chimes jangling in my ears. A couple of stitches on my chin were re-opened. "What kind of a note is this?" He held up my barely intelligible scrawl. "It reads like an episode of *The Edge of Night.*"

"Cut the horseshit. Re-do the suicide note," the driver said.

Stubby tore off another sheet, handed me a different pen. Parker Brothers.

I'd try to put some $50 words into this one.

Drugs. Figures. Maybe Brother Durgana's McGowan Street crowd were doped up on something, maybe not coke but something, and that's why they mindlessly prayed, waltzing around in threadbare robes, giving generously, they were mentally brainwashed and physically beaten, and through drugs their resistances were lowered. They had no collective wills. They were the walking dead. Okay, makes sense, and Ellen Reynolds broke free from all that, used my father's taxi service to make a quick break. Did his helping her cost him his life? Did she set him up?

Is Waterman a member of this cult?

Or perhaps Dr. Cohen's client Susan Whitfield is a player in this little drama. What's her role?

She knew Ellen. Did my father tell Ellen about abusing me and she inadvertently told Susan who told these fellas?

"Write the note. Quickly." A wash of teriyaki jerky smothered my face. "Mention the abuse. Mention it."

I couldn't.

We arrived at the same park that was just blocks away from Dad's. Cavanagh Hat threw the car into park, killed the engine.

Damn. The new note would be clean, look like it had been written at a table instead of in a moving car.

How could I admit, to paper, and the world, to read what had happened to me, how I felt betrayed by my father, by my own body, the dirty residual guilt that covered me and my thoughts, fears of sex, for years? My skin's full of fish scales that won't fall away.

The sheet of paper remained a snow-capped iceberg weighing me down.

Dr. Cohen reached for the paper, pen, and wrote hurriedly, saving me from re-animated trauma, Dad's hands, boxing gloves, pushing down the back of my head as he grunts and comes between my thighs. I don't know what she wrote. I didn't read it. I signed it. I didn't read it.

Stubby read it. Three, four times. Slowly. "That's better," he said.

The driver wiped at his nose again, smiled dimly. "Much better." He couldn't look at us.

A pulse ran along the doctor's jawline.

"I'm sorry." Cavanagh Hat's voice was cake crumbles. He rubbed at his nose once more. "You know I'm Jewish?"

Dr. Cohen spat in his face. "What would Dr. Jayson Garfein have to say?"

He let the spittle trail slowly down one of the lines bracketing his mouth, his chin. "He wouldn't think I was representing my tribe well," he said. "He'd call me a closet anti-Jew." Spittle hung from his chin, dripping, forty pieces of silver.

"Anti-Semite not anti-Jew is what he'd say." Dr. Cohen smiled.

So the driver did attend McGill. Dr. Garfein was Dr. Cohen's professor of psychology years ago.

"I told you, you talk too much." Stubby picked away at a balsa wood chunk of beef jerky stuck in his back molars. He seized the note from the driver, waved with his gun. "Let's go."

The ground, cold gravel, crunched, and the sky was clear liquid black, as an even colder breeze blew off the lake and over the Bluffs, stenciling our faces with thin portières of mist.

Pinpoint stars shivered above and on white caps of tidal waves.

The driver mumbled something about how getting me out of the narrative would ruin his plans. The pronoun choice was a little fuzzy. *His? As in the driver or someone else. What plans? Whose plans?*

White caps shivered with light.

It was too pretty a night to die.

My heart was in my shoulders and the back of my legs shook as I walked. Dr. Cohen, the two hitmen behind her, reached for my hand with steady fingers, stilling my trembling. I was a real mensch she said. She loved me. Stay strong. Don't let them win, don't give them your dignity.

If only my father had ever spoken such words.

The driver, Mr. Kerchiefs, sniffed and sucked back nasal drainage, and I knew he was about four paces off behind me.

The gravel turned from cold slivers to bald grass and then dirt and blackness. The mist on my face and arms felt heavier at the Bluffs' edge. Below, blue-black waves capped with bits of white light. Seagulls lapped at the white.

"You know what I love about the Bluffs?" Stubby was revving up to give a soliloquy, his words elevated. "Natural. Not a product of monopoly capital but of nature. True beauty. No members of the proletariat died to create this splendor." He paused. "That's far enough."

Did Cavanagh Hat have a gun? He had a machine gun at the office, but those were locked in the trunk of the Fairlane.

In the distance, a floating buoy blinked.

I tried slowing my breathing. Don't hand over your dignity. Breathe. Pain left my shoulders. *Breathe. You matter. Breathe. My legs were no longer shaking. Vulnerability is your strength. Breathe.*

"On three you take a powder. Got it?" Stubby.

Take a powder. Right out of Gold Medal fiction. Jim Thompson.

"I'm going to count to three. If you don't jump, I'll shoot you in the head. One—"

Two shots, bleating like one, crushed the night's stillness.

White light danced on triangles of waves.

And I turned, because I wasn't dead yet.

I had just seen the white triangles dancing.

Both hit men had dropped with the gunshots. Stubby was in a three-point stance, and Dr. Cohen kicked him before he could assess what the fuck was happening. She nailed him a beauty, right in the middle of his face, lifting him by the nose, sprawling back, head snapping, gun dropping, suicide note still gripped in left hand.

He held onto the wrong thing.

Before he could pick up the fallen gun, I had it in my mitts, breathing calmly, not quickly, and with both hands tapped the trigger, twice, red blossoms spilling across his chest.

He fell back, panhandler hands opening, wanting loose change.

He wasn't going to want a damn thing in a few seconds.

I smelled shit.

Stubby's breath was heavy and shallow, a hollow rustle of leaves, as eyes filmed over, losing their target, the dark, black sky.

Cavanagh Hat hadn't moved since he slumped to his knees, and then he slowly toppled on his face, a crumpled heap, his hat twisting in the Lakeshore breeze, blowing clear off the Bluffs.

He died without a word. No epitaph. The back of his head, grapefruit pulp.

I looked for the source of the shots. Couldn't see a damn thing in the shadows of trees and black sky. "Sal?"

"It's me." Stana's feet padded quickly in the dark.

I sure have a knack for being rescued by women. Anne Chevalier of the RCMP in my last case. Now Stana Younger.

I crossed back down to Stubby, his breaths asthmatic.

I looked at him.

His last gasp was a slashed whitewall tire.

I rolled the suicide note into a ball and threw it into the night sky.

The Bluffs took it.

"He's dead," Dr. Cohen said, matter-of-factly. I don't think her heart rate climbed over sixty. "You okay?"

"Do I *look okay*?"

"Stupid question."

"No, no." I touched her left shoulder and smiled my lopsided lupine grin.

The watery mist from the Bluffs smelled of spawning fish and my mouth filled with tears. "How did they know all that about *me*—about *you*—how did they?"

She hugged me.

Did Dad tell Ellen and she someone else? Did they torture Dad before shooting him full of hop and he talked?

Why kill him?

Dismantle the universe.

Dr. Cohen whispered that I shouldn't feel ashamed. To cry is to feel, a good sign. She's the one who should feel ashamed for feeling no fear.

Stana emerged from the black shadows, carrying my .45, the one from the glovebox of my Galaxie. Her hair was sweat stained, eyes full of worries.

"Thanks," Dr. Cohen said. "You're one hell of a fakakta cavalry."

"I got Hayden's note. And the Coffee Crisp." She kissed my cheek. She feared I'd had a relapse of bad memories and was running to Dr. Cohen's office for a therapy session, in search of much needed love and support, and when Stana arrived and saw us escorted by the two McGill baby-faced killers, with one of the fine gents trailing too close behind me, his walk and manner reminiscent of a certain Brother Thompson of McGowan Street fame, and his green-padded coat with the .45 pressing against her hip, she knew we were in trouble, grabbed the .45 from my Galaxie, and followed. "I wasn't sure the gun was loaded." She had no idea how to pull out the clip, but thank God she knew how to kick off the safety and blast the thing.

Damn she was good, awful good.

She rubbed at her shoulder. The gun had a loud kick, she said.

"You're not supposed to hold your arm stiff, bend the elbow."

"Do I look like the kind of person who's at home on a target range?"

Then Stana moved in the darkness, crossing over to the man with the grapefruit head, her figure blending with patches of black, and I felt the most connected to her I had ever felt before. I wanted to just hear her breathe, talk, breathe, and talk some more.

"I killed him, didn't I?" She bit her upper lip. "Shitshitshit-shitshit. I killed him, didn't I?"

"Dead as a doornail," I said. "Dead as a motherfucking door-nail."

Dr. Cohen laughed, throwing her head back. She smiled at Stana. "Dead as a doornail."

Her Cagney was better than mine.

AFTER THE POLICE BAGGED THE BODIES, the guns, the Tommies in the trunk of the Fairlane, stretched out more yellow tape, and asked enough questions to fill out the paperwork for a government grant, Top Cop Sal Lambertino and two lab guys followed us in Stana's car to Dr. Cohen's office. There I retrieved my gun from a lower-desk drawer and stood by the window as they dusted and Sal asked follow-up questions.

We showed him the posters, the Warhol-esque Star of David ditto run with artwork full of spots and comets of blood splatter.

"It's blood. I checked."

Sal lifted the bottle of hydrogen peroxide and handed it to me. "Your cut's reopened. You might want to clean it."

"Thanks, pal." I did so. Stana re-applied the bandage.

Sal told the lab boys take all the posters, run the blood through, see what we find. He sat in a chair across from Dr. Cohen. The room was high-key lit: desk lamp, two floor lamps, overhead fixtures burning brightly, chasing any shadows from the setting. For a moment, I thought I was in a goddamn Hollywood musical.

Dr. Cohen sat in her own chair, her wool coat snug tight, all but the very top button clasped. Maybe she was more affected by everything that went down than she let on. Her eyes were sharp points.

"So what they have against you, Doc?"

"Don't call her Doc," I said.

Dr. Cohen laughed. "And I have no idea what I allegedly said that I shouldn't have. *We know what you said.* That says nothing. I talk a lot. I say a lot." She shifted in her chair.

The lab boys dusted, took random photographs, and with a fluoroscope searched for traces of evidence in the killers' footsteps.

Sal wiped at the corners of his mouth, one foot pushed up against the edge of the desk, felt hat tapping out an errant rhythm on a raised knee.

He couldn't believe that Stana had killed a man tonight.

"I heard him count off, one, and I knew I didn't have much time to do anything else."

"Well, that's what you get for hanging with the likes of him." He pointed a stubby finger my way. "And I assume the other killing, yours Superstar, was self-defense?"

"Of course," I nodded.

"Sure."

"Hey, Chief. Check this." It was the heavier of the lab boys. He wore a dark suit, skinny tie, a homburg hat. He flipped a coin-size disc on Dr. Cohen's desk. It rolled up against an edge of the desk blotter. "The room was bugged."

"What?" Sal's slow rhythm hiccupped against his knee. The 2 and 4 hits shifting to 1 and 3. "Shit." He held up the disc, felt the pigeonholes. "Jesus Christ this is old. Prewar." He flipped it to me.

"Bugged?" I rolled the disc in my hand. It resembled a miniature mouthpiece to a telephone crossed with a diaphragm, a black bubble with ribbed aluminum ridges. *Shit. That's how the two hitmen knew about my past, my abuse at the hands of my Dad. How long had they been listening in on Dr. Cohen's sessions? More importantly, why were they listening? We know what you said suddenly took on a whole new meaning. They literally did know. They had heard it all. Who's they? Susan's family? Someone else? Someone connected to me? Did I reveal too much about Cassel and Steinmetz and Terrien and my first case and bodies buried in Vaughan, Ontario? Fuck.*

I pocketed the disc. They found two more. One inside a lampshade, the other behind a painting.

Dr. Cohen's face was absent of color. "My clients trust me," she mumbled, her eyes darting about, calculating, wondering how long she had been a victim of such surveillance. I thought of the cameras at The People's Way to Christ.

Sal didn't know what to say. Stana fidgeted with her handbag, lit a cigarette, blew smoke angrily in a corner of a ceiling.

Sal slapped his hands together, returned to drumming atop his knee. "So what have we got so far?" Let's quit worrying about what has taken place and do something to stop it, he said. They bugged the room. Who's they? What have we got, people?

The list was long. (1) My father was killed by drugs, perhaps for or over drugs, but the killers made a fatal fuckup: Dad was a lefty so the suicide wasn't a suicide. (2) A church/cult on McGowan Street, full of followers, people who have surrendered their possessions to allow their minds to be "possessed" by a charismatic charlatan, Brother Durgana, former stock broker turned all Elmer Gantry, is somehow part of the mix. The joint's crawling with surveillance cameras, there are no windows on the walls, and kitschy neon lights are everywhere; shit, surveillance cameras, people, hidden microphones: the two are related; I just know it; (3) Silverwood's Dairy delivered milk and butter to The People's Way to Christ. Were they delivering something else? Drugs? What's Bob Waterman's role, Mr. Company Man with his yellow polo shirts and blue Dickies and running nose? Allergies or fellow cokehead like Cavanagh Hat? Waterman found Dad. A coincidence? Or was he keeping company with somebody else? A woman? A cult? (4) Dad was seen by Mrs. Mary Hale taking Ellen Reynolds, a Saskatchewan runaway and member of the Métis, away from the church. Running from what? Toward what? What's Dad's connection to Ellen, the church, this case? (5) Ellen Reynolds befriended Susan Whitfield, of the famous Whitfields in Rosedale. The munitions engineer? His son, Deuces, is a stringer with the *Telegram*. Moreover, these floor plans—

"Shouldn't that be six—" Stana.

"Okay. Six." These floor plans. I unfolded the blueprints, spread it across Dr. Cohen's desk. It's of the church. The basement, as you can see, is circled.

"Is that an air-conditioning unit?" Sal.

"I think so. Maybe this has something to do with the midnight mass?"

Sal was no longer tapping his hat against his knee.

Stana jumped in. Her research this afternoon revealed that the Whitfield fortunes rested in armaments for the war effort, including an advanced form of creeping jelly, napalm in a grenade, that sticks to surfaces, climbs and burns.

"Where's this Susan now?" Sal's hat was pushed back on his head, a much better look than his bashing-about "Mr. Tambourine Man" pose.

"No fucking idea," I said. She's pregnant. Sought an abortion; (7) Is her father and his people the ones who know what Dr. Cohen said, bugged the room? Did they, after what they heard, want revenge on the good doctor? They're anti-abortionists? I don't know. Stana has a 4:30 p.m. appointment set up for us with the senior Whitfield, and his posse, tomorrow. A U of T medical student offered to provide the illegal abortion, but Susan changed her mind, after occasionally attending The People's Way to Christ with Ellen a few times.

"No shit." The brim of Sal's hat resembled a pug-nosed dog.

"No shit."

There's more. (8) Susan Whitfield hung with a group of Beat students at the U of T.

“Beat?” Sal wasn’t getting the vibe. His beard said Hemingway not Jack Kerouac.

“You know, like the writer, *On the Road*,” Stana said.

Nothing.

“It’s pretty good,” I said.

“Adolescent fantasy,” Stana said. “The women in the novel are just fuck toys for the boys.”

“Beat? Like bongo drums?”

“Yeah, Sal. Bongo drums.” I shook my head and Stana laughed.

The U of T kids were atomic-era products, calling themselves the Defeatniks, figuring the clock was about to hit midnight and then all would go ka-bluey. I was going to track them down tomorrow at the local coffee shops along Harbord Street. I needed to understand their philosophies, get a profile of Susan.

Stana was next to me, curling a hip into mine, bending slightly so that she could nuzzle against my neck and clavicle. She smelled of sandalwood. One of her hands traced my chest. “You doing okay,” she whispered.

“Comme ci, comme ca,” I waved my hand slightly. It was shaking nervously, much more so than I cared to admit.

(9) Gus. Gus Carhart. Our two baby-faced killers copped to killing him, but it wasn’t over cash and beef jerky. They killed him because they were dismantling the universe.

“Say what?” Sal’s face looked as if he had just walked out of a darkened movie theater.

“I don’t know. Those were their exact words—”

“That’s all they said. Dismantle the universe.” Dr. Cohen shrugged. Who’s universe, what universe, I’m not sure, she said. I don’t think they are either. “Call it a hunch.” She smiled.

“Drugs maybe?” I mentioned the perforated line of coke on top of the Fairlane’s bench seat, Cavanagh Hat’s running nose, Bob Waterman’s allergies, the church followers overall lethargy and lack of gumption.

"That's not a universe. That might be a gas station in a universe. But drugs isn't a universe," Stana said.

Nine items. How do they entangle, untangle, connect?

Tomorrow, and then tomorrow, and then Detroit. The Olympia. I was running out of time. *Dismantle the universe. How was Gus messing with their universe?*

"Ten." Stana extricated herself from my shoulder, stood straight. She wore a white blouse, black slacks, white low-heeled shoes. "The Army Surplus store."

"Oh yeah, ten. Army surplus." Pain returned behind my eyes and my empty stomach was full of coolant, my body trembling with air conditioning. "What about ten?"

The freckles in Stana's eyes danced. The lease for the building: Bolemac.

That was the name of the dummy organization of my first heavy case: the Stabulas girls, kidnapping, corruption, porn and gambling at Maple Leaf Gardens. Bolemac was where Smith and his potato-chip eating sidekick Bullard hid pots of money. Smith was now, because of that case, in serious trouble with the law: racketeering, gambling, extortion charges. He was also suffering from bleeding ulcers. Were his hands in more dirt? I couldn't quite figure the connection, but I recalled the cache of arms at his modern, post art-deco mansion in Rosedale: the room full of tear-gas canisters, potato mashers, Thompson submachine guns, and AK-47s. I wonder if he also housed bugging devices and some creeping jelly grenades. Let's just say, if he were into army surplus, I don't think it's for the camping gear or the joys of kayaking.

Sal sighed and picked up the phone. He asked for the boys in the lab.

Stana returned to nuzzling my chest, bending slightly, hair fine, sweat behind a right ear. "You look beat," she whispered.

"Maybe I'll read some Kerouac."

She smiled.

"You were good back there." I tucked a wisp of auburn hair behind an ear. "I never got a chance to thank you—"

"Redemption, remember?"

"I'm sorry I said that," I whispered.

"You're not going to fucking believe this." Sal dropped the receiver back in the cradle. It hit like a rim shot. He waited another beat. "Eleven. That was Anne Chevalier on the phone. RCMP." He held up a hand and spoke hurriedly. The two dead were college students at McGill: one Barry Kunz and one Ivan Sevrier. Believers in a free Quebec. Libre, baby. N'oublie jamais. Card-carrying members.

"Oh no," I growled, recalling their tossed-off comments on imperialism, monopoly capital, and Western storytelling.

"And let's not forget, 'Ode to the Scarborough Bluffs,'" Dr. Cohen said.

"Here we go again," chimed in Stana, shaking her head. My last case was full of so-called terrorists who ended up being posers, one of them from Kirkland Lake, Ontario, not Quebec.

But these two guys were the real deal, hardcore types dedicated to Quebec independence, Anne said. They were two of the culprits involved in dropping a few smoke bombs at the Montreal stock exchange last month. And when a multi-nationalist came to McGill to give a lecture, Kunz welcomed him in bare feet to protest a sweatshop the guy had opened in Peru.

"Twelve." It was Dr. Cohen's turn to hold up an authoritative cop-like hand. "Ivan Sevrier. Susan knew him."

Christ.

She had mentioned him, by name, in several of her therapy sessions with the doctor. "I remember the name because she made fun of it, saying one of her friends had a real commie name, that's how she phrased it, a real commie name, Ivan. As in the Terrible or the Bear." He was a part of Susan's inner circle and she liked him a lot, said he had integrity and spoke with his eyes. "They were always sincere."

"Uh-huh."

"He was also a member of the Defeatniks."

THE SKY WAS AN AMBER ORANGE and dust from a ribbon of road drifted into the car covering my hands, the steering wheel, the inside windows with silty chalk. Tall grass bent in the shape of curved, shadowy letters, Hebraic markings in a strange land.

The building, a block and a half long and shaped like a gold brick, glinted dark yellow. Instead of curtains, Hebraic letters draped in the long, angular windows.

I knocked on the door.

Sun on shoulders and neck, the sky above appeared to be crying. It was as if my body were under a blanket. I was a kid again.

A rabbi opened the door, his eyes wide-set, face, clean-shaven, even though he was sixtyish and I expected him to appear bearded.

"Things aren't always what they seem."

I smiled.

"Hayden Ira Fuller?"

Before I could respond, he handed me another Hebrew letter, and I wanted to spell something with all the letters I'd seen, but I didn't know what they meant.

With a hooked finger, he beckoned me to follow. He was dressed all in black, looking Medieval. Me, I was casual: black leather jacket, tan chinos, a chambray shirt, boat shoes. I never wear boat shoes.

But I was happy to be here, to come out from under the blanket into orange light.

Suddenly, I knew I had a lot of time left: life, hockey, love.

"You do." The rabbi followed my thoughts, eyes locked on mine.

"Is Dad here?"

"He is."

I was looking forward to seeing him, talking for a while about the past, about Mom's death, about the past twenty-four hours, about Ellen Reynolds, about my disparaging memories and how unkind I'd been in my heart toward him.

"He can't stay long," the rabbi said, handing me yet another letter.

I studied some of this stuff for my bar mitzvah. But that was years ago.

Another room. White furniture, walls, carpeting, Venetian blinds. Chandeliers hung from the vaulted ceiling giving off bright white light. A white coffee table. White glasses.

Dad sat in a canvas chair, one leg resting on top his knee, his face dotted with salt-and-pepper stubble, eyes weary but full of playful possibilities, jokes to tell. He was in his Silverwood's uniform but the blue-and-gold piping was now all white on white.

He wasn't holding any letters.

Hebrew or otherwise.

He stared, beaming at me, and I felt loved. No words. And then he was gone.

The room, white as ever.

"I told you, he couldn't stay." The rabbi rubbed together hands folded in front of him.

"Yeah, you did."

My voice was happy and content. I hadn't heard those tones in a long time. Something seemed meaningful about all this, attainable.

The white room turned dark green, and the grass outside was now inside, swaying.

The letter in my left hand became the Talmud; the letter in my right the Torah. And as the grass weaved about the room, lifting and falling, falling and lifting, we danced, the rabbi and me, dancing with the rhythms of the tall grass.

—

SHE WAS ON TOP, pushing my hips into couch cushions, lips

gracing mine. "Shh—"

"What about Dr. Cohen?"

"She's asleep."

Stana's fine hair filled my eyes, lips, and I wanted to take all of her into my mouth, like Diego Rivera had wanted to do with Frida Kahlo's ashes, dying and living, sex as death, as beautiful as death, as sad as living. Resignations of desire filled me.

My gun was on the coffee table next to the couch, watching over the two of them, allegedly asleep in my room, but now Stana was here, watching over me, wanting me. She arched back, breasts raised and I kissed her nipples, took in a breast, another, wanting to take in all of her. "She'll hear us," I murmured.

"I switched glasses."

Dr. Cohen, knowing that Stana was upset over killing Sevrier, had mixed up a sedative for her, only Stana got Dr. Cohen to drink the one Stana was supposed to.

The tip of her nose glistened in the dark room, and I was hard in her hand.

I pushed against her hand.

"Easy, easy." She guided me in.

She moved up and down, taking me quickly to the edge, and then just as quick that edge ebbed away, my body becoming grimy fish scales.

"Relax." She pushed deeper, pressing arms into my thighs.

"I can't. I can't."

I wanted to, and then I slipped out.

Hair in eyes, nipples under my chin, she reached for me, and said don't worry about pleasing her, just have fun, and go when I'm ready to go.

My body just wouldn't cooperate, I wanted to say.

I was struggling to breathe.

"It'sokayit'sokayit'sokay."

She kissed the side of my neck, holding me, holding herself, holding on to us, what was left of us, of me, of my sexual self, holding, holding.

And then I came.

In her hand.

AFTER A FRIED EGG SANDWICH, black coffee, and an orange, I wandered around U of T's Registrar's office and asked about Susan Whitfield. Was there any support for such a troubled person, was she seeing a therapist? They didn't seem to know she had stopped attending classes. A young woman, a non-trad student and part-time secretary wearing a black pantsuit and leopard-spotted bandana, knew of Susan and her friends and gave a list of names and locations they frequented. I slipped her a ten-spot and followed the thread.

Sharon Dafoe was the first name on the list. A tall angular blond, whose hips entered the room before the rest of her, she was a barista at a local coffee shop at the corner of Bloor and Spadina, several blocks west of my old office. She wore a cashmere sweater, orange with black trim and black buttons, and tight-fitting capri pants. She didn't want to talk, but when I flashed my PI license and said it was me or the po-lice and their white interrogation room with bright lights on Bay Street she opened up.

Susan was, in a word, weird. Sharon's fingers stuttered as she spoke, and one leg under the table was crossed over the other. The sleeves of her cashmere sweater were pushed passed the elbows.

I sipped at my au lait and waited on significant details.

They weren't quite the flash of Sputnik's orbital arc, but they were pretty damn significant.

First off, Susan's brother was a real asshole. Just a jerk. And part of Susan's problem was listening to him too much. He guided her in everything from the fashions she wore to the lipstick across her lips to the books she read to the courses she took at U of T. And what he did to Colin Thompson—

Thompson. *Brother Thompson?*

I leaned forward.

She played with an earlobe, smiled thinly.

The coffee shop was full of Formica tables and along each wall were six or seven mannequins, mainly women, some naked, some wearing the latest hats designed by Coco Chanel, some looking on with approval, others with mockery. It was a little unnerving.

Thompson hung with the group, the Defeatniks, but he was a bit slow, okay, borderline, you know, retarded, and Franklin W. Whitfield II sets him up with a prostitute. Colin's, you know, twenty-four and never got laid, so Whitfield, the big-hearted guy that he is, lines up a rendezvous and you can imagine the failure that happened, the humiliation. She held a stiff arm in the air and let it fall straight down. On her pinky finger was a ring, green, with a bright yellow spot in the center.

"Was Whitfield in the room, dusting for fingerprints while Thompson and the woman fucked?"

One of the mannequins looked outraged over my f-bomb. Another one appeared to be smiling. She was the one that was naked.

But she had no nipples. What's up with that?

"Everyone knew about it, that's all I know, and Whit ridiculed Colin later that night and shit. The guy was a real dick. And that's all I'm going to say about him." She crossed her arms, bit her upper lip, and her eyes smoldered as she leaned back, worrying that she had already said too much. "Just a piece of work." She adjusted a feathered earring in the other ear.

How come Whitfield acted as if he didn't know Thompson when Stana and I first came upon the Gus kill? Why the subterfuge?

I flipped through old notes. Franklin had referred to Brother Thompson as a "nutter" but didn't claim any prior friendship or acquaintance.

However, he did tell us to investigate Thompson. To take him seriously.

Susan often talked about death. She was obsessed with it, because she believed that it held something better, something beyond the known. And she didn't like the known, her everyday reality.

"Her brother picking out her lipstick—"

"I guess." Sharon lifted a flutter of fingers to her neck. She was wearing a silver necklace that glinted every time she raised or lowered her chin. It was a philosophical position, Sharon said. Susan sought the spaces between the known and unknown. "She called it living in the in-between." Sharon tapped her fingers. The nails were chewed down.

"Hmm."

"Dimension V." As in the Venn diagram, you know, it's like living in the in-between, the space between the expected and the unexpected. "At least that's what she told me."

I sipped more au lait. The milk was just so-so. It wasn't Silverwood's.

Dimension V was for Susan a zone without judgment, without the restraints of social order. She didn't believe in monogamy. She believed in freedom of choice and the pursuit of personal pleasure without the fear of being policed by the look of the other.

"And yet, she allowed her brother to pick out her lipstick—"

"We're all full of contradictions."

Dimension V. Is that the universe Ivan wanted to dismantle?

Sharon's lipstick was a striking pink periwinkle. I wanted to compliment her on how it brought out the hazel of her eyes, but kept my mouth shut. It might come across as a pass, and I didn't intend it that way. I just *liked* her lipstick. Stana didn't wear much of that stuff.

I scratched at a pimple along the stitches on my chin. The couch cushions were a little rough last night, and there was a jagged kink along the right side of my neck and jaw. "How did that philosophy go over with the Defeatniks?"

"It was way out. We all believe in freedom but not to that extent."

"Monogamy?"

"Well, no. Not really." The entire group was about free love. "But Susan was about the right for targeted killing."

"Targeted killing?"

"Killing people who have nothing to give to society."

Two of the mannequins were shaking their heads.

"Like the homeless, the infirmed, the retarded?" *We're not The Third Reich.*

"Susan was outrageous. We didn't take her seriously."

"Well maybe somebody should have." I rolled my neck, the kink wobbling, a flexing saw blade.

Susan was an abstract thinker, she talked in the abstract, she never *did anything*. Theoretically speaking, she believed in "targeted killing." She wasn't into pragmatism, prudence, or utilitarian philosophy. You felt like it. You did it. "Outrageous, as I already said." Sharon lifted her chin, the silver necklace gleaming, and then she looked off in the direction of a full arriving pre-lunch crowd. It was now 10:57, between classes. "But she could be a lot of fun."

"A regular riot."

"She was sweet. I can't tell you how many times she stayed up late listening to me and my man troubles—"

There was a story there that I knew if I stayed long enough I would hear about. *Edge of Night*, revisited. "So, Susan Whitfield was a bit of a nut. Murder Incorporated wannabe by day; Dear Abby counselor by night."

"Please. I'm doing her an injustice if all you get from our conversation is condemnation and judgment."

"I apologize." I looked down into my near empty mug of au lait. I was being an asshole. Again. My third face, I guess. "What did you Defeatniks believe?"

The main slant to their manifesto was heavily influenced by France's post-World War II existential movement: to be responsible for every action, every breath you take, every moment of the day; to seek out and attain social justice; to make the world a better place by questioning the policies of NATO and the Soviet Union; and bringing about an end to the threat of nuclear war through protest, poetry, and poetic art. "Make a change, you know?" She shrugged, her left cheek in her right hand, hazel eyes full of uncertainties.

"Uh-huh." Did she know Ivan Sevrier?

"Red Ivan? Yeah." Susan and Red Ivan really hit it off apparently. They both liked Pop Art and wanted to make art even more relevant than Warhol, more committed to social change, and not to the aesthetics of parody, camp, and kitsch. "Ivan, however, was not gay." She raised her eyebrows as if recalling a passionate, personal rendezvous or interlude. "Most people who are into camp are flamers. Ivan, I assure you, was not."

"Were they lovers? Susan and Ivan?"

"No, No." Sharon covered her thin lips, trapping a laugh. Susan had little interest in sex.

"She was pregnant—"

"It's no big deal to get pregnant." She tapped false fingernails on the tabletop. I wondered if she chewed her nails down out of nervousness and wore the extensions to curb the habit. Susan, Sharon said, was only into sex to meet the needs of others.

"Needs of others. Like putting on red lipstick for her brother?"

"I didn't think of it that way, but I guess so."

Ellen Reynolds? I showed her the picture. Sharon knew nothing. Never met her.

I didn't quite believe her. Her nails were tap-tapping. "A little Indian girl, huh?"

"Who got Susan pregnant?"

She didn't want to say, but I assured her that I was worried about Susan's safety, and I needed to put the pieces of this puzzling case together so that I can help Susan, maybe Ellen, my good friend Dr. Jeanette Cohen, and myself: I needed to find the killer of my father. If I knew who got Susan pregnant that might lead to a lot of somethings.

"Okay, okay." Her head drooped. He was an older man, a non-trad student. Fortyish, fattish, hung around the Half-Life, buying up drinks for Sharon's crew. They quickly developed this thing because he was interested in Dimension V, was a follower of Jean-Paul Sartre, having read, not once but twice, *Nausea* and *Being and Nothingness*, and listened to Susan's ideas on the spaces in-between.

"The Venn diagram?"

"Metaphorically, of course—"

"Right, right."

Susan appreciated his appreciation and slept with him out of appreciation.

"Uh-huh."

"Her brother really liked this guy."

"Whit?"

"Yes." She raised her chin, hazel eyes darkened by the long eyelash extensions she wore. "Whit loved talking to Gus about everything."

"Gus Carhart?"

"I think that's his name. Yes." She nodded, fingers tapping. "Gus was a radio operator during World War II and Whit enjoyed hearing old stories about those radios they used, and how you could hammer nails with the walkie-talkies and they'd keep working."

"I see."

Christ. So Gus knew Beanie Boy too. And Gus knew Deuces. The three of them knew each other. This was too many coincidences and when there are too many coincidences that adds up to murder. Call it Fuller's law: coincidences equal murder.

And of course, Whit and Gus bonded over Dimension V. Franklin told him all about it and Gus wanted to live in that space, that zone. He was fascinated at the possibilities of leaving his boring life as a Becker's franchise manager. They were, well hell, fascinated with each other. They should have been dating instead of Susan and Gus.

"I thought Dimension V was Susan's idea?"

Well, it was hard to separate out their ideas from each other. They were so on the same page, you know, simpatico.

"Oh, so, Franklin wore red lipstick too?"

That cracked her up. You see, the two concocted the idea of Dimension V in fifth grade. Well, he was in seventh, she fifth. They always played together, after their mother died. Suicide. She had pneumonia, insisted on staying home, hated hospitals, and one morning they found her in her room. The windows wide open. It was December. She was dead.

"She had a separate room from her husband?"

She was English.

I wasn't quite sure what that meant.

Dismantle the universe. Dismantle Whit and Gus's universe?

Anyway, Susan was lost without a mom. And it was during one of their elaborate year-long narratives involving characters re-worked from classic fairytales that Dimension V was born. "They had their own language and everything. Dimension V became their central philosophy, their rules to run by." Sharon gently tugged on an earlobe.

"I see." I traced the lip of my empty coffee cup. "Did *Gus* want the child?"

"He was furious when she sought an abortion."

"How about Mr. Lipstick? Did he want her to have it?"

"I'm not sure."

"Hmm." I stared off at one of the mannequins on the wall. Its eyes appeared to be smiling. "Was Gus furious enough to hurt Susan when she sought out a doctor's help?"

"No." She looked over at the people crowding around the glass display case, scoping out the desserts. "I better go." There were only two other baristas working.

"Could Gus have got killed because of his fury?"

"Gus is dead?"

Her fingers quit tapping.

I reached for them. "Yeah."

Her eyes filled with tears.

Matt didn't like Gus, saw him as an infiltrator, an old-fashioned square.

"Of course. Matt, the doctor?" I was guessing.

"Yes." She sat back, uncrossing her legs. "How did you know?"

"I'm a detective." I smiled my lupine, lopsided grin. "He has one of those Scottish last names. Ogilvy or something." I snapped my fingers. Again, I was guessing. There are a lot of Scots in Canada.

"His mother was Scottish. Father English. Clarkson."

"Right. Matt Clarkson with the Scottish Mom." I smiled. "Susan appreciate him too?" I shrugged. "You know?"

Her wet eyes now mirrored sadness. She smiled wistfully. "No. He's married to Angie, but he has a thing for Susan. Weird, huh? Unrequited."

I nodded.

And I knew.

"The best kind of love," I said.

She couldn't look at me. "So they say." She smiled, face down.

Neither of us could look at the other.

Her fingers were quickly tap-tapping and mine countered with the same melody, in a slightly different key.

MATT CLARKSON, BETWEEN CLASSES AT THE U OF T, was home for lunch, a Shopsy's bag of corned beef boiling on the stove top, his one-and-a-half-year-old on his left hip. A pacifier daubed her mouth and the hair around her ears was matted with muddy cereal.

I assured Matt that I wasn't going to report anything to the authorities about his practicing abortions, that's not what this was about.

He nodded, his mouth firm. He had small, deep-set eyes, and frail hair with a high forehead. Look, I need your help, I'm working on a murder case and a missing girl case. And yes, nearly two nights ago, I lobbed a phantom grenade in the direction of Toronto Maple Leaf CEOs Cal Bullard and Steve Smith.

"That was great." He hitched his daughter Denise higher on his hip and flipped over the bag on the stove top. "Great." He was at the game last night, figured Bower was guessing pass on my two-on-one when I put it under the bar, stick side.

Water boiled rapidly. Behind us a shower rushed.

"Tell me about Gus."

"An interloper." Matt's lips pinched into a frown of afterthoughts. "No, that's too polite. A stalker."

Gus sensed a weakness to Susan and used her brother Franklin to get close to her. He listened to Franklin prattle on about Dimension V, his affection for radios, and all the goofy experiments he did in high school, including one gem involving mice in a controlled environment: he fed both mice the same amount of food, but one grouping heard only R&B and jump blues, Big Joe Turner, Louis Jordan, all hours. The other grouping heard only easy listening: Patti Page, Pat Boone. The jump blues mice grew much more stout, stronger. The easy listening trio of mice remained svelte.

"That's crazy."

"I know it. But who would you rather party to?"

"Turner and Jordan."

"Exactly."

So, Gus listened and listened, nodded at all of Franklin's talks and pontificating, and the next thing you know he's dating Susan. Franklin told her to.

"Hmm."

And Gus's hands were always all over her, inside the back pockets of her jeans, on her left or right shoulder, grazing on the fields of her ass or breasts when he thought nobody was looking. I saw. Sharon saw. Hell, even Thompson saw, and I'm not sure he totally gets sex. "Anyway, one time, Gus just touched her breasts when I was looking and said, 'look what's mine.'" Matt shook his head. Susan didn't seem to mind. "I think she felt sorry for him. Slept with him because she felt sorry for him."

Sharon had said something similar. Pleasing others. Into sex for the other.

Matt placed Denise in a high chair, snapped the plastic belt, and slid the tray tight. Susan was such an activist, into the rights of women to govern their own bodies, but when it came to herself and men—he shrugged.

Denise squeezed the plastic turtle and ducky in front of her. As the toys squeaked she squeaked.

Matt mixed up some dry Pablum with warm tap water.

"She's a cute kid."

"Yeah." He looked at the floor, stirring. It needed sweeping. "Looks like her Mom."

Something about the way he said those four words implied a subtext not to pursue.

He sat next to Denise, hands atop gray Formica. I sat down too, placed my porkpie on the side. Shit, I forgot to shave this morning. I could feel my face pulling me down. I was very, very tired.

Supposed to play on Friday. Years ago, Rocket Richard spent all day moving his family from one Montreal home into a newer Montreal home, and then played hockey that night, scoring three goals at the Fabulous Forum.

I'm no Rocket Richard.

I'll be lucky if I keep Howe from scoring three. Shit.

Matt lit a cigarette, blew smoke in the corner of the room,

and the Pablum was now the consistency he wanted. I hoped to be a dad someday.

"How did Franklin feel about the pregnancy? Toward Susan, toward Gus—"

"Deuces? What does he ever feel, really?"

"You call him Deuces too?"

"Anyone with a roman numeral after their name is bound to be pretentious. I'm just bringing him back to earth. Yeah, we all call him Deuces." He took another drag and then launched a spoon of cereal Denise's way, but she pushed her head left, clamping her mouth tight. "Even after the pregnancy, Deuces kept buying Gus drinks. He was the only one allowed to buy Gus drinks. Gus insisted on buying rounds for everyone else, ingratiating himself to us—the poser—since he had a job in the, so-called real world." The spoon became a rumbling jetliner and Denise opened her mouth. "Good girl," he said.

She chewed, pleased.

Off to the left was the living room, stocked with built-in walnut bookshelves, crowded with books. The floor was yellowed linoleum and along the west wall there was a velour chair and threadbare couch with towers of more books taking up all of the places to sit.

Matt made like a dive bomber this time and Denise smiled and opened wide, her face dimpled.

I asked if he knew Ellen Reynolds. Showed the photograph.

He did. Saw her twice. One time on campus. She arrived with Susan to discuss the abortion. They had become fast friends, I guess, he said, and Susan was worried that the baby would be born retarded. I told her we could do a test for that, but she was unconvinced the test would be conclusive. You see, she said, two generations back there was a retarded child on her aunt's side and she was so sure it was her turn. It was like a panic attack, her fear, and Ellen was holding her hand. They'd met at that church, The People's Way to Christ.

"Uh-huh."

I guess Susan went there quite a bit. Anyway, we talked and days later, he said, she decided to keep the baby. Ellen was maybe fifteen or so, troubled, and quoted odd scraps of literature, not scripture, but lit, *white* literature, and breaking down words, their meanings, you know, as if she were a walking Merriam-Webster's. He thought it was odd to read that shit. "I mean, the girl wasn't white."

"She was taken from her biological mom. Brought up white. What do you expect?"

He nodded absently. "Sure, sure."

"Yeah." I wiped the sides of my mouth. "You mentioned Thompson earlier? How well you know the cat? Eccentric fella, wears aviator goggles, a green coat."

"Back then he wore hockey gloves. Seriously. All the time with the gloves. Not joking. It was his thing. Hockey gloves. Made it hard for him to open doors for women."

I laughed.

"Guy wanted to be a hockey player. Figured that wearing the gloves would make it happen, and that wearing the gloves was the way to love. We all *love* hockey players."

There was some irony there. I caught it.

"A lost soul, really."

And then he told the failed sex story, the same one Sharon shared, only this time the girl Colin slept with wasn't a prostitute but Sharon.

"Sharon slept with Thompson?"

"Yeah." He fed Denise a half-spoon of cereal. Took another puff off his Player's Navy Cut.

"Why?"

"Because Deuces asked her to."

"Okay."

He's a charismatic guy, Matt said, people do what he asks.

"Were *you* in love with Susan?"

"Yes." He didn't hesitate for he felt no shame over it. You had to be honest with your emotions. "But did I fuck her? No."

"Would you have killed for her?"

"Gus?" He laughed. "Why should I want to kill Gus?"

A bright surreal splash of white dashed by my periphery, across a living room bookshelf. "You didn't leave me a towel in the bathroom, hon," the white slash said, the tone wobbling slightly.

"There's some."

"A *dry* towel."

He had taken a shower himself and forgot to replenish the supply, leaving a wet towel hanging on the rack. She reappeared in the doorway, small splashes of water gathered at her feet. He apologized.

"I'm Marie," she announced, walking naked through the kitchen to get to the hall cupboard. Seconds later, a beach towel was in her hand. "Is this all we have?" She held out the towel. It was nearly as big as she was.

"I better do laundry," he said.

Water dappled her hips and gathered along the curves of her upturned breasts and nipples. "Yes, you better."

She shook her head, returned to the kitchen, pulled out the Shopsy's bag, and then wrapped the towel around her body. Now she looked like a stout tight end for the Toronto Argonauts. The towel featured a girl with a bucket playing in the sand. The sun was a poached egg. "Would you care for a cup of tea?" Her back was to me.

I don't drink tea, too English. So out of politeness, I just asked for a cup of water, with ice, if you have it.

"Matt didn't kill anyone." She handed me a glass, three cubes. She stood in a wide stance, like Stana, perfectly balanced.

She had deep-brown eyes and coarse hair with Joan Crawford shoulders and eyebrows filled in with black pencil, a lot of black pencil. Apparently, she had put *that* on before finding a towel.

"I didn't think Matt killed anyone, really." I passed the wampum belt with my words.

She smiled. "You threw that grenade at Pal Cal and Steve Smith. Tuesday night." She'd watched the game on TV.

"That's right."

"They deserved that. The crooks. Loved it."

"Thanks."

She tightened her towel and slid a corned beef sandwich on rye with mustard and a kosher pickle to Matt.

He ate quickly.

"Susan was weird." Marie's eyes narrowed. "She might have killed Gus. She was always talking about death and—"

"Targeted killing?"

"Why, yes—"

Matt dive-bombed once again, and Denise opened wide, her hands bouncing with delight.

"Don't do that." Marie swatted at Matt's wrist. "She might choke. Don't get her laughing."

"She won't choke."

Marie took the spoon. "Let me." Denise opened without the requisite sound effects when Marie handled the spoon.

I thought Sharon said Matt's wife was named Angie. I flipped through my notes. *Angie*.

Maybe Matt took his *wife* to the game. Marie, I guess, watched it on the tube.

Susan's ideas were, well, disturbed. There was one man, Marie said, a fellow traveler, Jackson Grayson, C-student, that she suggested we do away with. Like for kicks. She had been reading up on Leopold and Loeb and liked the freedom exhibited by their killing choice. And Jackson, a fraternity fella, business major, fit the bill.

I wrote the name down. Jackson Grayson.

He died later at a frat party, fell off a balcony. Accidental the police said. "But I always wondered. His blood alcohol was three times over the legal limit."

"Was Susan at the party?"

"No."

"She was writing a paper on Prospero for an English Lit class," Matt said.

"Right. She liked Prospero. Thought he was a metaphor for her life. Anyway, Franklin was there, the ringleader, Sharon, Matt over here, and Tom Frieze, an artist friend who Susan liked." She smiled. "I was there too." She paused. "And Angie."

"And you all have alibis?"

Marie nodded. "Many of our alibis are contingent on the others we were with. We were with each other."

"Uh-huh."

Matt finished his sandwich, pushed his chair from the table, and said he had to get back to the U.

"Why did you want to help her, Matt?"

"It's a woman's right to choose, to govern over her body's reproductive—"

"Sure, sure, but why you?"

Denise was now making with the robust whoop-whoop noises, wanting Daddy's dive bombers to refuel and return.

"She might be weird, but there was a vulnerability to her, a gentleness—"

"You slept with her, didn't you? You said you didn't, but you did."

"Free love is a part of our—"

"Don't be such a square, Hayden," Marie chided. Love is love and monogamy is a social construct to control us and maintain patriarchal order. "Almost all of us Defeatniks are in open relationships."

I wrote that down too. I was afraid to look at her. Open relationships? Shit. Loyalty is what love is, love that changes as you change, love that learns to walk three paths: together, and two separate ones. Respect the differences. That's what love was about. Maybe I am a goddamn square. So be it.

After they made love, Susan cried against Matt's shoulder, saying her parents never loved her, and her brother too often controlled her, and she wishes she were never born; if not for her brother's love, she felt no love; her mom up until the day she died never hugged or kissed her; her father was cold and aloof and when she wanted to speak to him she had to make a goddamn appointment, in her own house, to see her father, an appointment. Dimension V held out the promise of a better place than here. Her whole life was a search to find it, to slip into it, and travel faraway.

"Anyone opposed to Dimension V, wanting to dismantle it?" I rubbed at the sides of my mouth. "Something Ivan said, about killing Gus. *Dismantle the universe.* Make any sense to you?"

Matt shook his head. "We all thought Dimension V was a little crazy, but it was their kind of crazy, you know? Susan and Whit's. Our philosophy in the Defeatniks is to let people be. That was their thing. Dimension V."

"Ivan Sevrier? Susan sleep with him too?"

"Yeah." He was the one man she may have truly loved.

"He was a student at McGill—"

Matt smiled, hitching his backpack to a shoulder. Ivan traveled here on weekends—

"Recruiting for N'oublie jamais?"

"Oh, you know about that, huh?" He laughed. "We called him Red Ivan or Frenchie or Vichy. The Vichy nickname he really hated."

"I can't understand why." I made a face. And then tossed out *11/14/65, midnight mass.*

"Midnight mass." He shrugged. It made no sense. Christmas was six weeks away. Susan's religion was art. Through painting she felt as if she were inhabiting the world of Dimension V, finding a portal between light and shadow, the known and unknown. She talked about this all the time with Tom, Tom Frieze. You should see him. Has a studio near Massey Hall. He let her share studio space with him. *That* was her church.

Tom Frieze. I wrote it down, had to ask for the spelling. "But she went with Ellen to that church on McGowan Street with Brother Durgana. Went there a lot from what I understand. I'd call Brother Durgana a Grand Wizard, but I didn't see any robes."

They have robes, Matt said. Susan showed him a photograph. Black robes. Hooded. They wear them for religious ceremonies.

"Really?"

Marie picked up Matt's plate; it was patterned with heels of bread that resembled a sad face. "Susan was full of contradictions. If she did go to the church regularly, maybe she was punishing herself, getting even with her father, who is a known atheist." Marie tapped Denise's nose and wiped cereal off her chin. "I don't think Susan liked herself very much."

What about Sharon sleeping with Thompson? Did she like herself?

Or Deuces telling Susan to sleep with Gus. Did he really like his sister?

I wondered if Thompson left his hockey gloves on while doing it. He wasn't sporting the goggles back then. That was a later affectation, a different mask to hide behind.

"The whole midnight mass thing just doesn't fit." Matt tapped me on the shoulder on the way out the door. "Got anatomy class to get to."

"Sure."

The fourteenth of November wasn't Christmas, he said. "And I don't think their church is Catholic—"

"It's not a typical church, that's for sure," I said.

And then again, nothing about this case was typical, nothing at all, I pondered, as Marie, and not Angie, directed a thumb-sized piece of crust into Denise's waiting mouth.

—

HANDS WERE EVERYWHERE.

Some were pointed, stretching to sky; others clasped together with thankfulness. One set was a boxer's fist, heavy, a knuckle caved in; but the biggest pair of hands, on a silver pedestal by the only window in the room, were a woman's, open, seeking alms.

Tom Frieze, prematurely balding, smiled at my appreciation of his sculptures, his head ducking slightly as he did so, embarrassed by my praise. About Susan, he held up a small hand and looked through my shoulder saying he didn't want to get too personal, she was a good friend, a great friend, but if he were about to reveal too much, for her sake, he apologized now, to her, in absentia. He respected private life, but he suspected, in the course of our interview, he would reveal things about her, himself, that he might regret. About her art, that he wanted to talk about and had a lot to say. Beginning last year he invited her to take up residence in his studio space, to develop her craft. She was a fine water-colorist. Her father did not approve of her journey in art.

"Why?"

"Impractical, he said. Get a real job. Make a difference."

"Social work?"

"No." He shook his head, his blue eyes bright pieces of jade. "Business. Make a difference in business."

"Sounds like an oxymoron."

Her father was one of the original Hidden Persuaders of advertising, playing on our fears, our desires, convincing us, after the war, to protect ourselves and our homes. We deserve it. We worked too hard to get what we got. We want to keep it, right? And to keep from losing it, to assure you are the protector your DNA wired you to be, be a man. Buy a monitoring system. Protect what's yours. From 1957, the era of Sputnik to the Cuban Missile Crisis, 1962, sales in his home security packages rocketed.

Monitoring systems. Bugs, microphones, in Dr. Cohen's office. His handiwork?

"I thought he was into weaponry, grenades full of creeping jelly."

"Yes, and guns." He half-smiled. "But monitoring systems too. Monitor, and then toss a grenade full of liquid napalm at your assailant."

That cracked me up.

"Recently," he said, "Susan tells me that her father was designing a fire extinguisher that's not quite a fire extinguisher."

"Huh?"

Instead of regular foam it fired some kind of advanced DDT, closing an assailant's pores, suffocating them instantly. "He's still working on the patent."

"Charming."

"A piece of work that family." He held up a hand and shook his head, his sandy-colored hair barely moving. "But I promised not to get too personal."

"Sure, sure."

I pointed at the sculptures, especially the glazed blue hands stretching for the sky. "You do good work."

"I'm obsessed with hands." He shrugged. Next to the eyes, the hands were the heart of expressions, revealing the root of our experiences, road maps to emotional truths. Hands, Mr. Fuller, can love, comfort; push away, threaten.

"Yeah." My father's hands were stubby, blocky, full of boxing-glove fingers.

One set of hands, on the far edge of a long white table, were saying no, the left higher than the right, warding off a possible blow. They were glazed yellow. "This is my favorite, I think."

"Yes." He couldn't look directly at me. Tom was quiet, withdrawn. For a fella in his late twenties, he had a much older face: heavy, fallen apple cheeks, blue eyes shadowed at times by a scaffolding of a protruding forehead and bushy eyebrows, and a nose that belonged on Emmett Kelly, the clown. He half-smiled again at my smile, and I felt a twinge of guilt for he saw that I saw that he was quirky, slightly goofy, but an intelligent, sensitive artist, nonetheless.

I meant no disrespect.

The problem with Susan, he said, was that there were three Susans: the outgoing one that hung with the Defeatniks spouting outrageous ideas in vain attempts to one-up theirs; the submissive Susan that followed alongside her brother who controlled and subdued so many of her natural impulses; and the third Susan, an insightful artist who shared his studio loft. That one was smart, vulnerable, introspective.

I wiped at the edges of my mouth and briefly saw the two of them in the space, working. Drop cloths on the floor, she quietly painting, he shaping a hand, dry clay on the outside edges of his own. Now, the sun filtered through the only window, the light turning a glowing white by the brightness of the nearly translucent walls, the cabinets, and the long, long table housing supplies. The room smelled welcoming. It was a relaxing room. And I felt like confessing, talking over things I had only told Stana and Anne Chevalier and Dr. Cohen.

"What about all the talk of killing Jackson Grayson?"

"Just talk." His hands hugged elbows tight to the white smock he wore. "Her first face. The one that tries to impress and push away others." That's the face she wore with her father.

"I heard about Daddy and Susan having to get appointments to see him. In her own home."

"Yes." He shook his head. "I don't think he ever wanted children. DDT in a fire extinguisher. That was one of his children."

"I get you."

"Do you?" He half-smiled again.

"But Grayson did die." Fell off a balcony or was pushed.

"He did." Tom pressed his hands into his thighs. The one window in his loft was tall, narrow, letting in the white light of the sun. Voices of children in a park on Queen Street diffused the room with a spirit of playfulness.

He noticed that I noticed and appreciated that together we liked the sounds. He was very aware.

"Children," he said. "Play is what art is all about. To push, to experiment, to take risks." To play with the same exuberance, the letting go of expectations that young children have, before goddamn puberty and self-consciousness sets in. An artist for Tom must be free of judgment.

"Dimension V? Is that why she wanted it, to be in that zone, free of judgment?"

"Dimension V? Drugs, sex, free love, rebelling against your father? That's not how you find it." He pointed at his heart. "It has to come from here. It's an inner peace."

I nodded.

"When I first saw you, you gave me that half-smile so many do, a smile that says I'm weird, strange, eccentric, possibly even a lightweight—"

"I don't see you as a lightweight, Tom." I took off my porkpie, studied the brim. "I'm sorry if I gave that impression."

"It's okay." He smiled wanly, eyes downcast, sad. "I'm used to it. Most people see me that way. I assure you, Mrs. Frieze does not, but most do. And in a way, I've courted that. I like people to underestimate me, and then I can surprise them with my art, my hands." He held them up and was about to say something, and then broke off his flow. "People can't surprise me, you see?"

"Yeah. I do." It was his armor against being hurt by the hands of others.

There was a long pause. But when he worked with his hands, on his art, all of his self-consciousness, fears and doubts were gone. "I suppose you feel something akin to how I feel as an artist in playing hockey."

That's why I took to the game, I think. Yes, I was very, very good at it. But I felt safe on the ice. The game has rules and patterns of improvisational behavior, movements that lead to a certain set of definable, agreed upon outcomes. I was looking forward to Friday night at the Olympia.

Miriam had the levaya under control. I had scribbled two sentences together for a possible eulogy, but my mind was on this case, and Howe, and Detroit, and not words I couldn't believe in.

"You're an artist of the ice."

That made me laugh. Tom had a way with *words*. He said "of" instead of "on". There was a poetry to that choice.

"I wasn't being funny," he said. Play created flow for him, and he was sure for me too, and flow created joy, contentment.

I was never more content than when I played hockey or lobbed that phantom grenade in the direction of Bullard and Smith. "Did Susan ever attain that in her art?"

"Rarely." She was good but almost always self-conscious. Sometimes she attained freedom to just be.

"Dimension V freedom?"

"I don't subscribe to the principles of Dimension V. It's—"

"Narcissistic?"

"Yes." He dropped one arm to his side, a hand still clutching an elbow. "The V for them meant Virtual."

"Not Venn, as in diagram?"

"No." He laughed. "Virtual. A world that isn't quite real but for them is." He smiled, resembling a wounded soldier after a fierce bout of trench warfare. Maybe the clay dotting the left side of his chin furthered this impression of a muddied man. Susan, he said, occasionally freed up a space for herself away from her brother, but too often his presence invaded her work.

"What do you mean?"

"Let me show you."

We crossed over a series of clay-dotted drop cloths to the long, low white table. He opened a large shallow drawer and pulled up a portfolio bag, unzipped it, and gently removed a host of water colors.

All were dotted with rain-drop splatters of blood. Some of the splatter were fat coins, others dots of confetti. I couldn't help but think of bloody Stars of David in Dr. Cohen's office: *We know what you said.*

"Oh." He smiled, his lips pinched in bemusement. "The blood. Her signature. Literally." Susan believed in completely giving of herself in her work and the dots of blood represented the life she'd given and given up to create.

"Her form of Dimension V truth, I imagine."

"Yes. One of their bullshit mantras: *Expect the Unexpected.*"

Christ. Deuces must have coined that.

"I told you her father was an original Hidden Persuader of the advertising age. It rubbed off on his kids. A lot of the finer points, nuances, to their project involved pithy advertising slogans."

"The pause that refreshes, huh?"

"I prefer Pepsi."

That cracked me up.

Her brother drew the blood from her arm, using a syringe, a vial, whatever, and from that small drawn amount, she'd "clip it" to her art.

"Her brother?" Always the brother, lurking. Drawing her blood. A regular Dracula.

He shrugged disapprovingly. Susan and Franklin had their own language, 100 or so words that no one else knew but them. Hell, they often completed each other's sentences, said what the other was thinking or said the same things on the exact same beat. Always in rhythm. They even had a self-invented sign language. Very quid pro quo.

"So Franklin told her to sleep with Gus. Who did she tell him to sleep with?"

"Franklin told her to sleep with Gus?"

"Yeah. That's what I hear. Gus. Owns a Becker's. Dead. Killed for beef jerky. Allegedly."

"He's dead?"

"Yeah." As a doornail, I wanted to say, channeling my inner Cagney.

"She slept with Gus?"

I flipped through my notes. Yup, that's what Matt suggested. "Wasn't he the expectant father of her unborn child?"

"She never said a word about Gus to me. She liked the doctor, Matt Clarkson. But Gus?"

"I thought Franklin liked Gus."

"Franklin liked Gus. Yes." He shook his head. "I didn't even know she had a thing going with Gus."

"Then who's the father of the unborn?"

"I think Ivan. That's who she loved." He shook his head. "Matt, she had a thing for, but Ivan—Ivan she loved."

"What about Thompson, the guy with the goggles—?"

"Thompson? He wore hockey gloves. Always. When I knew him." He smiled. "Hiding his hands, afraid to touch, to be touched—"

"Right. Thompson and Sharon Dafoe?"

A sordid thing really. Franklin set that all up and we all listened. Well, I wasn't there, but everyone else was.

"At the fraternity?"

"Yes." Franklin had talked Sharon into sleeping with Thompson, a kind of vestal virgin thing, I guess, I don't know, but it was all arranged, and Franklin set up a secret radio sound studio in the bedroom, one of his father's security systems, microphones under the bed, and they all listened in, in another room, listened to Thompson's struggles. I think he came really fast or couldn't come. One of the two. Sordid.

Microphones under the bed. Microphones in Dr. Cohen's office.

"They all listened in?"

"Yeah. Big joke, huh?"

I'd heard that Tom was there. From Matt. Or was it Marie.

Now he's saying he wasn't.

"Who's they?"

Gus, Jackson Grayson, Matt. Angie. Others, I can't recall all the names. "Anyway, I got the story from Susan so she must have been there."

"She wasn't. Shakespeare paper. Prospero."

"Oh, yeah. That's right." He half-smiled.

Grayson kept teasing Thompson afterward, calling him Short Dick. "How he knew the size, I don't know." He held up a hand. But Grayson wouldn't let it go, saying did you touch her tits with the hockey gloves, shit like that, and Thompson fled crying, and wasn't seen again by the group. Ever. He quit hanging at the Half-Life. A no-show. He quit hanging at the frat. He had been their mascot. He wasn't smart enough to attend the U of T, but he earned his mascot keep at the frat by sweeping floors, cleaning the kitchen, running errands for the fellas, buying cigarettes, condoms, that kind of stuff.

"Quid pro quo, huh?" I'm surprised the frat didn't make the poor bastard dress as Elmer the Safety Elephant. Rule Number Two: Don't Run out from Between Parked Cars.

"I guess so."

From frat mascot to gun-toting custodian at The People's Way to Christ.

"Sharon had no idea they were transmitting the escapades through speakers for all to hear." He shrugged. "She hasn't been a part of the group either, since that night."

Shit. I had to talk to her again. She pointed fingers at some, especially Deuces, and away from herself. There was no prostitute.

I turned to the water colors. Under the blood splotches was some really fine portrait work with the horizon line high or low in the composition. None of the portraits were T-framed. They were all off center, destabilized, giving an aura of urgency and uncertainties.

One man, with dulled red hair, stared openly beyond the

space shared by the artist, eyes vaguely brutal, face somewhat immobile, lips slightly parted.

"That's Jackson Grayson."

The guy who *fell* off a balcony. "You think Thompson came back and pushed him? Killed him?"

"Yes." He shrugged. "But the police interrogated him and let him go."

"Inconclusive I assume."

Another nod.

One canvas was blank except for the blood splatter.

"That's a self-portrait," Tom explained, his words soft puffs, a candle going out.

"There's nobody there."

"That's her. Invisible."

I snapped on my porkpie, adjusted the brim, unsure of what the blank sheet meant.

"What do you like about this one?" He gestured with an open hand to a third work.

A girl and Franklin W. Whitfield II waited by a bus stop, a brown bag on the bench behind them, the sun no longer visible, the street dusky.

"A lot of blue in the image. And yellow."

"Right. Look closer."

I did. The brown bag on the bench was actually a dark, almost earthen blue. It matched her blue dress, his blue blazer.

He smiled, eyes looking through my shoulder. "And?"

"Uh—the horizon line—"

"Forget the horizon line—"

The twilight's blue, the street's blue.

"Good." Notice, he added, the yellow tie, yellow belt, yellow hat band. Yellow shoes. She has yellow hair ribbons, yellow handbag, yellow sash to her dress. Yellow heels. "The accessories match."

Quid pro quo?

"He insisted on that. In real life."

Franklin was a controlling force, a regular Svengali. When they partied together, he insisted that her accessories correspond with his choices. "Hence the blue bag."

A sign of subconscious protest on Susan's part? A lunch bag is never blue.

Maybe, he said. "But in his world. In his sick world. A lunch bag is blue."

Franklin was two years older than Susan. He called all the shots. "Is it any wonder why she disappeared. Wouldn't you?"

"Uh-huh."

"See anything else?"

"The bus hasn't arrived. They're waiting. She's waiting for something, someone to take her away from all this."

"You've been there. Haven't you? Wanting to be taken away from all this?" His blue eyes probed, seeing the buried shadows of my heart.

"Yes."

"I have too," he said.

Could her escape involve the cult on McGowan Street led by the charismatic Brother Durgana and his promises of a simpler life?

"What about the hands?" He tapped his lower lip, returning our focus to the canvas.

Neither set were in a proper resting position. His index finger was sharply pointed at her, his thumb stretched at an adjacent angle, giving an imperative command. The fingers of his other hand were curled worms.

Both of her hands were snowballs, tightly packed.

"He's trying to tell her something," he said.

"I'm more interested in what she has to say," I said.

And we stared at the hands, and then I said something about the hands that he creates, the hands that once scared him, scared me, that we now have control over. "It got better for you?"

"Yes."

"Your father?"

He nodded.

"Mine too." I pushed back my porkpie. "Mrs. Frieze, the sex—?"

"It got better too."

"My sex life's not so good."

"It'll get better."

And then I pulled up a chair, removed my hat, and we talked, an hour, an hour and a half, about all that was broken.

SHE HAD BEEN A VERY BUSY GIRL. Those were her words, not mine.

We were rushing along the Don Valley Parkway, eating burgers, sharing French fries with gravy, and balancing cups of soda between our legs. Our meeting with the Whitfields had been pushed back from 4:30 to 7:30—big business meeting, teleconference for Whitfield Munitions with a bunch of CEOs or some damn thing.

First off, Bob Waterman's not a cokehead. Stana checked with Silverwood's. Two days ago, he'd taken time off work to get tested for allergies, his back a scratchy road map of various allergens: food, pollens, molds. Black mold was the one.

"Black mold?"

"Yup. He's going to get a new office."

"Cool. Good for him." I wiped gravy off my lower lip. "So, he's no cokehead. And it wasn't coke that killed my father."

Forty-five minutes ago I had called Sal from the burger stand and he said the blood results had come back on the Star of David posters: AB. I told him to run an HCG on it. I had a feeling the blood would reveal that it came from a pregnant woman, Susan Whitfield.

The autopsy results on my dad were also in. He had a massive seizure followed by a heart attack. In his blood stream were high levels of chlorpromazine, an anti-psychotic, better known by its brand name Thorazine. "Used on schizos," Sal said, calming them, taking away the highs and lows. *Does it taste metallic?* My sources have said so. *Does it affect muscular movement?* Yes, I believe that's one of the side effects that the lab boys listed. That and weight gain, cowboy. *The folks at McGowan Street walked with baby steps.*

"Thorazine, huh? Same drug used on the church followers—"

"Probably."

"Wow."

Now, Stana wiped gravy away from the corners of her mouth, licked the top of a finger.

Secondly, she said, Anne Chevalier called the *Telegram* and wanted to meet with us and Dr. Cohen tomorrow to talk over our case.

Chevalier of the RCMP. She helped crack my last case involving domestic violence, a possible terrorist threat, plastic surgery, and murder. Perhaps this case posed yet another threat to national security? N'oublie jamais.

Late this morning Stana had also surveyed the Army Surplus store, familiarizing herself with a kayak paddle, compasses, K-bars, and Sterno kits. Two men in wool coats, felt hats, and glasses bought some heavy rope and roadside flares. Nothing else or suspicious to report but those two fellas, wannabe secret service agents, or in all likelihood stage managers on the lookout for supplies for an updated *Hamlet*.

Oh, and in the back of the store, she said, the door, black, heavy with chipped paint and peeled-back strips, was stenciled in a florid fluorescent orange: "Keep Out." Rising up from the basement, low voices, and the rhythmic strum of a wonky machine. It had an inconsistent beat. Speeding up, slowing down.

"Like it was hand cranked?"

"Sure. Maybe."

"Like it was a ditto machine?"

I had to find a way into that room. Maybe it was full of guns and 1940s-era creeping jelly grenades to be run by N'oublie jamais into Quebec. Ivan was with N'oublie jamais. Was the universe he wanted to dismantle English and predominantly Protestant? Maybe. But I was beginning to feel that something else was going on in that basement and the French revolutionaries were a sideshow, a strange coincidence. This case wasn't about them.

Just a hunch.

But what was it about? A strange brother. A sister. A murder at a fraternity. The murder of my father. "A big mashugana, that's what this case is."

Stana sighed, and I changed lanes.

And remember Brother Durgana, how he knew so much about us, reading our auras? What if he had access to our prior conversations with Dr. C, what if he were behind, or at least involved with, the bugging of her office?

Another hunch, but they were adding up to something.

Stana's eyes expanded, her chin lowered. "Time for another conversation with the brother."

"Yeah." I laughed. "I'm glad he's not one of my relatives."

She wiped a spackle of gravy from chin, her fingers lingering over my cut, the dirty bandage. "How's the chin?"

"Okay." Sure the adhesive tape looked like a streak of heavy mud, but the pain was gone.

"Mashugana, that's like, what? A big storm?" She smiled.

"No that's mishagoss. This is like a storm, but of the mind. Crazy. Bizarre. Dimension V shit. And how does that damn cult fit in? We know Susan goes there or did. Does?" I shook my head.

"I didn't see her in the crowd I interviewed yesterday."

"Maybe she was in the church when you were interviewing?"

"Maybe."

"Maybe they're hiding her—"

"Maybe."

"Maybe I'm losing my fucking mind."

"Maybe."

That cracked me up.

The streetlights of the Don Valley glared above like the lights we stare into while waiting in a dentist's chair. Stana was turned sideways in her seat, huddling her shoulders closer toward me. The duct tape buckling against the broken part of the passenger window wasn't keeping all the cold air out. I had the heater on full but the air was just warm. I needed to add anti-freeze.

"There are so many loose strings. I can't tie it all together." *Gus and Deuces and Brother Thompson all knew each other and they had acted as if they didn't. Why?* I hit the steering wheel hard with my hand, and the car lurched left, then right. "Sorry." I apologized, biting my upper lip.

I filled her in on Colin Thompson and Sharon Dafoe, the recording, the ridicule, so many of the suspects present, listening in, and Grayson's later needling of Thompson and a fall from a balcony. Thompson could have got even, killing Grayson, pushing him off, or just nudging him. The guy was loaded. A woman could have done it. Sharon. I'd have to have a follow-up conversation with her—there were too many gaps in her narrative. If she'd made love to Thompson because Franklin told her to, could she also have been compelled to commit murder, nudging Grayson from the balcony?

And what about the microphones? The Whitfields specialized in home security systems. Deuces placed listening devices under Sharon and Thompson's bed; did he and the Whitfields also bug Dr. Cohen's office?

"I thought you thought Durgana bugged the office?"

"Maybe the good brother and Frank Two are in it together." With my left hand I felt the dimpled dome bubble in my pocket.

"Maybe."

Finally, there were a few other suspects: Matt, Angie, Gus.

They were there. Susan wasn't present, but could someone have done the "targeted killing" at that frolicking frat for her?

She was busy writing about Prospero.

"Angie talked to me," Stana said. This afternoon she visited her at the Free Clinic on Parliament Street. Angie worked there as a nurse, receptionist, doctor's assistant. It was a small, understaffed clinic.

"Sure."

Angie didn't give a damn about the Defeatniks. Thought they were self-absorbed posers. *Where's their fucking bongos?* "She must have uttered that refrain ten times during the course of our interview." *Where's their fucking bongos?*

"That's a gasser."

Now Susan. Angie hated that chick. Not just because she had slept with her husband (after all who hadn't? Sharon apparently), but get this, Stana said, when Angie slept with Susan, Franklin watched. Took pictures. Pentax. "She remembered the brand."

"Did he use a filter? I might have gone for some bounce light."

She punched my shoulder.

"I mean, who watches his sister having sex?"

Stana shook her head.

"Sick. Who does that?" *Quid pro quo. Did she later watch her brother fuck somebody? Gus?*

Stana reached for another fry, placing a hand under it to catch gobs of gravy that might add to her fashion statement. She wore a dark green dress, green pumps, and a big necklace full of white shells and smooth stones. Angie felt manipulated by the two of them. She swallowed the promised freedoms of Dimension V, resigned herself to Franklin's controlling charms.

"A common theme to Mr. Whitfield's escapades. Sharon, Brother Thompson, and maybe even Gus felt a similar vibe. He uses people."

"At the *Telegram*, you'd have no idea. He's so—"

"Obsequious?"

"Yes." She smiled. "I see our games of Scrabble have helped your vocabulary."

She always beats me at Scrabble. I hate Scrabble.

"That's his persona. His mask. His second face. His real face, his third, is on display away from the paper, away from his father, in the world of the Defeatniks."

"I guess so."

The duct tape buckled heavily with wind.

I still had to take care of my father's burial, and now the car window, and oh, by the way, suit up to play in Detroit on Friday. Shit, I needed a daily planner like the business cats carry around in their lapels.

Manipulation. Psychological abuse was Deuces' game. That was his will to power. And how about Susan's will to power? Isn't that the real reason she ran away? The pregnancy was the final push toward autonomy and freedom, a life outside the one brother and sister had created together, the fallen paradise of Dimension V. He was Adam to her Eve. She wanted to bite a different apple.

"Crazy," I said, channeling my inner 1950s Marlon Brando.

One night at the Half-Life, Angie recalled Franklin ordering Susan off the dance floor. Her green handbag didn't match the blue band of his fedora. "And get this, no one objected. They all agreed with Franklin. That's how *charming* he is."

"Suave." It was a similar story Tom Frieze told and the subtext to Susan's water colors. We hit the Bloor off-ramp. I couldn't believe a brother forcing his sister to fuck somebody else while he took pictures. Hard, lurid memories filled my head, me naked on the couch, forced at gunpoint to perform. Stana made to watch. My last case. Exposed before her. Weak. Inside. Outside. Ashamed. Survive, her eyes said. Just survive. And I did.

And then the other night.

"I'm sorry about—"

My hands were firm on the steering wheel as paper cups blew up against a curb in Jamestown.

She gently topped my hands with hers. Her fingers, warm; mine, pale white, the underbellies of dead fish. "We'll get it right," she said.

My eyes filled with appreciation.

"I think we ought to interview Angie again, with you there," Stana said. She felt Angie was holding back, she really hates that whole crowd, bongos and all. "Smith owns the surplus store. He wouldn't broker a deal with separatists, would he?" Fuck, his best friend was a munitions engineer, arms manufacturer. Could he be procuring guns for N'oublie jamais?

"I don't think so."

If dismantling the universe involved guns against the English, the Protestants, the United Empire Loyalists forget about it. Smith would never be a part of that program.

"Well, he's procuring something for himself." She gave me her smart-ass look, eyes widening with mirth, the tip of her tongue sticking out of the side of her mouth. After casing the surplus store and coming up a big zero, she visited Smith. He was talkative. Played with his glasses the whole time. Said the store was a tax break. "Called you an asshole about forty-two times."

"I'm glad he remembers me."

Following the interview, Stana drove her car down to a curving cul-de-sac, walked back, hid behind a long line of maple trees, and waited. Within twenty minutes a Ford Econoline van, white, arrived, off-loading two young women, fourteen or fifteen year olds, wearing padded jackets that resembled life preservers, big white boots, and fishnet stockings.

"Fishnets?" Like Ellen, the day Dad drove her away.

"Uh-huh." And, she said, these two girls were among the people she interviewed at The People's Way to Christ yesterday. They stayed about forty-five minutes. She handed me three photographs. "The blond in the white Bolshevik hat drove the van."

Sharon Dafoe.

Shit. She said she'd quit the Defeatniks over their sexual hijinks and now she was pimping for Durgana. No wonder he got such a good deal at the surplus store. I sifted through the photos. "You have been busy," I said.

"The church and Smith—and the midnight mass?"

I shook my head, confused, hitting the steering wheel, three quick taps. "I think N'oublie jamais is a dead-end street, a coincidence. A parallel world that has no meaning in the world of this case." Ivan Sevrier, Red Ivan, the fella you made into grapefruit pulp, was in love with Susan Whitfield. That's why he was in Toronto. Often. Sure, he did a little recruiting, but hell they called him Vichy. He wasn't making any inroads here. He was here for her. Not guns. He loved her.

"Then what did he mean with his toss-off comment, 'dismantle the universe?'"

"I don't know." I shrugged. "Maybe he wants to dismantle Dimension V? Maybe he hates Deuces?"

"Ivan's the father of the unborn child?"

"Yes."

"But what about the other fella, his sidekick?"

Neither of us could remember his name, the Marxist-Leninist cat who thought the Bluffs were beautiful because monopoly capital played no role in their being. Did it matter that he was forgettable? Once a side man always a side man. "A friend who made trips with his pal, occasionally."

"But why kill Gus?"

"For Susan?"

"Why?"

"I don't know." All I knew was I was holding the wrong threads; the surplus store was involved but not in the ways we suspected.

Sharon Dafoe was delivering girls from the church to Smith's home in Rosedale. Bolemac, Smith, owned the surplus store. What was the church, Durgana, getting in return besides a 25% discount to buy aluminum canteens and Sternos? "It feels like a dead end." Hopefully our meeting with Frank One and Frank Two would yield something new.

I felt the ribbed ridge of the microphone in my pocket.

"Frank One and Frank Two?"

"You know, like Dr. Seuss?" I said.

"That's good." She gathered up the photographs, looked away. "What about our case?"

"Huh?"

I could barely make out her eyes in the dim glow of the dashboard light.

"I took my vacation." She smiled awkwardly, pressing lips together. "Two weeks. I was thinking of going to Detroit. With you."

I smiled my lopsided grin. "For a vacation?"

"Yeah. And we'll work on your case—"

I wasn't ready to share what Tom and I talked about, but this was a giant step. "Detroit and then back to Montreal?"

"Yes. Detroit, and then back to Montreal."

She kissed my cheek, catching the side of my lips.

I tasted gravy.

It tasted sweet.

THE ROOM WE GATHERED IN was straight out of Tennessee Williams. *Suddenly Last Summer.*

It was part 1950s modernity with its tulip-shaped lamps, low-flung coffee tables, wide-flared chairs with metal triangular legs, and a hi-fi unit complete with Julie London records. And it was also part primordial ooze with a far wall that didn't appear to be a wall at all but a series of heavy plants, casting Neolithic shadows on all our faces. Its trees, heavy, stout, and full of elephant-trunk branches, weren't like any species of tree found here. A thin ribbon of water flowed inside this dense heat of green, and a slither of snake scarfed a rodent the size of a chameleon. On the table in front of us were three or four vases full of what I assume were orchids, a light bluish pink, giving off a fragrance that didn't quite fit in with the snake still slowly swallowing. Next to the vases were two black-cylindered fire extinguishers and a pair of sealed envelopes.

Temperature wise, the room was a goddamn blast furnace. My shirt was wet, collar stiff. I loosened it.

Julie London was the only nice touch to the joint.

Frank One sat back against a high, King Arthur throne, a clear break from the room's modernity and jungle themes, and a sure sign that he saw himself as special. He sat with assurance, straight, all angles and sharp lines, manicured fingers poised in front. His skin was the glaze of fresh frost, with a large cocoa-puff of a mole on his right cheek. Nothing bothered this cat. He wasn't sweating at all. And he had his jacket on. My jacket was draped to my chair, my Arrow shirt becoming see-through.

His son, Frank Two, appeared snappy in his freshly pressed charcoal suit, standing behind his father, like a member of the Queen's Royal Guard or some damn thing. He too wasn't sweating. Shit, his double-breasted jacket was fully buttoned.

At one of the table's short ends sat Steve Smith, Leafs CEO. His body drooped like a fallen leaf in *Macbeth* gone to sere. His Lombardis gleamed back images of trees and underbrush. I couldn't see his eyes.

Shaved off was the Errol Flynn mustache. I guess he wanted to strike a more innocent look for the jurors. Libertine of the Year, 1965, wasn't going to cut it.

"What's he doing here?"

"A family friend." Frank One smiled, his teeth very even. He and Smith belonged to the same country club. Whitfield had stock in the Leafs and "well, Steve came to me hours ago, saying that you, Miss Younger, were lingering about outside his Rosedale home—"

"I was spying," Stana corrected, shifting in her rattan chair, trying to get comfortable. She'd already downed the glass of water in front of her and the freckles of her face were aligned with the fresh dots of freckled sweat. Her green dress was a little darker, it seemed, than a few hours ago.

"Yes. So you were." He nodded. "I appreciate your honesty."

"I don't," Smith said. "I could have you arrested for trespassing." His security cameras had picked her up. Forty-five minutes of loitering. Apparently, he had purchased one of Frank One's monitoring systems.

Was he into microphones under beds as well?

Smith removed his glasses, wiped sweat off the stems, pushed them back on, shadows of trees filling his eyes.

"Those girls are underage." Stana leaned forward.

"Yes." He smiled. "You have a devious mind."

I reminded him of my first case: hidden cameras, a porn racket involving underage girls.

"And may I remind you, Mr. Fuller, that was Landover Leeds's peculiar obsessions. Nick Stabulas's sickness. The charges leveled at me involve blackmail and extortion, not sleeping with underage girls." He sighed. "And let me remind you further, they're just, as they say, charges."

"Uh-huh," I said.

The girls Stana saw were young entrepreneurs, working with Smith, in conjunction with their church, to market pies (blueberry, caramel apple, peach). He was giving them advice on a business plan on how to label and push their brand.

"Pies?" Stana looked skeptical.

"Pies. Blueberry, peach—"

"Yeah, yeah, I got it."

I was kind of looking forward to a slice of caramel-apple.

"Who goes to a business meeting in fishnets?" Stana tapped her lower lip. "Fishnets, really?"

"They're young. They'll learn appropriate attire—"

"These are a group of girls who usually wear canvas: tops, pants, dresses. Dull, canvas."

They also walk dully. Loaded with Thorazine?

Frank One held up his hands, tired of the banter. "I assure you, Mr. Smith has assured me that he has acted appropriately. He can show you their proposal—"

Smith reached for a briefcase by his feet, slid the locks open and pulled out folders full of pie photographs, pie recipes, and an assortment of memos and correspondences.

Stana flipped through the evidence and said nothing. Slid the stuff back across to Smith, his phosphorous fingers tapping together with victory.

"We done here? We cleared up our little differences of opinion?" Frank One's eyes were the brown of lentils, his face wide, Eastern European. I'm sure Whitfield, like Fuller, was a created name, an attempt to fit in. This guy wasn't a descendant of the United Empire loyalists, more like a member of the Balkan powder keg, 1914. "There were no underage girls involved in anything sordid."

I knocked back the last of my water, played with the brim of my porkpie. "Nothing sordid, huh?" I pulled the microphone disc from my pockets, tossed in on the table. "Three were found in Dr. Cohen's office. Three." I pointed at Frank One. "You're into monitoring systems." I pointed at Smith. "You're into voyeurism, hiding behind a two-way mirror while folks lap dance." I pointed at Frank Two. "And you. You're into planting bugs under beds and listening to people fuck."

Frank Two moved away from his father, bumping the edge of the table, his upper arms tensing in the sleeves of his sport coat.

"Now, now." Frank One held up a large hand. He rolled the disc between fingers as if he were about to do the Van Heflin coin trick from *The Strange Love of Martha Ivers*. "This isn't one of ours. It's inferior." He snapped the dome bubble from its ridged ribbing. Pulled out the transistor. "It doesn't even have meshing for noise reduction. No ambient noise filter." He smiled, lumped all the pieces together. "Our microphones are half the size of this and much more efficient." He saucered the lump back to me. I pocketed the mess. You better look into someone else, he said. All of us in this room use Whitfield products.

"Sure, sure. Brand loyalty, huh?" I wasn't buying it. "What about Brother Durgana?"

"What about him," Frank Two asked.

"He *loyal* to your brand?"

"He likes pies," Smith said. "That's all I know. Pies."

Frank Two returned to his proper place, standing behind his father's right shoulder.

"What about the floor plans? The floor plans that Ellen took and handed off to Susan?"

Stana pulled them out of her purse with the rings-of-Saturn handles.

I spread them across the table. Showed them the circled air-conditioning unit.

"That's where they're going to build the lab." Smith's hands flashed over the plans, a contrail of phosphorous. "That exact spot. Ovens, everything. Unfortunately the central-air unit blocks out the flow of ovens—"

Smith knew Ellen. She was one of the original founding members of the group to bake pies. It was her idea to make it into a business. "Who says redskins lack drive, initiative, huh? Bigots say it."

The irony was lost on Smith.

Why was Ellen wearing fishnets? The day she disappeared. Fishnets.

Something wasn't right about all this.

"How often did you meet Ellen?"

"Three, four times. At my place." He folded his hands in his lap. "And then she became disillusioned. I don't know why." He sighed. "Disappeared."

I folded up the floor plans. Handed them back to Stana.

"I have to admit. I thought your general demeanor the other

night, the lobbed grenade was in poor taste. On Remembrance Day?" Smith smiled when giving you a beat down. "Respect our troops, the men who served—"

I remembered Smith's father, the first owner of the Leafs affectionately labeled the Old Man, and his militia during World War Two and the guns and grenades and AK-47s in Smith's cubbyhole in Rosedale. "Point taken—"

"I thought my son's write-up, if I may piggyback on my good friend Mr. Smith's comment, my son's outrage in the *Telegram* over the event was extremely impassioned, well-written." Frank One smiled again, looking over his shoulder at Frank Two.

"Point taken back," I said.

"You don't have to be insolent." Frank Two's cobalt eyes were full of napalm.

"No. But I choose to be." I pushed back my porkpie.

Frank One held up both hands. He seemed to like doing that. Maybe he ought to moonlight as a traffic cop. "Head strong." He gestured again. "Steve? You're free to go. I think we've cleared up our little dispute with our guests. I have other things to discuss with them."

"Yes sir."

I never saw Leafs CEO Smith follow the orders of anyone so willingly. Maybe Frank One was paying his legal bills.

Smith gathered the folders, his briefcase, pushed himself from the table, and moved toward a large marble black door, feet faintly splashing with hollow echoes.

Frank One smiled awkwardly. "He's a little too enchanted with that church." He shrugged. "I appreciate him wanting to help the kids, be a mentor, but—I don't want him to hear my proposal to you."

Smith knew Ellen.

Frank One wanted to hire us to find his daughter. She was trapped in that cult on McGowan, he said. Steve thinks they're eccentric; I think they're a cult. He shrugged again.

Frank Two, his angular face with the aquiline nose, plunked a cassette recorder on the table's marble, pushed down a button and a woman's halting voice waltzed around the room, taking its time finishing sentences.

Daddy? Frankie? This is—Susan. I'm in the healing hand of our Lord—God bless his—ministry—his work—his healing power. I'm fine? Yes, fine. Love you. The monolog ended with a familiar scripture passage, Matthew 13:45–46.

"The pearl of heaven again." Stana tapped her chin.

"Pearl of heaven?"

She explained the passage to Frank One and he rose higher in his chair, his upper lip curling under the lower. "Does she sound okay to you?" Stana asked.

"No." She sounded as if she were reading from cue cards.

"Cue cards written in French," Stana added.

"The life has gone out of her voice," Frank Two said. "Like she's a prisoner of her mind."

A Venus fly trap closed slowly on a black bug the size of my first car. "How did you get this recording?" My tie was now in my pocket, my shirt three buttons undone. Sweat was even behind my ears. I could feel it. I sat forward in my canvas chair to keep from being stuck there like a fly glued to a strip.

Frank One wasn't shifting at all, his head didn't dip left or right. His chin was forever raised as if holding up a spackled crown.

"I recorded it." Franklin Two's lips slightly parted as he breathed.

The snake in the garden was still swallowing the rodent-lizard.

Frank Two had bought the gizmo from an army surplus store. It had a small suction cup on one end that sticks to a phone's receiver and the other end's jack slides into an RCA plug on a cassette recorder. He had applied this gizmo to the phone in his bedroom in case Susan called. She had been missing for over a week.

"An army surplus store or *the* store, the one next to The People's Way to Christ?"

A different one, he said, but I didn't believe him. Anyway, Susan called. Wanting money.

"Uh-huh." I rubbed at the edges of my mouth and flashed my lopsided grin. It's the same squirrely look plastered across my PI license. It's my don't-give-a-damn trademark. If I were a movie actor, I'd be the Robert Mitchum of the matzo-crackers set. "You've edited this, Prospero."

He grimaced, wanting to stay cool and loose in front of his dad. "I have. Edited it," he admitted, quietly.

"It plays like a soliloquy. Not a conversation—"

"For the sake of brevity, I thought—"

"That's right, Prospero, you thought. Yes, you thought. Mixing up the elements, using your hoodoo magic, removing the context in which the words were originally spoken, obscuring truths."

"I obscured no truths. I told her I loved her if you must know."

"Recording. Editing. You're good with technology, aren't you, Prospero? Placing microphones under beds and listening in with a host of friends—the Defeatniks—while a young man, a little slow on the ball cavorts with—"

"This isn't about my son or how he carries and comports himself with his so-called friends." Franklin One held up an abrupt hand. I'm surprised a scepter wasn't in it.

"You mock me again, I'll lay you out," Frank Two said, the twist of his Rolex gleaming.

"That gizmo, Mr. Whitfield? That part of your *brand*?"

"I've never seen it before," the father said.

"Right. And what's to stop Sonny Boy here from using microphones you've never seen before, bugging Dr. Cohen's office, writing anti-Semitic impulses on paper, paper with blood splotches on it, splotches reminiscent of Susan's signature on her art?"

"What splotches?" Frank Two.

"The design's the same, Deuces. On her watercolors in Frieze's loft and on the Stars of David found in Cohen's office."

"Susan's behind the bugging?"

I folded my arms and laughed and mocked his spin on things. "Sure, Susan's behind the bugging."

"Enough." Frank One spoke as if he *did* carry a scepter. They had a boxing ring in the basement, next to the bowling alley, and he invited us to take up our scrap at some other time, but right now petty differences had to be set aside. "Susan is lost. She has been lost from us for some time. She may be behind all of this." He sighed, his lips pushing together awkwardly.

Franklin Two and I said nothing. He untangled the twist to his Rolex. I put on my porkpie.

"Sharon Dafoe. That mean anything to you?" She was a member of the Defeatniks, slept with Thompson on your orders, and today was seen bringing girls in fishnets to Smith's home. All the players in this story mix and mingle in incestuous ways. What's your connection to her, today?

"Huh?"

I could see the retreat in his eyes.

Dafoe and you, Thompson and you, murder and you.

He prattled on about unfortunate coincidences, unrelated events, pies and fishnets, Sharon and Colin and Sharon and the pie girls, and his sadness over what happened to his friendship with Colin, the fraternity's mascot.

"Mascot? So what, did you dress him up like Elmer the Safety Elephant? Rule Number One: Look Both Ways Before You Cross the Street."

"Droll. Very droll, Fuller."

"And why on that first day, the day of Gus's murder, did you act like you had no prior history with either of them?"

I was waiting to hear this.

On top of the hi-fi unit were a series of framed family photographs. In one of them, a young eight-year-old Susan, in an orange swimsuit, sprinkled the plastic pool with water, the hose gripped with both hands, gingerly spilling. Ten-year-old Franklin, hands on hips, stood idly by. His skin was the white of cocaine powder. The tops of Susan's shoulders were sunburned.

"Look." Frank Two glared. "I've done some things I'm not proud of, things that I regret. I didn't acknowledge Thompson because I was sad over how I treated him. I denied him, okay. You want me to be biblical? *I denied him*." But, I'm still a man of integrity, a man of action, a doer, he said, playing with the flex band of his *prestigious* Rolex. He assured us that he had not been idle. Since his sister's disappearance, he had been asking questions of the police, Dr. Cohen, fellow Defeatniks, that chi-chi artist Tom Frieze who has a misguided thing for her, and more importantly he's been in talks with Tod X, a deprogrammer who recently left the US, the slums of Chicago, to emigrate to TO. Tod X had tackled the Moonies and other cults, infiltrating their ranks, finding lost men and women, and recusing them from these organizations' realms of brainwashing. Forty-seven cases so far. He was finishing up matters on a case in Northern Ontario and would be lending a hand to tackling The People's Way to Christ tomorrow.

Tod X was really a kind of secular priest, Stana said, performing secular exorcisms.

"You could say that," Frank One nodded, his face rippling with a patronizing smile. "You could. But I prefer to say he's a man of justice. Highly principled who frees people from their prisons."

Only to return Susan to another prison: her brother and Dimension V.

Tod X left Chicago after the assassination of brother Malcom, Franklin said. American Whitey, Tod says, has enslaved us for nearly 350 years, going back to 1619, but when we start killing our own, special visionaries, then it's time to start living elsewhere. Canada. Canadian Whitey's not so bad. "Those are his words." Frank Two now held up his hands like his father before him.

Uh-huh. What would the Indians say about Canada's human rights record? Ellen was taken from her home, in the middle of the night, by cops with guns on their hips, taken from her Indian mother and given to a white woman.

"How's what he's doing not kidnapping?" Stana shook her head, the white-shelled necklace around her neck a heavy pendant. "These *kids* are over twenty-one."

"Yes. But he has the permission of the parents. These kids are sick. Their minds trapped—" They're being *rescued*, not kidnapped.

What was Susan's life like with you? Filling swimming pools. For you. Following your orders, Mr. Accessories. A kind of internment camp, pally.

"Brother Durgana is a charismatic ne'er-do-well. A dangerous man. We know who the good guys and bad guys are here." Frank Two exhaled sharply. "Tod X will infiltrate and bring her back."

"Speaking of good guys and bad guys, pally, who would want to dismantle your universe?"

"Huh?"

"Dimension V. Ivan wanted to dismantle it." I was guessing, rolling with a hunch. "Why?"

Frank Two shrugged, looked away. "Everyone wants to be king." He smiled.

"So you're the king?"

"Of Dimension V. Yes."

"What about Susan?" Stana leaned forward.

"She's lost. In that cult."

"And you're sure she's there? In that church?" Sweat from her hair dripped small coins on the table, the lines of her clavicles were glistening. "We've looked into them. I interviewed several of their members, followers, excuse me, is the nomenclature they prefer. Followers." She wiped sweat from her brow with a chamois cloth of a hand.

"We're pretty sure she's there," Frank One said, his chin raised, the crown on his head straight. "Keep gathering evidence." When Tod X arrives tomorrow we were to share our intel with him and join in his pursuit of Susan.

Frank One handed me an envelope. It was heavy. $1,000 down for our efforts and expenses. 5K if we bring her back, alive.

Stana whistled when I handed her the money to put in her handbag the size of a milk crate. "What do you all know about Brother Durgana?" She lit a Parliament. If she tossed the butt over her shoulder, I'm pretty sure the whole place would go up in a blaze. She exhaled stiffly.

"A punk. A mediocre stock broker." Franklin One didn't pull punches.

"Knows his scripture," chimed in Frank Two.

"Oh?" Stana took another short drag, tapped the cig on the side of the ashtray. "So you've been to his church?"

"No." He laughed. "No way. But he's called here." He shrugged. "On Susan's behalf. Asking for donations."

"How much did he get out of Susan?" I asked.

"Bilked her for ten thousand, in securities, family trust stuff," Frank One said, his lips a hard line. "The balls of that man. The balls." He looked in the direction of Stana and waved apologetically. "Pardon my French."

"I like the French," I said.

"The balls," Frank Two echoed his father. "The goddamn balls."

"Now *you should* apologize." Dad pointed at Frank Two, smiling at Stana.

Tersely and somewhat reluctantly Frank Two did as he was told, eyes on the floor.

Stana tapped her cigarette against the ashtray's floor. She wanted to explore Susan's story, why did she leave the family, her life of privilege, access, and entitlement, for a group of marginal loners who wear canvas-cut clothes and meditated for hours every morning in threadbare robes. She was running from something to something else. "What are these two somethings?" She picked at a sliver of tobacco off her lower lip.

"I think you know, Mr. Microphones Under Beds."

Frank Two no longer smiled, but his voice was full of calm milkshake-smooth contours. "Susan was unstable. You have to remember our mother committed suicide when she was three. Susan didn't have a woman to guide her, to give her advice on lipstick and how to wear heels, how to talk to boys. Anyway, my sister was always temperamental. Flighty." He shrugged.

The speech was a total phony, rehearsed, so sincere as to be insincere, lacking urgent impulses.

One time, after watching a Frankenstein double feature with Karloff, Susan killed the family dog Ruffles. Poisoned him with anti-freeze and then sought to re-animate him, attaching electrodes to his paws and other extremities, and generating energy from a car battery. The car running, of course.

"Of course."

"I don't need to tell you how it turned out."

"No Zombie Jesus rising from the tomb, huh?"

"Zombie Jesus? You fucking Yid!"

Between breaths, I was out of my chair, across the table, and on him, tackling him to the floor. I hit him once with a left, and he turtled, covering his face. Stana screamed behind me, and if Frank One were carrying that damn scepter he'd be whacking me with it, but he didn't need a scepter. He had a gun instead.

The hammer cocked. I felt the edge of the barrel behind my ear.

"One more punch, Mr. Fuller, and I pull the trigger. You know I have a lot of friends in this community, friends like Toronto Maple Leafs CEO Steve Smith, who will accept my behavior, my cries of self-defense."

I climbed off Frank Two, stood tall, dusting off my suit.

Frank One nodded briefly, uncocked the .32, and returned it to an outside pocket on his jacket.

He ordered his son to apologize for the ethnic slur and me for the Zombie crack

Frank Two wiped his chin, the fraternity pin on the lapel of his suit jacket polished brightly with privilege. It had a gleam equaling that of his Rolex. "This is yet another one of his grenades. First at the Captains of Industry, now at the principles that this country lives by."

"We're not a Christian country," Stana corrected. "We're products of the Enlightenment."

"What about Susan's talk of targeted killings?" I snapped the porkpie tight on my lid.

We all returned to our chairs, none of us apologizing.

"I assure you my daughter never talked of targeted killings."

He sure liked that word: *assure* and making *assurances*. There was nothing sure about this case. "Uh-huh." I adjusted my sleeves. "And I suppose Jackson Grayson just happened to slip off a little old balcony after drinking too many Molsons."

"That's what the police report said." Frank Two.

"Hmm. I have at least three witnesses who can verify that Susan spoke of targeted killings. Sharon Dafoe for one. The girl you asked to sleep with Hockey Gloves. Matt Clarkson for two. And Tom Frieze for the trifecta. Win, Place, Show, baby."

"Susan targeted Grayson. She spoke of killing him," Stana said. "And then there's Gus." Stana was now standing, her white beaded shell necklace tossed over a shoulder. "Who you, Deuces, ordered Susan to sleep with, and did she order Red Ivan to kill Gus because she was so disgusted with what she'd done?" What was left of her cigarette vibrated, a hummingbird at her fingers.

"Susan talked murder but it was abstract for her. Theoretical. Never practical."

"Uh-huh."

"She also had to make appointments to speak to you, her own father, in her own house. Goddamn appointments?" Stana crushed the cigarette in an ashtray. Smokey the Bear would be proud.

Frank One pushed away from the Arthur chair and pounded a fist on the table. "I haven't been the best father." He shrugged. "Okay, damn it. I admit it. And I'm probably responsible for my children's eccentricities. My neglect. But Susan liked to push the envelope through talk, never action. Your Zombie Jesus utterance, Mr. Fuller, would have pleased her to no end, because it the kind of thing she'd say—disrespectful, unconventional, iconoclastic."

The ass-end of the rodent-lizard still protruded from the snake's mouth. Another animal squawked a death yawp. The ribbon of water appeared motionless, clogged.

"So. I failed them. Me. This—" He fanned his hand over the two black-cylindered extinguishers on the table. "This is my children." He held up one of them. It was a new weapon that he and his team had perfected, a modified version of 2,4,5T, a defoliant mastered in the Netherlands in 1963, and adjusted here into a foam spray. Spring a load of this on someone's face, and they'll suffocate to death in seconds, he said. Blocks the pores. He snapped his fingers. And. He snapped them again. And shrugged.

"Pillars of salt, huh?" I said.

"Yes. I suppose so. It makes people into pillars of salt. I don't know if we can market it that way—" He laughed, his Hidden Persuaders chuckle. "I might be an atheist, Mr. Fuller, but I know of the traditions on which this country was founded, Enlightenment or no Enlightenment." He smiled wanly. He had read the good book. "I never joke about Jesus." The Lord's aligned with power, he said.

"I've read the good book three times," his son said in the spirit of one-upmanship. Twice to get the nuances. A third time backwards, literally backwards from Revelation to Genesis, each sentence, backward. "That's the best way to memory retention."

He was serious. "Is that Dimension V logic?"

He said nothing.

"My children are very intelligent," Frank One boasted. Both scored off the charts on IQ tests, genius levels, 160 to 170. Sometimes, he ruminated, it was better to be only an ordinary genius, finding simple solutions to problems, making the clear direct choice. His children did create their own world for themselves, starting with the death of their mother, and perhaps even before that. Dimension V was part of that imaginary vision.

He lightly touched the extinguisher's nozzle. "My obsessions, shortcomings, are what should be on trial here, not my children." He smiled. "I love them. I don't model good behavior, what with the appointments to see me and all, but I do love them."

Stana sat down. "So what's next?"

"Wait on Tod X. He'll call you."

I gave them my home number and that of my father's house. I felt a need to return to Gradwell, to breathe in his scent to get the scent. My desire to find Susan was growing, but my desire to know my father was getting lost. I needed a returning, a countermovement. Gradwell might give that to me.

Frank One reached for another envelope leaning up against one of the cylinders. He undid the short clasp and slid two black-and-white photographs in my direction. Stana placed them side by side. The photographs were blurry, rushed by the circumstances of their shooting. The subjects wore black robes, triangle hoods with slits for yes. One photo, a long shot, showed followers meditating in the McGowan Street sanctuary. And very similar to what I saw on my first visit here, they were caressing the floor with their hands, silently praying. Neon lights and imagery surrounded them, and even in the sanctuary's dim shadows, the threadbare fabric revealed curves of breasts, patches of pubic hair, the dangled lines of manhood.

In another photograph, a medium close-up of two people, one had a hood, laughing behind it, eyes crescent moons. The other, hoodless, appeared to be wearing nothing. Wiry wisps of chest hair circled his nipples. Aviator goggles were pressed tight to his face, making his eyes amber. Colin Thompson.

A neon image of David glowed behind them. Too bad we couldn't see David's PF Flyers.

"Prepping for some kind of ritual," Stana said.

"Appears so." Frank One.

"Sacred or profane?" Frank Two.

"Both?" Stana offered.

"How'd you get these?" I turned the photographs over, checking the paper.

"They arrived in the mail, shortly after Susan's disappearance." Frank Two. "Four, five days ago."

Written on the back: *You will not harken to me. I will punish you for your sins*—Leviticus 26:18. The handwriting wasn't my father's; it didn't match what I found hidden in his switch plate.

Stana tilted her head right in conjunction with the lilt to the words. "The quote's not quite right," she said. "'I will punish you *seven times* or *seven-fold* is what it should say, modifying sins."

"Catholic school," I said, pointing at her.

"And Jesus was never a zombie," she gently scolded.

I apologized to her. To Mr. Microphones, forget about it.

Frank Two studied the back of the photographs. "She's right. The quote is wrong." He rubbed at the fuzz on his chin, his face grimacing.

A wrathful, vengeful God. Stana believed in the God of Love, the New Testament God. But these folks on McGowan were into fire and brimstone, Old Testament punishment, Sodom and Gomorrah, floods, Cain and Abel. Isaac and Abraham, kill me a son.

Is that what we had here? Cain and Abel, but instead of brothers we had a brother and a sister? Cain and April?

I flipped the photos back to the mass of black hoods. Anything else accompany these photos? Blackmail requests?

"None." Frank One held up both hands as if directing traffic. The only requests he had for money were from Susan, twice calling for donations to the church. And in both conversations, she mentioned becoming a part of heaven.

"That's what she said. *Becoming*? As in morphing into, transforming herself into?"

"Yes." He looked puzzled. "And?"

"I don't know." I pushed back my porkpie. The language was alarming. She was sloughing off her old self, leaving Susan behind, her life behind, her actual life. Becoming a pearl. In heaven. Now. In heaven. Dead. In heaven. Now.

"Has she ever been suicidal?"

"My daughter?"

"Yes." Frank Two said, looking at the cylinders on the tabletop. When she was seven she stabbed herself with a knife, trying to join Mommy, wherever she was. Two months before discovering her pregnancy, she had OD'ed on alcohol and pills and had to be rushed to the emergency room. After that stay, she started going to The People's Way to Christ temple. "Do they even call it a temple?"

"I know they call *it* a church," I said, looking at the black robes crowding the photographs.

"Tod X will be here tomorrow," Frank One reassured us. "He'll have a plan. Sit tight. By a phone."

We know what you said. Could it be these black-robed people with their vengeful gods?

Franklin Two placed the cards with my phone numbers inside the lapels of his crisp sport jacket as shadows of trees shrouded our table in the shapes of fighting dinosaurs, tearing away at one another.

My money was on the triceratops.

I sat in Dad's chair, my arms resting on the slick worn leather, a Rémy-Martin shot on the coffee table by my side, my head tossed back, taking in the ceiling's patterns, water stains resembling the Great Lakes. I was half-drowning in Lake Huron.

Dad's scent was all around. A mix of aftershave, beer, sweat, and Ajax cleanser. He always scrubbed away at his hands after each day's work, washing off the dirt of empty milk bottles, metal trays, and the truck's grimy steering wheel.

Next to my drink was a dog-eared copy of *Playboy*, featuring Maria McBane, and *More Joy in Heaven*, a sad gangster love story that Stana had me read three years ago.

When did Dad start reading?

Maybe they were Ellen's library books.

I wiped edges of grit from tired eyes. Two hours ago I had dropped Stana at my Houston Crescent home to watch over Dr. Cohen, handed her my .45, and gave her instructions to call if there were any problems. The Cerlons across the street and the Capetellis next door were good people. If you need help right away ask them.

I sighed, imagining going under, the water stain swallowing me, how easy it all would be just to let go.

Once I arrived here, an hour or so ago now, I called Anne Chevalier. Couldn't reach her. She was on a stakeout. Then I called Sal from Dad's chair. Lab results had come back: the blood splatter on the Agitprop work was that of a pregnant woman. HGC confirmed it.

Sal thought I sounded funny, asked if I were okay. Searching for memories or trying to lose a few I said. There was an awkward pause. "You're not in your dad's house?" "Yes." "It's a crime scene." "Yes." "We're not having this conversation." Another awkward pause. "Take it easy, Superstar. Rest."

Susan Whitfield. Dr. Cohen's client was possibly involved in harassing, threatening, ordering the good doctor's targeted killing. Maybe I needed to quit being so damn chivalric in my relationships with women, always seeing them as victims of bad male behavior, and maybe Susan wasn't merely a victim of her brother's Prospero–esque machinations, but a woman full of her own particular menace and desires to destroy others. She was a client of Dr. Cohen's. She could have easily planted the microphones.

We know what you said. Who's the we of that utterance? Susan and her brother? Susan and that black-robed cult on McGowan? Susan and her card-carrying N'oublie jamais boyfriend Ivan Sevrier (who with the help of Stubby Face killed Gus)? Susan and Gus whom she slept with because her brother told her to? Susan and Tom. Artists who shared a vision and a loft? *We.* Susan and Matt. He cared about her enough to kill for her? *We.* Two people or a club? *We.* A combination. Two people within a club: Susan and Brother Durgana and all the followers of The People's Way to Christ? *We.*

Did this we want to dismantle Frank Two's universe, Dimension V?

And what about Ellen and Smith. What really happened there? Too many pairs of fishnet stockings.

I pushed back my porkpie and swam to the shore, clambered out of Lake Huron.

Next to the Callaghan book was an even more worn copy of Hemingway's *The Old Man and the Sea.* I flipped, forward to back, deckle-stained pages. Dad loved jam and crackers before turning in, and this one had some red residue at the lower end. I flipped sticky pages, backward to front, and a folded recipe card fell out. It was full of writing.

Dad's writings.

I really love the style. Like reading a newspaper. Clean. And I can see the story. Like a movie. But I'm not sure about the whole fish thing. Sometimes you just got to let things go. The past is the past. To be a good fisherman is to know when to stop fishing. Move on. I wonder what Hemingway would of thought of Koufax? The guy wins game seven on two days rest. Arm sore and all. Complete game. I mean, DiMaggio was smooth, elegant, but nobody is as dominant as Koufax. And he's a Jew too. I don't think Hemingway liked Jews. It's in the prose. You can feel it. Couldn't finish The Sun Also Rises.

Maybe I don't like Jews either.

Maybe that's my problem.

But I didn't finish The Sun Also Rises.

So that should count for something.

I never liked myself.

I re-read the card twice and knocked back the two fingers of Rémy-Martin. Then I pushed myself off the chair, ambling to the kitchen. The milk was past its date. In the fridge: Kraft cheese, orange juice, Hebrew Nationals, and Hershey bars. I pulled a slice of cheese from an unsealed wax package. One of the corners was a little dry. I ate it, folding it in half first, like I used to do when I was a kid.

The dishes were still dirty in the sink and the ends of the curtain by the window were stained with smudged fingers. Dad must have used them as a makeshift towel.

I laughed.

That was so Dad.

No tea towels anywhere. No big deal. Use the kitchen curtains.

The cabinets housed a half-dozen plates and plastic cups. Yogi Bear was on one of them. Next to a tall angular cabinet full of dust mops, brooms, and cleansers was a dumbwaiter with a rope and pulley system. Dad had converted it into a makeshift laundry chute. I checked around inside its door and smelled cheese.

I picked up something that resembled a lemon slice of plastic. A piece of hardened cheese. It nicked one of my fingers.

Ellen was hiding in the dumbwaiter when Dad was murdered. He had stowed her there safely from the killers.

Christ. She had seen, heard, from her place in the dumbwaiter.

The phone rang.

I wandered away from the opened dumbwaiter and the glass of orange juice on the kitchen table to the beer sweat of the living room. "Fuller—"

"Hayden?"

Stana's voice was crisp and slightly elevated. An ice chest had just arrived at my front door on Houston.

"Did it just arrive or have you just now noticed it?"

"Both I think."

"It's an either-or question, Stana."

"It wasn't here before, when you dropped me off. It has arrived since then—"

"So in the last two hours."

"Roger that."

Her nervousness had somehow converted her into a member of the Royal Canadian Army.

She had nudged, all right, *kicked at*, the chest, heard water and chunks of ice sloshing about.

"Good. So that means it can't be a bomb."

We were on the same page. She wanted to open it, it might be an important clue, it might—

"It might also be something you don't want to see—"

"I'll risk it."

Always the reporter. Two-week vay-cay or not. "Okay." My heart was in my shoulders. "Be careful."

The lid unsealed with a long breath, and then pockets of silence, followed by a scream.

I couldn't make out what she was saying. She handed the phone to Dr. Cohen.

A pair of hands, Dr. Cohen said, matter-of-factly, hacked off at the wrists. Bones were exposed, bits of muscle, blood drained. The fingers, slender; the nails, pink; the pinky adorned with an emerald ring; the stone set inside the ring, yellow.

Sharon Dafoe.

"Jesus Christ, Hayden. Is this a typical couple of days in your line of work? A shootout on the Bluffs, a pair of hands on your doorstep?"

"No. I usually have time for some ballroom dancing."

"I better call Sal," she said.

"Yes. How's Stana?"

"She's been better." Stana was in the bathroom, tossing up the burger and fries we ate hours before. "Why Sharon?"

"I was going to ask you the same thing, Doc."

She was hesitant, halting.

"Susan? Your client?" The blood splatter was from a pregnant woman, AB blood. Your client was, in all likelihood, terrorizing you; she's a part of the "we" in *we know what you said*. Susan and Ivan were lovers. Sharon knew something. Susan had Sharon killed. "I'm guessing, of course. Or Susan did it herself."

"I don't know."

Tom Frieze, a fine artist, who specialized in rendering the beauty and horror of human hands in all of their complexities could have done this, but the symbolism, the hacked-off hands, was too obvious. Contrived. Yes, he shared a studio space with Susan, and maybe he was part of the "we," but I couldn't believe it about him, not after our two-hour conversation at his kitchen table. I preferred to think of this as but a clumsy attempt to divert suspicion on him.

I wasn't going to say a word about Tom's hand sculptures to Sal.

What if Ellen were a part of the we. Ellen and Susan? "Have Sal call me here."

"Right." Susan sure did love Sevrier, Dr. Cohen recalled. She thought he was funny, sincere, but to be a mastermind behind the killing of my father? No, Dr. Cohen just couldn't believe that about her client. No way.

Then I told her about Dad and the Thorazine OD and the church's followers and their baby steps.

"That's definitely a side effect of chlorpromazine," she said. "But I still can't believe that Susan could—"

"There's a lot of things that I used to believe in that I don't no more."

"Sounds like you're ready for another session—"

"Maybe." I smiled.

Her pause told me she could feel the smile through the phone. "My sessions with Susan were more about finding her own island of existence. That's what she called it. Her own island of existence."

"Dimension V?"

"Yes. I believe so." There was a long pause. "Don't give up on believing, Hayden. Please."

"Sure, Doc. Call Sal."

I dropped the receiver in its cradle and wandered back to the kitchen and the cup of orange juice waiting for me. It had got a little warm so I dumped it in the sink and poured another.

I must have sat there for an hour or so, holding what was left of my Yogi Bear cup of juice in one hand, smoking Dad's stale Rothmans with the other. I found the cigs in back of the silverware drawer.

I finished the orange juice, mind numbed.

Stubbed out the last cigarette.

Smokey the Bear would be proud.

Yogi the Bear would wonder where the fuck's the picnic basket.

I don't remember leaving the kitchen table.

—

IT WAS A DARK, DEAD SLEEP.

The kind you don't remember and wonder if this is what really happens when you just quietly slip away from it all.

Black stillness.

And then, thankfully, you wake up, free to listen to hardbop jazz, breathe in the warm sun.

But there wasn't any sun. It was black beyond the kitchen curtains, 10:17 by the clock over the sink.

A black sky.

I rubbed at my eyes, half-smiled at her face.

It was a nice face, a little heavy on the lower cheeks, nubs of dark hair peeking out from under her Montreal Canadiens toque, green eyes, a gap between her front teeth. The dent above her upper lip looked as if it were pressed there by an angel.

She half-smiled back at me.

"Ellen?"

Dressing Room

The kiss was just a little off, she said.

It was full of neon, bright and glaring with no real substance behind the kismet, puffed afloat with vapors and clouds of gas.

It happened on her seventh and final week at the church, three days before she jumped in Ira Fuller's milk truck.

For her first three weeks in the city, spring of 1964, Ellen Reynolds lived in a youth hostel, finding part-time work at Dominion's, stocking shelves late at night and later working in the bakery, making donuts, butter tarts, cakes, and pies. Only fourteen, she lied and said she was sixteen, and her supervisor, a heavyset man in thick glasses and a pock-marked face, believed her because he wanted to believe her and because she flirted a little, telling him he walked with confidence and wore way cool shoes. Wing tips, he said. Her foster father never wore such things on the farm in Melville, Saskatchewan. *Wing tips*. She wrote that down. She liked words.

Unfortunately, her own words were forgotten except a few like maybe, maashcoat, and the odd phrase her mother said, pe-nepuea pchi feey, come to me my little girl.

Money was thin along the lakeshore, below minimum wage, and Ellen eventually left the hostel, finding shelter in a variety of abandoned buildings in Toronto's downtown hub around Front Street.

One night she met Scott Cameron, a pug-faced, freckled fella with lopsided ears, in a bus station diner. She was eating fries, drinking coffee. His approach wasn't subtle. "I got a fifth of scotch. You wanna go home with me?"

She had met a variety of such fellas along Yonge Street shoeshine parlors—a past she didn't want to revisit, now, with me.

"Why don't we just drink here?" she said.

"Why not?" He tilted his head left, banking on his elusive Paul Newman charm. He looked a little like Paul, the eyes a piercing blue, the hair curled, tight and sweaty. He removed the fifth from his beige jacket. It was a weird jacket. The collar curled up and opened into a tulip of a turtleneck. He topped off her coffee with two fingers, and they sat and drank for a while.

In the books Ellen was allowed to read, she supposed his smile would be labeled "rakish." There was a romantic aloofness to him, a sense of knowing yourself, how to be all the things Ellen wanted.

They walked back to his place, a long, narrow room above a pool hall. He had an athlete's glide and she felt a little dizzy, leaning against him, breathing in Aqua Velva and garlic.

Scott worked at an Italian restaurant and couldn't splash enough cologne to drown the garlic away. All day he found himself covertly sniffing fingers, wishing remnants of grease and garlic could vanish. They couldn't.

That made her laugh.

He was vulnerable.

In his flat, he watched TV while she read books, novels mainly written by whites, and together fixed easy meals: Shake and Bake chicken, mac and cheese, bacon and eggs. Occasionally, she brought home a pie she'd baked at Dominion's.

Twice a week they made love as pool balls thudded across tables downstairs.

She was fourteen. He, twenty-two and thought she was sixteen.

It wasn't really love.

She felt obliged to cooperate. Often, as he came, kissing her, he'd whisper, "I love you." She didn't believe in the possibilities of those three words anymore, so she responded with a tap-tap on the tops of his firm arms.

"Why'd you leave. Run away?" He asked one night, slowly lighting a crumpled cigarette.

Her foster mother had taken to hitting Ellen when she appeared less than thrilled completing a chore or errand. "It's in your shoulders, your eyes, all the times, the eyes. The devil."

I stayed with Scott out of convenience, a roof, food, she told me. "I feared going to the CAS—they'd probably send me back to Saskatchewan, and I didn't want to milk cows anymore." Her pattern was to run from trouble rather than confront it. She was aware of this, but inside, she knew, "I'll always be running."

So, one day after meeting Brother Durgana outside her Dominion's, Ellen decided not to return to Scott and to run somewhere else.

Durgana wore a long black leather coat and his hair was thick and curly, much curlier than Scott's, resembling a woman's wig. It was so full. He handed her a pamphlet to The People's Way to Christ. His eyes were blacker than coal, a description Ellen had probably first come across in an old 19th Century novel, and his eyelashes were long and lush. He was pretty. For a man.

"What a beautiful face," he said to her, "bristling with God's presence." He smiled, teeth perfect. "You have an old, old soul."

If you could have one wish to make the world a better place what would it be?

"For everyone to get along." She was surprised at how the words spilled from her. "For *all* to be okay, equal." *Mothers shouldn't have dominion over their adopted daughters.*

The latter thought she said out loud for he picked up on the theme. How do we seek and find such non-dominion?

He paused, tapped his chin, nodded, full of confidence and a non-threatening self-awareness that she found disarming. He was a spiritual man who felt no need to apologize for his particular disposition. Jesus walked into the desert with no possessions and fed the needy, helped the infirmed, gave comfort and advice to the lost, especially like the woman at the well. Remember her?

Ellen had read the bible only sparingly, because the mother who smelled of Avon products, insisted she read it. Ellen didn't recall the story of the woman and the well.

"How do you need to be fed?"

"With acceptance, appreciation, love." The words were just there, across her lips, all self-consciousness gone.

And then he talked about the pearl of heaven.

AT THE CHURCH, THEY HELD SERVICES eleven times a week, with three-hour meditations every morning, exercises in the afternoon, and evening devotions at night. On Thursdays, the women and men did their spiritual ruminations in separate quarters.

Once a month they washed each other's feet: an act of intimacy and humility, laying one's self bare before the Father and Son and Holy Spirit.

Ellen never felt more invigorated. The Word filled her with purpose. The people here truly believed and didn't use God to control her. She no longer hated her mother, herself. "I wasn't the devil's child." She couldn't quite look at me when she said that.

The only thing that was tough at first was giving up bubble gum. Since she was nine years old, she had enjoyed perfecting balloon-size bubbles, but at the church such practices were deemed extravagant, lacking in simplicity and a proper focus on the spiritual.

Within eight days, Ellen was baking the occasional set of pies for Friday night desserts, cutting back on the sugars for a tart flavor that fit with Brother Durgana's philosophy of simplicity and struggle.

Her cube, that's what the girls called their quarters, was shaped like an igloo and housed with three other transient runaways including Susan Whitfield, a rich heiress (do heiresses still exist, Ellen asked me, or was that simply a 1930s-word I'm using to describe a rich ingénue?). Susan, recently pregnant, was the leader of their dwelling. She taught Ellen the church's central hymn, a lament for a life left behind.

This Ellen could relate to as a Métis girl who no longer could recall her own people's words for bird, fish, deer. And because of Susan's privilege, she was allowed to leave the compound for day trips into the city, to visit doctors about her pregnancy or her therapist, Dr. Cohen, about her condition.

Ellen accompanied Susan on these visits.

On those days Ellen blew large pink bubbles that popped the air.

She felt a little ashamed for how much pleasure it brought her.

One time, at the Half-Life, a bar on Spadina, Ellen met Ivan Sevrier, Susan's beau, who spent the whole afternoon pontificating ("Does the root of this word, Mr. Fuller, come from that blowhard Pontius Pilate? To pontificate like Pontius Pilate?") about being French and what a second-class status it was to be so in Canada, for to be bilingual meant being French and having to learn English; it never worked the other way around.

She wanted to tell him, how do you think it feels being French and Indian and having a white man with a gun on his hip take you away to a woman who smells of tuna casserole? But she said nothing. Ivan's words, however, sounded forced to Ellen, like a rehearsed mantra, part of a manifesto. "Oh, Vichy, don't be so pompous," Susan teased, apparently agreeing with Ellen, but loving her beau nonetheless, kissing him on the cheek.

Ellen wanted to be loved like that.

Near the end of her second week, after baking pies for the tenants, Ellen met Steve Smith, CEO of the Toronto Maple Leafs and owner of the Army Surplus store next door. Smith was tall, angular, maybe even a little withered. He looked like Ichabod Crane, a story Ellen read in seventh grade, and he admired her pies and approached her about a business plan.

His bleeding ulcers made his breath bad, so he often pointed his words away from her, at a corner in the room, the ceiling, but he really liked her pies—the best he ever tasted—and sought a way to market them, creating what he called a brand. "Get the pies out in the world. We need a name." He snapped phosphorous fingers. "Something catchy."

"Melville?"

She was born in Regina but taken to the "suburbs" of Melville.

Melville Pies. He adjusted his glasses. That was okay, but not loud enough. Melville, huh? He snapped his fingers again. "How about the White Whale, the Whaler?" Eating one of her pies was like going on a quest, conquering Moby-Dick. *White Whale Pies.*

White? Was he aware of the irony? Was he not seeing her?

"Sure," she said.

The next day, at his home in Rosedale, they drew up a two-week marketing strategy, involving radio spots, billboards, newspaper ads. Smith, with a floor plan of the church spread across his mahogany desk, discussed converting the basement into a chef's kitchen, a row of ovens, sinks, refrigerators. The central air unit, which he had circled, would unfortunately break up the track of ovens, but we do what we can.

Susan, who cleaned Smith's Rosedale home twice a week, warned Ellen to look out for Smith riding his hobby horse: *Find your purpose in life. Your role.* He drops that little aphorism into every conversation. Susan laughed with a veil of smugness. Sure enough, that day Smith said it. "You are a nurturer, you give to others rather than yourself. Your pies are a gift of giving. Know your role."

It was all pretty cornball stuff, but she liked Susan's prior use of the word hobby horse. Ellen first came across it in Laurence Sterne's *Tristram Shandy.* And whenever Smith said the expected turn of phrase she tried hard not to laugh, or wind a family clock like Walter Shandy.

On the way to his car, Smith placed a hand on her shoulder. It was cold, surprisingly heavy and resembled glowing ash. "Next time you come, make sure you wear fishnets."

FISHNETS? ELLEN'S MIND WANDERED from the book Durgana forced all his followers to read: Norman Vincent Peale's *The Power of Positive Thinking. Fishnet stockings?*

"It's nothing," Susan said. "A fetish."

"What's that?"

"Guys who feel threatened by girls make them wear odd, sexy clothing to make themselves feel less threatened and in control."

"What?"

"Surely you've met guys who made you over into a fantasy. Ever put on a wig for a fella?"

She had. And she'd been labeled a cute little Indian girl so often she couldn't fix a number to the encounters.

Susan smiled, playing with the rough-edge collar to her canvas top. The lighting in the room was soft, a little foggy, making her dirty blonde hair turquoise. "It's a way of getting off."

Ellen was confused. How was this behavior part of a spiritual path? Why would Brother Durgana have such a friend?

Susan shrugged, played with the ridges of her canvas collar, and nonchalantly, as if washing her hands, said at the end of her Rosedale cleaning sessions Smith handed her a new pair of fishnet stockings and then escorted her to a back room, dark and cool, full of Toronto Maple Leafs memorabilia, classic photographs by Harold Barkley, and there removed his slacks, his briefs, and jerked off all over her netted legs.

"Gross." *And you allow that?*

"It's nothing." She tapped her lower lip, and once again played with her scratchy collar, while walking to a narrow night stand between their beds. A Coleman lantern sprinkled broken bits of light on a blond Jesus. Susan opened a drawer that took some work to budge. "And he gives me things."

Things? What did Susan need with things, Mr. Fuller? Susan had things when she lived with her father. Maybe her break from privilege wasn't as strong as it needs to be?

Maybe, I said.

But who am I to judge, she said. Shit. Sometimes while baking pies in the church basement Ellen subtly chewed Dubble Bubble, hoping the cameras wouldn't catch her or that Brother Durgana might not smell it on her breath.

The drawer was cramped with jewelry, bracelets, charms, including a horse with blue marble chips along its mane.

"You're not allowed to have this stuff." Ellen's voice quivered.

Both girls wore canvas clothes, sported short-cropped hair, no makeup: signs of foregoing the trappings of consumer excess for a life of spiritual simplicity and a quest for oneness.

"Oh, come on." Susan dangled the charm with blue marble in front of Ellen. "You want it. You do."

Seize it, her eyes said, seize it, girl.

Ellen did.

FOR SEVERAL DAYS ELLEN KEPT THE CHARM buried in the pocket of her canvas pants, fingers gracing its smooth surface, as if it were an element of the earth that one needed to live by.

Eventually, troubled over Smith and Susan's behaviors, she walked into Brother Durgana's office. I'm always available, he had told her when she first joined and took their covenant.

He wasn't pleased.

"You should knock—" He scrambled, inadvertently knocking over a figurine of a man fishing, and quickly reached for the small ear pieces in front of him. He quickly inserted them in his ears, a thin smile crossing crimped lips.

The room was dimly lit. There were no windows which always struck Ellen as odd.

She didn't understand his frustration. It was okay if he had a hearing problem. Why be ashamed? The church had taught her to accept all differences and to find your own inner qi, the life force, and to celebrate the beauty of each individual before God.

I'm part Indian and I'm beautiful.

He had taught her to say that. *I'm part Indian and I'm beautiful.* "But why only *part* Indian I wonder now, Mr. Fuller. It's as if there's a benefit in not being full Indian."

"Yeah, *part* cuts a couple of ways—" I struggled to say more.

"Anyway, back to the story—" She apologized to Durgana once again for not knocking, and a placid expression filled his face, a fresh coat of paint. "No harm." A shell on the beaches of Normandy, 1944, had punctured one of his ear drums. He had got pretty good at reading lips. He looked away, his eyes back on the bloody beach, as he picked up the fisherman figurine and placed it back in line with the others: angels, ballerinas, dancers.

One of his ear drums? But he had two ear pieces?

Yeah, I guess so, she said.

Hmm.

Anyway, Brother Durgana agreed that humility was central to a Christian life, and in this case, he wasn't very accepting of his own body's limitations. However, the hearing loss did encourage, in a small way, his stand to seek out a life beyond the body, beyond sex.

"Do you miss it?" she asked him.

"Of course." But his past loves weren't really about love. They were merely pursuits of carnal pleasures.

She nodded and spoke to intimate moments with Scott, her desire out of thankfulness to please him, but those encounters left her often feeling diminished.

"I understand." The coat of emotional pain had now firmed up his face, making Brother Durgana appear like the church leader she had come to expect. He smiled, placing the fisherman now at the front of the group, ahead of the angels. "How goes the pie campaign? Take lots of notes?"

"It goes." She had a folder full of marketing stuff resting on a mahogany table in Smith's home. She looked away.

"Good."

"What do you really think of Mr. Smith?" She spoke into her hands.

Smith was a weak man. Extremely so. His spiritual center was full of black haloes, but he genuinely cares about helping people, yes, the girls here. The light of Christ still walks with him, despite his darkness.

Ellen said nothing.

"We must learn forgiveness, Ellen. Forgiveness is God's love, it is the path to the greater good, outside of judgment. *He who's without sin cast the first stone.*"

"*Now go and sin no more*," Ellen countered.

"Ah, you have been reading your scriptures." He wagged an admiring finger at her. "But in this case, walking in God's light, Susan has already forgiven him."

Apparently, Susan sought Brother Durgana's counsel over Smith some time ago.

Ellen smiled thinly, a hand on the smooth charm in her pocket, its chips of blue marble, feeling with reluctance that things had shifted between her and the church.

THREE WEEKS INTO OCTOBER, the shift became seismic.

Ellen was in the basement, mixing up pies for a special Friday night party, when through the vent, voices: Smith, Brother Durgana, and a third man.

Ellen wasn't trying to follow the contours of words, but when

Smith said let's do something "outside the boundaries of the acceptable" she wondered if the discussion were about her and Susan and fishnet stockings. She moved directly under the vent.

Brother Durgana, his voice barbwire fishing tackle, said, "Sure we can. Why not? As long as it's biblical." His voice was now cooling and full of distance. It was a timbre she had never heard before. "We can do it in a special service."

Do what?

"Biblical *and old.* A gesture," said the Third Man. His voice was full of stadium lights. He was clearly the leader.

"Can I watch?" Smith.

"Yes." Durgana, breathing naturally. "But you can't be a part of the service."

"This is my call," said the Third Man, reminding Brother Durgana of the church's hierarchy. "Yes, you can watch—from a distance."

"Sorry. I guess I didn't know my role." Brother Durgana laughed, Ellen was sure, in the direction of Smith.

Papers shifted, chairs scraped the floor, sliding up against the table's edge. "I have the perfect subject." It was the bright voice again of the Third Man. "Two subjects, actually, for such a ritual."

She could feel his smile through the words.

"A new chapter to the Book of Revelation. Our own Revelation." His tone was laudatory, self-assured, menacing.

"I'm not sure." Brother Durgana padded about the room, sighing. It was an unbalanced walk she recognized, the right steps heavier than the left. "It could be dangerous."

"Dangerous? Where's the fun without the danger?" Smith.

"Absolutely. Where's the fun?" The Third Man, his tone ironic, words full of quirky sideways glances.

Yesterday, Brother Durgana had kissed her, a neon kiss.

She had been tidying his office, dusting his desk with Lemon Pledge, when he walked in, right step heavy, left step light, seized her shoulders, and kissed her twice.

Did he feel he had a right because she's part Indian?

It was a neon kiss full of half-lived lives.

Her eyes were flames of forgiveness.

And then he left the office.

Now he was pacing, his left leg trying to lighten the right leg's load. "We have to be careful—"

"Agreed," The Third Man said, his voice a dark curtain closing the conversation.

WHEN SUSAN HEARD THE STORY from Ellen she laughed. "You must have read too many comic books as a kid."

"I heard them through the vents." *Two subjects, special ritualized service, a new kind of Revelation.*

"It's probably some kind of flashy sermon Brother Durgana is cooking up—"

"No. The tone was—"

"Conspiratorial?"

"Yes."

"It's nothing." Susan smiled vaguely.

It was a look Ellen had seen on her face all too often recently.

It was like she was becoming neon.

They, Durgana and Smith, had already approached Susan about it and the Revelation idea and she had agreed to do it. "I'd tell you about it, but I can't." She smiled again, face full of deferred feelings. "You'll find out. After Remembrance Day."

"Who's the third man?"

"The Third Man?" Durgana and Smith, there was no third man, she said.

"I heard three through the vents."

"Only two approached me."

"How long after? Remembrance Day. How long?"

"Shortly." She shrugged. "I have to do this for me. It'll take me where I want to go. Spiritually."

And then Susan hummed the hymn of lament, its discordant chords for the first-time filling Ellen with dread.

The fifteen-year-old hummed along, afraid to do otherwise.

THE FEAR DIDN'T LEAVE HER, she told me, voice heavy, and she slept broken dreams all night. In the morning, the women gathered in the sanctuary for three hours of devotions and silent meditation.

They were there without Susan.

Brother Durgana was vague about Susan's whereabouts, and as he tugged at his left ear chastised Ellen for listening in on a conversation, eavesdropping by the vents. "I saw you," he said, his black eyes full of the distance she had heard in his voice the day before. The cameras had captured her every gesture and attentive lean.

"You were also chewing gum."

Ellen's mouth was suddenly dry.

"The ritual you heard about you'll experience—soon."

"When?"

"Soon."

His aloofness alarmed her. She had lost his good opinion, and that turn of phrase made her face burn, thinking of Darcy in her favorite book *Pride and Prejudice*: "My good opinion once lost is lost forever."

Brother Durgana wasn't Darcy, and Ellen clearly wasn't Elizabeth Bennett.

Why did she care for this white man's good opinion?

But she did.

She hated having her good opinion lost.

"In the interim, as Susan prepares for the ceremony, you'll be cleaning Mr. Smith's Rosedale home. Today." He smiled, but it was like one of his neon kisses, floating in a mist of vapors. He looked through her shoulder. Smith's on the path of repentance, he said, help him find it.

He handed her a pair of fishnet stockings, quoted Luke 15:7: "There should be more joy in heaven over one sinner who repents than over the ninety and nine just persons who need no repentance."

FORTY-FIVE MINUTES LATER SHE STOOD WAITING in Ira Fuller's milk truck.

He made deliveries on Thursdays, often teasing Ellen, roughing up her shorn hair and telling her to stay in school, get an education, you're too young to surrender your life to God. And then, as his own kind of repentance, he'd hand her a pint of chocolate milk.

This particular day, he was wearing his Habs toque pushed so far back on his head that it looked like a red, white and blue yarmulke. A cigarette dangled in his mouth, smoke curving by his eyes. "What's with the stockings?"

"Fringe benefits and some bullshit about repentance." She looked away. "I gotta get out of here."

She mumbled, hesitating to form the words, about a ritual to take place after Remembrance Day, a profane ritual moving beyond the acceptable, and how the whole joint was giving her the creeps. *Should a fifteen-year-old be wearing fishnets?*

Ira knew to ask no further questions, threw the truck into gear, and pulled away from the church. His face was scruffy, he hadn't shaved that morning, and all of his fingernails were dirty.

Two calls later, empties rattling in the metal trays in back of the truck, she confessed she had nowhere to go. "Look at what *they want me to wear.*" She didn't trust the Children's Aid Society; they'd send her back to Saskatchewan.

"You hate farming?"

"No, my mother. Foster mother." She looked away. "Her. Her I hate."

She thought she had gotten over it, through the Word, but lately harsh feelings curled out from the shadows of her heart.

Ira didn't say anything, his upper lip curled under his lower teeth.

On the way to his next call, a series of apartment dwellings, she told him, a foster mother who tried to beat the red devil out of her with a leather belt, her foster father's. People around her, her minister, her friends, teachers, unable to ask about her sullen moods outside the home.

"Unable? Maybe they just didn't know how?"

"Or didn't want to bother—"

"I doubt that." He now gnawed at his upper lip, the sun creasing his eyes, one ear poking out from under the toque. "You don't need to go back to *that* or the church." He sighed. "We'll figure something out."

He lit a fresh Rothmans and offered her one.

Ellen was technically a minor, but Ira treated her as an equal. She accepted the gesture and lit her cigarette, careful to exhale smoothly.

That night they hardly said a word. He watched cop shows and she read. He asked her questions about the book and later ordered a pizza from De Luca's: half pepperoni and Kalamata olives (she liked that word and wrote it down—Kalamata. It took her some place beyond all this, a warm bleached bone of sand and sun and Dorian pillars). Her half pizza was pineapple and green olives. It seemed so boring next to his. She drank two orange sodas.

Afterwards she chewed three chunks of Dubble Bubble.

He asked her for one. It hurt his jaw so he stopped. Christ, won't this shit rot your teeth, he said. "They got a good dental plan at that so-called church?"

"I don't want to talk about that church."

"I'm sorry." He held up both hands.

"It's okay. It was kind of funny. So-called. That was funny."

He slept on the couch.

—

DURING SATURDAY'S HOCKEY TELECAST, he told her he wanted to read well; well, read better. He had dropped out of school after tenth grade and he always regretted that. As an immigrant, English wasn't his first language, and he often felt his mind didn't work fast enough, that contexts and situations took a degree of decoding, and he wanted to read with someone who, like her, studied and enjoyed the sounds, meanings of words, and maybe with Ellen's help, Ira could carry on meaningful conversations with his son who was an avid reader.

Ellen was embarrassed to admit that she actually liked white writers. She wanted, someday, to read words written by her own people, but for now her sense of selfhood was constructed by artists she felt aligned to in their fighting spirits and empathy for others. So, after a visit to the Public Library, she suggested they read *More Joy in Heaven* by Morley Callaghan.

Callaghan cared deeply for the people he wrote about and the irony of the title mirrored her own experiences navigating a space between the Indian and the white world. In her final conversation with Brother Durgana, he was quoting the *more joy in heaven passage* in Luke. This bemused her.

"I look forward to getting up to speed," Ira said, slightly smiling, looking away. "With reading comprehension."

"You don't need to get up to speed," she said. "You understand a lot." His empathy for her situation made her indebted to help in any way.

They read aloud during intermissions and for two hours after the game. Ira found the story moving: Kip Caley, a former gangster, can't escape his past. He serves eleven years for armed robbery, and then a priest, with the help of a group of civic leaders and reformers, gets his sentence commuted, and wind up, according to Ellen, using him as a symbol for their put-on charity.

"Kip's based on a real guy," Ira said, sipping a Molson Canadian. "A Norman, uh, Norman Ryan." It was in all the papers, in the 1930s, just before Hayden was born. A bank robber. Then he reformed, even had a heartwarming series on CFRB radio, celebrating his redemption and change, but all the time, get this, he was leading a double life, a gangster by night.

"A double life?"

"Yeah." Ira slapped the beer bottle on the table, harder than he meant to. Foam spilled over the bottle's lip. "Like me," he said, confessing to doing to Hayden greater cruelties than what the Government and Ellen's foster mother had done to her.

And then he cried.

Ellen wanted to forgive him but couldn't.

She quietly chewed her gum.

They sat, the TV turning to bumble bees.

Eventually they returned to the book, finished it, and Ira cried over the death of Kip's girlfriend (Julie reminded him of his own wife, Rebekah, and the sacrifices she made, her unconditional love for him, her death from cancer). Christ, I cry over everything, now, he said. A regular waterworks. Call Ontario Hydro.

Self-deprecating humor is charming. Self-deprecating. A kind of clever humility, really. She wrote that down.

The haphazard police busted in and shot Julie, in a crossfire. The police busted in and took Ellen, from her mother.

Unlike Smith, and his little aphorisms and promises of future moneyed privileges, Ellen felt that Ira was a real man of repentance, someone she was comfortable around. "I loved your dad," she said.

Yes, he had abused his son, but with him, now, she knew she was safe. He had changed.

They talked about the Jewish faith, suffering, and living in God's law.

Together they also baked pies—his favorite being blueberry—and she taught him how to make the pie filling less runny by adding three tablespoons of quick-cooking tapioca.

"I loved your dad, but not in a sexual way, but with affection, and love." He read with enthusiasm, wanting to learn, and when he pushed his Habs toque down over his forehead she knew he was really becoming the Old Man in Hemingway's novel. There was a vulnerability to his earnestness, a life of regrets.

He knew he couldn't take back what he did, and for this he was truly ashamed.

He owned it. She admired that.

Over three days they read *The Old Man and the Sea.*

On the fourth day, sixteen days after moving in with him, Ira was dead.

IT HAPPENED BEFORE DAWN.

She was asleep and Ira pushed her awake, yelling at her to hide *now*, in the kitchen, the dumbwaiter.

He gave her a slice of cheese, closed the door, and moments later was scuffling about in the living room, getting knocked over into the furniture.

Payback was the word Ellen heard again and again and again. Payback.

Susan's voice was hazy and full of doubts.

The other voice was French, Ivan's.

At gunpoint they forced Ira out of his clothes, and with what must have been a hand over his mouth, they shot him full of heroin, his last words mumbled murmurs.

Not heroin, Thorazine, an anti-psychotic. "Thorazine," I said. "Ellen, they ever make you take pills?"

Once a day. Vitamins, they said.

Uh-huh. *To keep you in line, slowed down*, I said. *Thorazine.*

"But I heard Ivan say uncut—can Thorazine be uncut?"

Maybe he thought it was H, but it was Thorazine, I repeated. Thorazine.

Ellen wanted to pull on the pulleys and sink to the basement but she scrunched inside the box wishing herself small, invisible.

It was over quickly.

Susan sighed and angled herself to the kitchen, leaning left. Ellen watched through a slit between the dumbwaiter's door frame and the door.

Susan ran a hand through what was left of her hair. She was buzzed, her hair now dyed a dark, dark black, licorice nubs.

Below the dumbwaiter, heavy footsteps trudged the basement, pulling an old bed's abandoned box springs from the wall, knocking over crates, kicking about old hockey gear. "She's not here," he shouted up the stairs.

Susan collapsed against the Formica table, her stiff arms anchoring her. She lit a cigarette, hands shaking. "Okay. Try the bathroom—behind the shower curtain."

Susan disappeared from view. Smoke filled the kitchen.

Ivan reached the landing and took his time getting to the bathroom. His steps were heavy Frankenstein feet. The whole house appeared to shake, and Ellen's heart pounded her neck, shoulders, chest.

The fridge door opened, closed.

"She's not in the bathroom." He was now headed to the spare room, Rebekah's "office," fitted with a Singer sewing machine, dozens of fabric remnants, patterns for old clothes, a rocking chair, and a lamp to read by. Ira hadn't changed a thing in that room since Rebekah died.

"That's because it was his penance of remembrance," I said.

Ellen nodded.

Susan stared at the dumbwaiter.

At the slit between jamb and door.

Into the slit between jamb and door.

Ellen's breath stopped, her heart punching away, the cheese slice dampening against skin.

Susan opened the door to the dumbwaiter.

Ellen said nothing.

Susan smiled and held a finger to her lips.

"Nothing here," a voice in the spare room shouted.

"Nothing here, either," Susan said, before closing the dumbwaiter's door.

Third Period

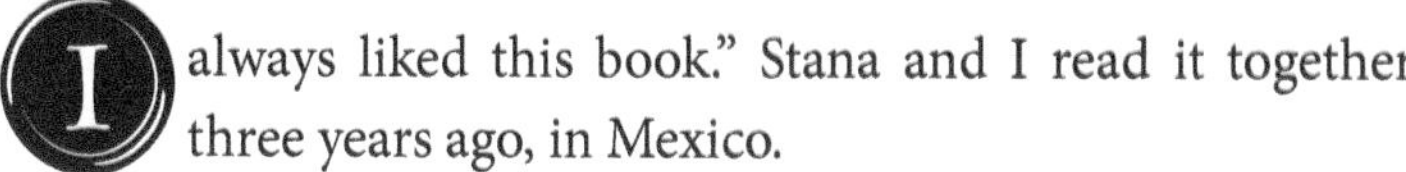

I always liked this book.” Stana and I read it together three years ago, in Mexico.

The hands on my father’s clock stuttered as if each tip had been coated with fly paper. It was 11:07. I tossed the Callaghan novel on the table next to it.

“I need to take the book back to the library,” she said. That and the Hemingway. They were signed out in her name. She smiled thinly. “That isn’t why I came back, but—”

“Sure. Overdue library fines are a bitch.” I smiled.

“You have your dad’s humor.”

I’m not sure I saw that as a compliment. *Color of the day* and all.

She gathered up the two books, stacked them neatly in front of her. She wore an argyle sweater. A weird choice: business-school conservative, not the look I expected.

Boundaries of the acceptable, post-Remembrance Day rituals, two subjects. What did all that shit mean and why was my stomach full of crumbling rocks? What do these things have to do with photographs of followers dressed in eerie black robes?

I pushed back my porkpie, poured us each another cup of coffee. It was strong and just breathing in its scent sharpened my own.

“Why didn’t you report my father’s murder?” I sat in his chair.

“Look at me. What chance do I have in a white world?” She

tugged at the sleeves of her sweater. "They'd probably find a way to blame me." Or send her back to her white mother. She had a history of running. Her first instinct is flight. "I just don't trust the system at all." So she ran and ran and ran. "I think I'll always be running."

I nodded.

"I really, really, really liked your father." She smiled awkwardly. "Loved him, like a daughter should love a dad." She never knew her own father. And her foster father? Forget about it. She shrugged dismissively.

"Sure." I tented my fingers together. "You ever see those black robes? At the church? Looks like a Klan rally without all the bleach?"

"I've worn those robes—"

"For what?"

"They're sacred. Special services. Rituals. Like Easter."

"On Easter you wear black?"

She nodded slowly, her eyes searching for something on the ceiling. Maybe she wanted to slip into Lake Huron too. The dark robes, she said, were a reminder to all followers that we can, at any time, slip back into our fragile pasts, allowing the darkness of temptation to return. Those robes are a plea, a kind of atonement, that we must be ever diligent about letting the dark sides of our nature win. We all walk in darkness and light.

"Uh-huh." I rubbed at the sides of my mouth. "Ever participate in a midnight mass?"

She laughed, a gap between her teeth, green eyes filling with light. "Midnight mass. Isn't that a Catholic thing?"

How many times had I heard that on this case? And yet "Midnight mass: 11/14/65" *was written* on an envelope.

She removed Dad's Habs toque and rubbed nubs of blue-black hair that resembled broken teeth on a comb. "We're not Catholic."

"What are you—exactly?"

“Multi-denominational. Of the way, but not the only way.”

“Sounds like ad copy—”

It was. She smiled at her Buster Browns, dotted with spots of salt and sand. Smith came up with that, part of our brand. She placed air quotes around the latter word.

“The pie lover.”

She rubbed at an elbow, adjusting the bunched-up lump of wool. “Yes.”

“*Beyond the boundaries of the acceptable.*” I shook my head, played with the brim of my porkpie. “That sound Christian to you?”

“Not the way they said it. No.” There was too much menace behind the words, leaking through the vent, the promise of the dark eclipsing the light.

I handed her the creased photograph I'd been carrying for two days, a portrait of her and her uneven bangs. “This mean anything to you?”

“I need a new hairdresser?” She laughed, deep and low, at her own joke. I liked it.

I pointed at the switch plate, told her how I found the photo.

“I didn't leave it there.” She plunked a chunk of Dubble Bubble in her mouth. And the photo's so old, Mr. Fuller. Look, I have hair. It was taken by Brother Durgana when she first arrived at The People's Way to Christ. “I'm fourteen in this picture.” She was now fifteen, fifteen and a half. “Look at all the pimples around my chin.”

“That's my father's handwriting—”

“Is it?” She didn't give him the photo. How would he have got it? “You sure it's his handwriting? It looks like a prescription written by a doctor, and anyone can imitate that shit.”

I rubbed at an itch on one of my elbows. A faint smile formed around my lower lip. She was right. It was an easy scrawl to imitate. “The Third Man. Through the vents. You didn't recognize the voice?”

It wasn't familiar. No. She blew a soft, small bubble.

Shit. So much of this case was pushing me into a dark corner. *Black robes. Biblical revelations. I couldn't connect the loose strings and time was running out.*

"Why did you take the floor plans, the blueprints of the basement?"

"Floor plans?"

"Yes. The one's to the basement—"

Ellen's lips crimped together. "*I* didn't take them."

"You didn't give them to Susan?"

"No." She absently traced a bulky triangle on her sweater. "Smith had the plans. Always had them."

"Uh-huh." *Smith.*

Susan must have got them from Smith. Why report something to Dr. Cohen that just wasn't true? Why drop Ellen's name off to your therapist? A setup, a false clue, a false lead. Why? Susan got them from Smith not Ellen.

"Did Susan ever say anything to you about dismantling the universe?"

"No."

"That phrase. You ever hear it spoken by anyone? *Dismantle the universe.*"

"No."

"Think. Think hard. Ivan said it when he was talking about being French and having to learn English?"

"I'm an Indian being forced to be white and I don't even say it." Hell, she noticed words, offbeat phrasings, she said. She would have wrote that one down. It had a rhythm, a poetry. And she'd never heard it until now.

"Sure."

"I've been circling the house for the last two days, hoping you'd return. To talk." She laughed, the crimp in her lips loosening. "And get the library books back to the library."

"Hmm." I smoothed out a crease on my chinos. "Where you

been staying?"

"Around."

"*Payback*. What's that all about?" She knew Susan, maybe she could guess at her motives. "Just give me your hunches. Like you did with the *doctor's scrawl*."

"I don't know." Her arms were bent at the elbows, half of each hand retracting inside the red sweater's cuffs. "She said it four times. At least four times." Ellen felt like Susan had to do it. She was being forced to do it.

"Payback? Not paying back my father, but paying back some-one else, like a brother maybe?"

"Maybe."

"Just maybe?"

"More like yes. Definitely." She smiled, her lower lip a loose rubber band. "Most definitely."

"She ever talk about her brother?"

"I saw him one time. At the Half-Life, bossing her around for not wearing the right accessories. Accessories? We had to wear drab canvas clothes at the church, but still he thought her watch band should match the color of the canvas."

"Crazy."

"Susan often joked that she was in *retreat*. The church was a *retreat*. From *him*."

She flipped the photograph, a third time, as if it were a giant coin she was about to toss in the air and call tails. "Midnight mass. 11/14/65." She ran a thumb under her lower lip. "That's in forty minutes. Tonight."

"What?"

Midnight mass.

Ellen talked quickly, her voice falling dominoes. Look, you go to a Christmas service celebrating Christ's birth on Christ-mas Eve. You celebrate the 25th on the night of the 24th. Thus, if you're celebrating God knows what on the 14th, then the ser-vice, the midnight mass, would be the night of the 13th, today, not the night of the 14th. The 13th at midnight.

Fuck. I hadn't thought of it that way. Nobody on this case had.

Half dollars of sweat formed in my hands. Franklin W. Whitfield II told me to sit tight, he had hired Tod X, the great deprogrammer out of Detroit to rescue Susan from the prison of her mind, starting tomorrow, but what if tomorrow were too late and Franklin knew it, what if the whole Tod X sideshow was just that, a sideshow, a distraction to keep all of us at bay while he finishes, *tonight*, whatever he has planned to do to his sister, without Tod X's interference?

What if he never contacted Tod X?

Quid pro quo.

How many times had people I interviewed uttered those very words to describe a brother and sister relationship?

Quid pro quo.

Brother and sister had imagined a whole separate world, seeking a kingdom beyond all this: Dimension V. Brother and sister developed their own Semaphore codes of sign language, spoke a private language. Brother and sister were in the habit of finishing off each other's thoughts.

Quid pro quo.

Susan had suggested a targeted killing of one Grayson Jackson but couldn't make her theoretical proposition a reality. Franklin could, and did, shoving a liquored-up Grayson off a frat house balcony.

Quid pro quo.

A debt was owed. To pay back his targeted killing, Susan had to kill someone her brother targeted: my father. My father was but a set of accessories, another element in Franklin's control game. *I killed for you, now you must kill for me.*

And now at midnight something horrible was going to happen to Susan. She was about to become a voluntary victim that will take her beyond the boundaries of the acceptable and into

Dimension V's aesthetics of dismantling the universe.

Maybe she was suicidal and this was her way out.

I dialed my RCMP hotline, was placed on hold, and finally patched through to Anne Chevalier, one of their top agents in the field.

Her words were hurried, elevated, she was on a case. "Don't you have a game Friday?"

"I'll be back—"

"The grenade toss? That was five stars out of five."

I could feel the warmth of her voice. On my last case, we had faced death together, tackling a faux N'oublie jamais terrorist cell and sharing personal secrets (my abuse at the hands of my father; her closeted sexual orientation), and because of that a mutual respect and admiration embraced the words between us. We liked each other. We trusted each other.

"Listen—" I filled her in on this case, all about Ellen, what she'd heard, and how in less than thirty minutes I feared a black mass was about to descend on the cult on McGowan Street.

She was already on it and in position, surveilling the very The People's Way to Christ as we now talked. An inside follower had sent her photographs of people in dark robes and details of a possible black mass, Satanic ritual, tonight. Anne had three operatives positioned in the sanctuary, in stand-down mode.

"Careful. They have cameras everywhere. They'll see every move."

"We know about the cameras."

She apologized for cutting me off and spoke softly, giving directions to one of the operators inside. She was communicating with her team via radio transistors in their ears. "Look I have to go. Radio silence begins in a minute. I'm going to leave the car. Move to a position on the street."

"Right."

She said she was so sorry to hear about Dad. She knew my feelings for him were a mixed bag, but he was still my father.

"Yeah. It's a complicated bag."

And then she was gone.

I dropped the phone in the cradle, turned to Ellen, my mind floating away from all of this as thousands of camera bulbs flashed. "You ever see a control room in the church, a control monitoring hub?"

The Whitfields had made a bundle of post-war money specializing in security systems to protect families from burglaries, break-ins, home invasions. "The cameras? They're everywhere. Where's the control room?"

Ellen didn't have access to everywhere, just the basement, the sanctuary, her own cube, and Brother Durgana's office with no windows.

No windows. I snapped my fingers. "I bet reception is better without windows, without interference—"

And then I knew.

Dimension V.

Franklin W. Whitfield II was living it, in it. A watcher, he watched his sister fuck, listened in while Sharon fucked Thompson. And now he controlled the world through his Dimension V compound and its opticon gaze.

The Army Surplus store. The basement with a ditto machine.

"You ever see Brother Durgana rub at his ear, tug on a lobe?"

Her eyes creased. "Yes." Many times.

Yes. Me too.

Brother Durgana wasn't wearing hearing aids; he's fitted with radio transistors, like Anne's operators in the field. Brother Durgana is constantly being monitored by Frank Two, told what to say, what to think. "I always felt his words were too eloquent, refined." As if he were an evening news anchor reading from a teleprompter.

Ellen agreed. After all, his kisses were neon kisses. It was like he were a mask, a living mask.

"That's right. A mask. And the face behind the mask is Whitfield's."

The Third Man is Whitfield.

"Think back. The voice through the vent, the voice complaining about Susan's accessories at Half-Life. One and the same. Whitfield. Deuces. Frank Two."

"Maybe. Yeah. Maybe. The voices were very similar."

I pulled down my porkpie, called Stana; she picked up on the fourth ring.

"I wake you?"

"No. Just a little queasy. Slow moving."

"I'm sorry about the hands—"

"Yeah—"

"I have Ellen Reynolds here in Gradwell. I need to roll on the church. How long till you and Dr. C can get here?"

Fifteen minutes, she said. "And it was fucking horrible. The hands—"

"I know. I know." I'm going to leave in ten, I said. Watch over Ellen.

"On our way."

I smiled at Ellen, my lopsided lupine leer.

The RCMP had the church on lockdown. I was about to lock down Dimension V.

I don't think they knew about the Army Surplus store and there was no way to reach Anne.

I zipped my leather jacket, holstered my snub-nosed .38. "He'll be *watching the festivities.*"

"I want to go with you."

Her face was delicate, the dent above her upper lip, angelic.

I held her close. "It's too dangerous." She smelled of coffee and orange sodas and bubble gum. She was *only* fifteen. I leaned my forehead against hers. "Stana is a great gal." I lifted Ellen's chin. How horrible it must have been to be trapped in that dumbwaiter while my dad was murdered. "I'm glad you were a part of my father's life." I shrugged. "Dr. Cohen's a little stiff, but you'll like her. She's a fighter, a survivor like you."

"And you. You're a survivor too."

"Yeah." I played with the zipper of my leather jacket, setting it half-way. "Can I keep the book?" I pointed in the direction of the coffee table. "I'd like to read it again."

"It's due next week." Her lips crimpled together.

"I'll take it back to the library. I promise."

She separated it out from the Hemingway, slid it toward me. "Make sure."

"I will." I held up a hand. "Now you've got to promise me something."

"Quid pro quo?"

"Oh, God, don't say that."

She laughed.

"We have so much more to talk about—wait for me, please. Don't run. I'll be back."

"Why did Susan not kill me?" Her eyes were wet.

"I think it's a sign that she's not completely under her brother's control." I smiled again. "I think Susan genuinely liked you." I kissed her forehead. "*I* like you."

We separated and she walked to the far end of the coffee table. There she picked up the Habs toque.

The clock stuttered. 11:42.

"Promise to wait for me? Pinky promise?" I was still holding up my left hand.

"Pinky promise," she said, flipping the Habs toque, catching it by the inside. Ellen had wanted something to remember Ira by, that's why she took the toque, but she changed her mind, had to return it. Circled the house for two days. *It was meant for me.* He was going to give it to you after Tuesday's game at the Gardens, she said.

I held the toque lightly in my hands.

"Look inside—"

My face felt akimbo, a Picasso painting. Along the toque's

tag, in black magic marker, Dad had scrawled: "For Hayden, one tough Jew."

THE ROOM WAS BLUE, underwater moonlight.

He sat, his back to me, behind a long, hard table of black marble with blue lights burning, buried inside, casting indigo hues throughout the room. Above him was a row of eight monitors. Dark-hooded followers moved in a solemn processional down carpeted aisles.

A second camera, medium-long shot, captured a flash of gray-white centered on the carpet between curtains of black hoods. These two were without clothes. She, her breasts full, dimples along her hips, was probably about four months pregnant. They had shaved away her pubic hair. He, sporting amber goggles, walked without shame, his erection sharply pointed.

Susan and Colin.

The sanctuary's neon lighting was of one subdued, uniform color, fighting to match the underwater moonlight in Frank Two's lair. A giant headset covered Dimension V's King, a heavy crown. The headset had a Martian-like antenna and headphones resembling a pair of unopened Swanson's frozen dinners. Frank Two whispered words into the microphone curled by his mouth.

Brother Durgana, tapping at an ear shrouded by an oversized Ming the Merciless hood, repeated the maestro's words.

So, in this time of trouble, war in Vietnam, protests in Quebec's business district, people living outside of wedlock in our new, so-called advanced permissive society, we make this offering. Oh, Lord, keep us humble before you, keep us, through your grace, free from falling into the darkness of addiction and pleasure and violence. We are all eyes stuck in the needle. To be free we must become camels, innocent of sin, we must give something back to you, to crawl through the needle's eye, Oh, Lord. We must atone and make our covenant with you. We offer this sacrifice in the spirit of Abraham and Isaac. We are forever humble, your lambs, bloodied for you.

"Nice speech, dickhead." I pushed back my porkpie.

Frank Two's shoulders froze, locking into his neck.

Colin and Susan stopped at the edge of the sanctuary's platform. The Latin-filled curtain draped behind Brother Durgana, as he raised his arms to God, his black robe with a red cross on his chest, resembling the garb of a crusader. He shook his fists and bowed to his knees, before God.

Next to the podium was a bone-white pedestal. On it, two fire extinguishers, loaded up, no doubt, with the Whitfield munitions variant of DDT and 2,4,5T.

Brother Durgana rose, readying to make Colin and Susan into pillars of salt.

"Game's over, asshole."

The snub-nosed .38 was clamped in my hand.

Frank Two turned slowly in his chair, the size of something you'd find in the cockpit of an Avro Arrow fighter jet. A big Saran Wrap grin stretched across his face. "Game: a very apt word." He chuckled. It was a little wet. "But *asshole*? Really? My, my, my such language. So refined." He took off the headset, placed it next to him. "I think I preferred when you called me Deuces." He laughed, an empty rattle this time, lacking genuine enthusiasm. "You chose the wrong option, shamus. You let the pursuit of knowledge cloud your judgment. You bit the apple instead of following the Word. You should have gone to the church to stop this from happening, this mass. Not stop here to talk to me, the prime suspect, the genius behind it all." He beamed. "You want my knowledge." He beamed again. "And I'm glad. Because a genius likes to talk about what makes him a genius." He was still beaming.

It was pretty good, as far as beaming goes, full of conceit and glee. He must have been practicing that look in the mirror or something since he was five years old. "Oh, I'm not worried," I said.

To his left was a wall filled with a cache of arms: AK-47s; Thompson submachine guns; tear-gas canisters, and so-called grenades, liquid napalm really, his father's brand of creeping jelly, hexagonal, egg-shaped things with small broomstick handles.

A lot of ordnance for such a small room.

On the typewriter table to his right, by a pair of metal folding chairs, wasn't a typewriter at all but a ditto machine. Apparently Roy Lichtenstein lived here too.

I pointed at the ditto machine. "Why'd you have those bloodied posters, Star of Davids, posted in Dr. Cohen's office?"

"To throw suspicion on me and my family, of course. Or to throw you off. Or," he beamed again, "to fuck with you. I don't like Jews."

"Right. We played this act before. At your Dad's. This one ain't going to end well for you, pally."

"Words. Words. Words."

"Yeah, yeah, yeah."

He was awfully confident for a fucko who left the door to his basement hideaway unlocked. Sloppy. Nabbing him was far too easy. Frank Two never heard me coming because he was too absorbed in the show he was producing in the sanctuary. His addiction. The cobalt blue of his eyes matched the blue steel, technological vibe of this room and the one next door.

Blue.

Underwater moonlight.

On the white shelves were several closed cardboard tubs labeled C17H19Sin2S. I pointed in their direction. "Uranium isotopes?"

"Funny, Mr. Fuller, but you can do better than that." He smiled. "What killed your father?"

"Thorazine."

"Chlorpromazine. An anti-psychotic. Keeps our followers following. You get my drift?"

"I get it." Something to control *them* by. Blue is what *con-*

trolled him.

The primary color in Susan's art. They matched. He was living in Dimension V's blue; her art suggested a need to catch a bus, to get away from it.

"Dimension V, huh?" I pointed at all the monitors, the gizmos, the weaponry, the room's somber glow.

"What of it?" He crossed arms over his freshly pressed blazer. Underneath the blazer and his glistening fraternity pin was the collar of a new crew-cut sweater. He truly was in a celebratory mood.

"It's over."

He looked at his watch. The crystal too was blue.

"Over? Indeed, it is." He uncrossed his arms. "But not the way you mean." He couldn't stop beaming. "You can't stop it, now that it's started."

Durgana placed his hands on Colin's naked shoulders, said a few words, and then he moved to Susan's shoulders, mumbling similar words. He asked them to rise.

"Wanna bet?"

I knew about the RCMP, positioned, ready. He didn't. Fuck him.

"Put the gun down, Hayden."

That's why the door was open. CEO Smith came to watch and he now had the drop on me. Shit.

A hammer cocked. Jasmine perfume. *Not just Smith.* "I'll shoot in three—" A woman's voice.

I dropped the gun. Turned.

Sharon Dafoe.

Tall, angular, her blond hair curling up and back from a black beret, full of fashion élan and danger. She wore pink periwinkle lipstick, an orange wool coat, and white go-go boots right out of Christian Dior, topped off by a bizarre set of space-age hoop earrings that resembled flying saucers right out of Ray Harryhausen.

"It's Angie's hands your friends found. Not mine."

"She was getting too close." The Saran Wrap smile stretched even further on Frank Two's face.

Smith deliberately bumped my shoulder as he passed, trying some kind of macho assertion thing that just wasn't working. He was now rubbing at his shoulder. "You're a nosy fuck," he said, parking his bony ass on a metal chair in front of one of the eight monitors. He removed his Lombardis, cleaned the lenses with a thin square of cloth. "And now, shamus, you're going to be dead." He pushed his glasses back in place and leaned forward in his box seat to see the human sacrifice. "Angie always talked too much," he mumbled. "A real know-it-all broad." He dismissed her with a phosphorous swipe of a hand.

"I was the sawbones." Frank Two. On point. Always. "She was alive when I hacked off her hands." He smiled faintly. "Style points, you know? Like the etherized frogs we cut up in biology? Their hearts still beating?"

How long did it take her to die? "How do you sleep at night, Deuces?"

"Oh, it's Deuces now?" A faint chuckle slithered through his lips. "I sleep. I sleep fine, shamus." He glanced at the back of a hand, checking out his manicure. "I sleep fine. It's the other guy who stays awake worrying about what I'm going to do."

"Yeah, you're a real mastermind. A wizard of weird." I shook my head. "I understand how you could talk someone like Colin Thompson into being part of a human sacrifice—he probably figures he's going to a place where he can be playing hockey, but your sister, how did you convince her?"

"It was easy," he said. "She'd be done with me."

He didn't laugh this time. His tone, matter-of-fact, flat. *It was easy.*

And convenient. With Susan out of the way certain truths could be buried.

"Truths? Like you and Terrien and Steinmetz and their bodies buried in Vaughan, Ontario?"

My first case. He had been listening in on the goings on at Dr. Cohen's. He planted the bugs.

"Of course I planted the bugs. And you got really close to that truth. You're a worthy adversary." He pointed a proud finger. "Worthy. I admire you. Holmes and Moriarty. Only in my world, I'm Holmes." He laughed. "I win. Holmes always wins."

You see, he said, without an equal, all of this is no fun. He needed me. He heard of my exploits in Dr. Cohen's office, solving two prior sensational cases and wanted to lure me into his game. That's why he killed my father, to get the chess piece he wanted. Initially, he bugged Dr. Cohen's office to keep tabs on his sister, but when he heard of my cases against corruption and porn at Maple Leaf Gardens and terrorist threats and drugs involving a faux N'oublie jamais, he'd discovered his adversary, and what made me tick, and how to *play* me. "I need competition. And you gave it to me."

He arrived on the scene at Becker's, after the Gus kill, not as a reporter but as a psychologist, to see if I were truly committed and I was. He let me boss him around then, an act, a moment of humility topos. "I can only be as good as my opposition," he said. "And you're very good."

Sharon shifted the white purse on her left arm. It was heavy and resembled a large kidney. "You're such a fool, Hayden." She shook her head. "All a woman has to do in front of you is emote and your chivalrous streak kicks in. Everything I said fooled you."

"Everything you said fooled him because I was doing the talking." Frank Two's grin was now a twisting snake. "I helped write the script she spoke." Sharon was wired and had a transistor in her ear the day I met her at Half-Life. "I was in the room *with you*. At the coffee shop."

"How'd you know I'd interview Sharon?"

"I planted enough clues. You played the game according to

my rules." He inhaled, sniffed, shook his head.

"And I'm not a victim of unrequited love." Sharon adjusted her beret. "So touching when you held my hand." She laughed. It sounded like a whimpering animal caught in a trap. "I don't hate Franklin. I love him."

"Good for you," I said. "Where's the bridal registry. I'll send a gift."

"Let's not be too hard on him, Sharon." He raised a hand and clapped softly. "He's been a fine, fine challenge. I mean it, Fuller. You're good." For the third time, he looked at his watch. Maybe he was real proud of his Rolex portfolio. Blue chip stock and all. Me, if I had the money, I'd invest in Tim Horton's.

Without the aid of Frank Two in his ear, Brother Durgana now spoke some facsimile of Latin that was probably stats off the back of a hockey card.

A lot of hockey cards.

"The posters. That was me. Well, me with a delivery made by Kunz and Sevrier. God rest their souls. Good people. Sevrier had a real sense of humor. Anyway, the switch plate and the photo? That was me too." He held up the other hand, smiling with Saran Wrap blue. He swapped out Dad's oversized plate with a regular-sized one. I noticed the different textures of wall stains and found the photograph with the cryptic clue that Frank Two had planted. "I wrote that note. Me. The genius. You even solved the world play. 11/14/65. Tonight, on the 13th, not tomorrow, the night of the 14th."

"That was Ellen. You remember her?'

"Yes. A mousy thing." He had watched her on eight monitors, watched her in the sanctuary in her threadbare robes, watched her shower in the basement. "That was another one of my wonderful ideas." He smiled. "Showers—"

"Why am I not surprised?"

"Very sexy." He shrugged.

"She's fifteen—"

He shrugged again. “How old were the girls who posed for Renoir? I’m an artist.”

“Bullshit.”

“Let’s not quibble. I was just beginning to *like* you.”

Big joke.

“And the photos of the obscure black-robed rituals?” *He had sent those t*o his father, clues to aid and abet the game. Tod X. Pure invention. Never called him.

“The game?”

“I invented it, Fuller. Me. All the rules. All of them.” The church, its philosophies, teachings, all his vision. Everything Brother Durgana ever said of importance were his words, Frank Two’s words. He was—

“A god? That’s what Dimension V is all about isn’t it? Becoming God?”

“*Vengeance is mine, sayeth the Lord*. And indeed, it’s mine, oh brother, it’s mine.”

“Vengeance? Oh, you’ve been wronged, haven’t you, poor boy. Mom’s suicide—”

He dropped his hand with sadness. “That was hard—”

“Bullshit. You killed her. You killed your mother, left the windows in her room wide open, middle of winter, and her pneumonia worsened and she died.” I was guessing of course, but my instincts are usually pretty damn good.

“You figured that out too.” He chuckled to himself. “Damn, you’re good. Bravo. Bravo.” He stood up, applauding rapidly.

“I get by.”

“Mother wouldn’t let me be me, to fully be me.” He shrugged absently. “She was always curbing my, shall we say, Dionysian impulses.”

“Thanks, Nietzsche.”

“Oh, you’ve read Nietzsche?” He sat down.

“Yes.”

“I underestimated you.”

"You also killed Grayson Jackson. Set up the Gus hit? Why? And don't give me this shit about testing my psychological mettle. Why'd you kill Gus?"

"Because I could."

"Uh-uh. There's another reason—"

"Could you two philosophers take your lecture notes outside? I want to watch this." Smith pointed at the screen, the couple sprinkled with holy oil or some damn thing. Colin's painful erection glanced across Smith's Lombardis. "Look at the boner on that guy—"

"Do you mind, Steve?" Frank Two pointed at Sharon who was opening her long coat, the gun trained on me the whole time. "Manners."

Smith bowed his head abjectly, raised a phosphorous hand. "Sorry."

"Why have Susan *kill* my father?"

Unlike Sevrier and Kunz, Frank Two was pleased to fill in this case's loose ends. If he could he'd *only* talk in paragraphs. After all, he was a genius.

You see, he said, he was losing his sister, he had to get her back under control, and that targeted killing did the trick. The death of my father was to lure me into the case. Sure, Ira had taken Ellen, but he wasn't being punished for that. No. He was being sacrificed to bring me onboard and Susan back to the fold. Quid pro quo.

"Uh-huh."

"Uh-huh, uh-huh, uh-huh. Don't play the laconic tough guy with me." He pinched his lips together. "Those killings are nothing compared to what I'm about to unleash. My greatest accomplishment." Another glance at his watch followed by a short lecture: two minutes ago, it started. You're a good dick, shamus, but you never figured out the floor plans, did you? Just a loose end? Something to do with ovens and baking pies? Wrong. Central air. It was all about the central air. "I had Susan give a big, big clue to Dr. Cohen. The floor plans. You missed it, dropped the goddamn ball."

He had planted cyanide pellets in the central air's cooling system; rigged to a battery and timer, the pellets were set to dissolve at 11:58, a minute ago, and now the room was filling with poisonous gas, in seven minutes, tops, following the ritualized sacrifices of Colin and Susan, everyone in the room would be dead, a black plague of biblical proportions.

Neon glass, faces full of boils.

His voice was elevated, like a poet hitting a rhetorical flourish.

It was a lousy poem.

Frank Two shifted about in his jet fighter chair. "Just sit back, enjoy the show, and then, I'll kill you." He sprinkled some powder on the back of a hand. Smiled. Inhaled it up his nose. "Consider this my Sherlock Holmes affectation." He laughed again. "You don't have much time before I kill you. Laugh."

"Like you killed Gus, because he knew. Knew the truth."

The chair stilled.

"Susan and Gus were intimate, pal. He figured it out." Gus wasn't the father of the unborn child, neither was Susan's real love, Ivan Sevrier. Susan was so afraid of the child being born with a mental defect that she contemplated an abortion, because you, you, pally, are the expectant father. Gus knew that. Gus died because he knew that.

"Yes, Gus did. And so I am the father." He smiled. "I told you, you were a smart guy, Bravo. Bravo. You're going to be dead in a few minutes but bravo, bravo."

Smith, eyes on the monitor, applauded in unison.

Sharon was holding a gun, so she applauded with her hazel eyes.

"*Dismantle the universe.*" I snapped my fingers. "Ivan wanted to dismantle the universe, your universe, kill me because he knew how important I was to you. That's why he took us out to the Bluffs. That wasn't part of your plan. That was his plan to ruin yours. He knew the child wasn't his and he wanted to get back, get back at you for what you'd done to Susan, dismantle your universe. Payback."

"Yes." Frank Two smiled. "Yes. His job was to scare Dr. Cohen, plant clues that were a part of the game, not kill her, or heaven forbid, you." He laughed. "A moment of excess. We all have them."

Brother Durgana carried one of the extinguishers as a sacred object, cradling it to his chest. The couple, he said, were granted a goodbye kiss, forming a dual covenant between themselves and our god.

He muttered some other words about Abraham and Isaac and Tinker and Evers and Chance.

I hoped the RCMP informant told them about the cyanide. My instincts told me she had.

"Go ahead and kiss," Brother Durgana said.

They did.

A neon kiss full of underwater moonlight.

"I think he's coming," Smith said. "Oh my god, he kissed her and just shot his load—" He slapped at an upper thigh.

"He's not a sophisticated man, Steven," Frank Two reminded the CEO. "Colin's a little, shall we say, slow."

"Slow. Did you see him jizz?" That cracked him up for some reason. He was now slapping both thighs.

Frank Two nodded briefly at Sharon with his eyes.

"God. Jizzed all over her. Christ. I remember what it was like to have—"

Susan shot him twice in the head.

His jaw and half his face were gone.

"Fuck," I mumbled, looking at Smith's crumpled remains slumped up against the monitor, his Lombardis resting on the lenses, a stem splashed with blood and bits of brain.

"He was beginning to bore me." Frank Two shook his head,

rubbed at the edges of his thin lips, removing traces of white. “This ceremony is about sacrifice, art, and beauty. It’s an artistic statement. Poetic. A returning. Adam and Eve. Forgiveness for biting the apple, making ourselves naked before God, giving of ourselves to Him.”

“So what are you, huh?” I stared directly into Sharon’s dancing eyes, catching her with my glare. “He nods with his eyes and you kill a man. Does he give you the same kind of nod when he asks you to put on a skull cap so he can pretend to be fucking his sister?”

Her eyes exploded, and then I had the gun, her wrist with the gun, twisting it, sending her toppling into Smith’s remains, the two of them commingled on the floor. She screamed at the brain matter now sloughed in her hair and stuck along the edges of her beret and orange coat.

I wasn’t about to ask her for the next dance.

Frank Two, in the commotion, grabbed a pair of creeping jelly grenades and was readying to toss them.

“Drop that shit, or I drop you.” I had Sharon’s gun in my mitts.

He did so, they wobbled like eggs, the short broom handle sticks slowing their progress.

I picked my .38 up off the floor, re-holstered it.

“You can’t stop the cyanide once it’s started, shamus. It’s taken hold. They’ll be dead in seconds.”

Sharon shrugged off brain matter, opened her coat further, adjusting her long skirt, and slapping away the crinkles of a slip showing through. “You picked the wrong building to come to.”

“She’s right,” Franklin said. “You should have gone to the church.”

“Uh-huh.” My money was on Anne Chevalier and the RCMP.

I was about to say, you two are under arrest, or some such damn cornball-style thing, when commotion broke in the sanctuary, police whistles and screams filling the screen, as various voices yelled freeze, police, don't move, and Brother Durgana, lost without Frank Two in his ear, dropped the extinguisher, and glanced about, seeking an exit, wandering around the platform, lost, waiting on the rapture.

"They'd all be dead soon," Frank Two said.

Susan wasn't lost. Nimbly she picked up the abandoned fire extinguisher, rushed Brother Durgana, pointing the nozzle at his face.

Colin didn't try to stop her. He was enchanted by her, her bravery, her beauty. You could see it in his face. You could see—

I'm pretty sure he thinks he's married.

Durgana raised both arms, trying to keep a final curtain closing down on him.

Ropes of foam folded around his hooded face.

He died that way, arms yelling stop, a pillar of salt.

Operatives and police, not in robes, rounded people up. Sal Lambertino, in his Sloan Wilson grays, and a fellow detective carried Susan off the stage, pinning her arms. Thompson tugged at the police's arms, trying to free her, as Susan kicked with her legs and succeeded in getting a hand loose, sending coded signals through the closest camera, fingers jittering lightning bugs, signs, signs, signs. Her eyes were lean, full of unspoken screams.

But the fingers spoke.

I had no idea what the gestures meant.

But Frank Two sure the hell did.

"She told them about the cyanide, didn't she? That's what she just told you." They'd found it. 12:03 and everyone's standing.

Frank Two's face melted into a distorted twisted mask and his voice fell into reedy mumblings, murmurs, and backbeats. He was talking in tongues, running from Dimension V's lost possibilities.

Suddenly his hands were clamped with two hexagonal eggs of creeping jelly. Before he could toss them our way I shot him twice in the chest. He flopped back into his jet fighter chair, the napalm jelly catching fire by his feet, crawling up his body, skin burning, the top of his head full of Medusa flames, the backbeat rush of broken scat still jolting along, faster, faster, faster.

"No." Sharon couldn't believe I'd shot the sonuvabitch and was slapping my face, my chest.

I shoved her away and pointed at all the ordnance in the room. Get it together.

There were enough explosives to make Dimension V go up like Dr. No's island.

I prodded Sharon upstairs with my gun as the blue room belched red, yellow, and orange, Franklin's backbeat stumbling and falling to a coke-filled end as the flames towered higher.

Sharon's shoulders trembled with tears.

Halfway up the stairs it hit me.

Some lucky fucker at Silverwood's had won the Smith death lottery.

The fire scowled and hissed as water punched down on what was left of the Army Surplus store. Ten minutes since the last explosion. All told there were seven.

Followers of the church were gathered up and herded into police vans and immediately placed in quarantine for debriefing, deprogramming. Tod X had offered his services and would meet them at the hospital. Dr. Cohen was on the job now, traveling with one of the paddy wagons to Scarborough General.

Ellen was gone.

Stana and I leaned under a lamppost, the slick streets capturing shimmers of our reflections. By one of the church's brick walls, two cats stretched their backs in the night, odd sentries to an even odder cult.

Anne Chevalier, in a trench coat and black fedora, her face and ends of her hair damp, took mental notes while I rambled on. Sal, on my other side, pushed back his gray felt hat, scratching away at an uneven patch of his Hemingway beard.

"You ever go to a barber, pal? You're always playing with your beard."

"I can't afford a good barber, not on what I make." He laughed.

I don't have many friends. He was fun to tease.

When Stana arrived at Gradwell, there was no Ellen, only the lingering smell of Dubble Bubble. Against an orange soda bottle, next to the Callaghan book, she found a note, hastily scrawled: "On the run. I think I'll always be running. Thanks for listening—and understanding. Love, Ellen. PS, tell Hayden don't be mad at me. I wanted to keep my pinky promise, but—"

If not for the note, I'd begin to really wonder about myself. Did the girl ever really exist? She was the living embodiment of ephemera. Even in her Buster Browns and argyle sweater.

Under Ellen's signature was an infinity symbol, hard blue lines on a white page.

"She's a survivor," I said.

"So are you."

Anne always had the knack for saying the right things. Her gentle hands were on my shoulders, stopping my trembling.

"Smith's dead, what's left of the corpse probably brittle bits of Melba toast by now." Two shots to the head. I held up my hands. "I didn't do it. Sharon did. Run a paraffin test on her."

"Will do," Sal said, eyes calm, full of untold stories. But he knew the evidence was probably gone up with the explosions.

"Last thing I need is the NHL on my ass, saying I killed one of their *beloved* owners. I didn't kill Smith. Believe me."

"I believe you." Anne smiled, her lipstick gleaming in the shadows of rain and hissing smoke and a black sky turned light crimson.

"Yeah. But that Sharon I don't trust." She let Deuces do the thinking, the talking for her. She spoke, via a radio transistor, *his* words when we met. What words might she speak on her own? I rubbed the sides of my mouth. I killed her boy. You never know what she'll say. "She didn't hate him, like she told me. That was part of the game, to draw suspicion on him, to make me hunt him down. That's what he wanted. An adversary." I shook my head. "Hell, they were lovers. That's the real story." The girl with the hands? Angie. She was putting shit together, figuring out the names of all the players. Sharon helped take her out of the play, and that makes Sharon an accessory to murder. "Deuces confirmed it."

"Right," Sal said.

"She'll say I killed Smith. Run the paraffin test."

"We will, we will. We got your back." Sal smiled.

But what good would a paraffin test do really? She could say, "Yeah I fired a gun, but I missed the target. Hayden killed both of them." Shit.

Library book. Library card. Maybe I could get Ellen's address from the library, charm the librarian. No, Ellen probably gave them a false address, like Francie in *A Tree Grows in Brooklyn* so she could go to a nice school. Ellen was always quoting from books. I bet she's read that one. If she hasn't, she'd love it.

I hope eventually she can find stories written by the other side of her ancestral identity.

"I did shoot and kill Franklin. With Sharon's gun." I shrugged, my head thin and light as if it were inside a helium-filled balloon, floating. "Four bullets gone. Two by Sharon. Two by me. My two were self-defense. He was about to toss some creeping jelly my way. Or maybe at Sharon. Who the fuck can tell with that nut."

"Right." Anne was done with the mental notes. She was worried about me. I was talking too much and my tone was slightly elevated and wobbly.

"Don't worry about the bodies," Sal said. "Nobody's going to find nothing in all that. I counted six explosions."

"Seven," I said.

"Biblical, huh?"

"No. Six-hundred and sixty-six would be more appropriate

for that crowd."

"How did they get all those people to follow along, to—" Stana's eyes were full of wasp tails. "I mean, we're talking human sacrifices here."

"Brainwashing?" offered Anne. "Maybe they were drugged."

"They were drugged. Loaded up on Thorazine." I rubbed the edges of my mouth. "That shit numbs you a little, slows your reaction time, but not—"

"—Sponsoring human sacrifices?" Stana shook her head.

"Right. That can't hook you. No. Charisma was the drug. Frank Two's charisma via Brother Durgana. That's what they were hooked on."

Stana kicked at a Styrofoam cup wobbling up against her feet. "Charisma." She laughed. "Brainwashing in a way, I guess. That seems too easy. The intellectual in me wants to make them responsible for their actions. But their choices were somehow removed—weakened—"

"Your next story, huh?" I kissed the tip of her nose.

"No. I'll be in Detroit." She smiled. "Well, maybe when we get back?"

"Sure. Write the story when you get back."

"What about my going to Montreal? With you?"

"Write the story."

"I'm coming to Detroit."

"No, stay in Toronto. Write the story. Three, four days, a week of follow-up pieces, tops, and then join me in Montreal. Vacation. Shit, Stana, you're a reporter." I pulled her close. She smelled of sandalwood and sweat. "Write the damn story. It's important to tell."

"You sure?"

I nodded.

It was important for all of us. And tell Ellen's story, caught between two cultures, forced to follow a chalky white path instead of diversity's roads, roads I hoped she was now running along.

"We didn't figure on the Dimension V angle, the next-door hideaway," Anne said.

"Uh-huh. Your leak didn't tell you about it?"

"Apparently not. She told us a lot of other things. A lot."

They *did* get to the cyanide pellets with over thirty minutes to spare.

Sal shook his head. "Creeping jelly, huh?" He pointed a heavy thumb in the direction of the fire still scowling away. "That jelly sure has a lot of creep to it."

"Yeah." I shrugged.

Colin was all right, Anne said. He was by Susan's side, helping her, healing her, loving her.

"Poor guy." I shook my head, kicked at shallow splashes of water by my feet. "He had no idea what was going on—"

"His love is real," Anne interrupted. "So's his loyalty to the girl."

"And Susan?"

Anne scratched at a spot behind an ear. Susan was in shock, but she seemed to like having Colin around. She recognized him, kissed his cheek twice, I can tell you that, she said.

"Like this," Stana said, kissing my cheek.

I pulled her even closer to me, my leather jacket and chest cradling her. "Susan was the leak—"

Anne nodded and looked down at five or six shallow puddles around her. After Susan and Sevrier killed my father, Susan just couldn't play any further with her brother's schemes and plans to create a Dimension V here and now on Earth. When Susan refused to kill Ellen in the dumbwaiter she decided to, metaphorically at least, kill her brother. That's when she called the RCMP and their counter-espionage wing. She remembered Anne from a *Toronto Telegram* write-up on my previous case.

Yeah, but, she couldn't really kill him, even *really* metaphorically, I said. She told you about the cyanide gas, but she didn't tell you about his secret lair in the Army Surplus store. She was giving him a chance, a few seconds lead time, to get away.

"I guess she still loved him," Stana said. "He was her brother."

"Yeah." *And my father was my father.* "What's going to happen to Susan?" *Murder charge, charges reduced for cooperating with the—?*

"I don't know." Anne shrugged, ribbons of water falling from her shoulders. "I don't know. I suspect she'll be psychologically evaluated first. I just really don't know."

"I'm not looking for—the whole vengeance is mine thing isn't my thing." I nodded and the lightness filled my face, opening my smile, giving me a feeling of thankfulness. "She's messed up." I shrugged. "But a hell of an actor. I mean goddamn. The performance she had to give." Appearing naked before a large audience, acting all in on the grand gesture of the sacrifice, waiting things out, knowing if the authorities didn't move quickly enough, she could become salt. That's brave.

"Well, what's next, superstar?"

"Detroit. Later today, tonight. Much later tonight." I sighed, rubbed tired eyes.

"Let's go home." Stana kissed me again, her hand circling my chest. "I'll make you breakfast in the morning," she murmured, a flash of freckles in her eyes. "Before you go to Detroit."

She directed me by my elbow to her car.

"We all done here?" I shouted over my shoulder.

Sal and Anne nodded and wandered off toward the flames and firefighters. Anne assured me she'd take care of NHL President Clarence Campbell. "He won't fuck with you."

I like how emphatic she can be. "Thanks." I turned to Stana. "Breakfast in bed, huh? Soggy eggs and Carnation Instant—"

"I didn't say in bed."

"No, I did."

"And I don't make soggy eggs—"

"Yeah, you do. You do. The worst."

"All right. I'm a reporter, not a chef at the Waldorf. How

about half a grapefruit and a Carnation Instant Breakfast? That sound do-able, Mr. Food Critic?"

"Vanilla. None of that imitation chocolate shit."

"Okay. Imitation vanilla shit. Got it." She smiled, gave me a full, soft kiss on the lips. "Now that I can't screw up."

"No. You're a great kisser."

"I was talking about the grapefruit—"

I laughed. I just wanted to sleep and sleep and sleep or drown into the black asphalt sky for a while. I was tired, trembling, and yet I felt good, awful good, just floating away, up, up, up.

I hadn't felt this happy in a while.

I wanted to drown and live.

"I should be in Detroit by 2:30 tomorrow, catch Coach Blake, get the pregame plans, you know?"

"I know." She smiled, lips parted, freckles dancing. "What time do you want me to wake you?"

"In the morning." I plunked my porkpie hat on her head, pushed it back so I could see her eyes. "It's a four hour drive to Detroit—so—I don't know." I smiled my lopsided, lupine grin. "Surprise me," I said.

"I shall," she said.

A Hayden Fuller Timeline

July 17, 1935, Hayden Fuller born in Cabbagetown, Toronto, Ontario, Canada.

March 17, 1955, Rocket Richard Riot in Montreal.

1957–58, Hayden's first season with the Toronto Maple Leafs.

April, 1962, wins Stanley Cup with the Leafs over Chicago.

Spring, 1962, begins a relationship with *Toronto Telegram* beat reporter Stana Younger and pursues a hobby in photography.

April, 1963, wins Stanley Cup with the Leafs; scoring the winning overtime goal of game two of the finals.

Spring, 1964, sent to the minors, the Rochester Americans of the AHL, for "moral turpitude."

Spring, 1964, retires from hockey following the end of the AHL season. NHL totals: 458 consecutive games played; 107 goals; 318 points.

Summer, 1964, earns his PI license after taking courses at York University, Toronto.

January, 1965, Sarah Kerr murdered (this was Fuller's first case).

April, 1965, events of *Cheap Amusements* take place. The novel introduces a recurring set of characters: gangster Babe Migano, reporter Stana Younger, and Toronto's Top Cop and personal friend, Sal Lambertino.

July, 1965, events of *A Fourth Face* take place. The novel introduces more supporting characters to Hayden's universe: his therapist, Dr. Jeannette Cohen, and the RCMP's head of counter-terrorism, Anne Chevalier.

Summer, 1965, Hayden, reinstated in the NHL, with the help of Anne Chevalier, following the events of *A Fourth Face.*

November 7–8, 1965, Hayden's father Ira is murdered.

November 11–15, 1965, the events of *Neon Kiss* take place.

November 11, 1965, Remembrance Day, Hayden returns to Maple Leaf Gardens, wearing Montreal Canadiens colors and is named the game's third star.

February, 1966, the events of *Day of the Dragons* take place in Bannerville, Ontario, Pop 1201, a small town some 85 miles northeast of Toronto.

February, 1966, Hayden contemplates retiring from hockey for the second time.

May, 1966, the events of "Shot, Reverse Shot" take place. Hayden lives on St Urbain-Street, Montreal.

May 5, 1966, Hayden wins the Stanley Cup with Montreal, figuring prominently in the last three games of the series.

May 6, 1966, Hayden retires from the NHL for the second and final time, and returns to his Bloor-Yonge PI office in Toronto.

June 6, 1966, Hayden and Stana get married at a small ceremony in Toronto. Sal Lambertino is the best man. Jean Béliveau and Frank Mahovlich are in attendance.

Late September, 1966, the events of "The Gray Hearse" (published in *Mag Pie Magazine* #19) take place. Sal Lambertino figures prominently. Stana announces she's pregnant.

December, 1966, with celebration for Expo '67 in the works, the events of "Four on the Floor" (published in *Groovy Gumshoes*, 2022 edition) take place.

April 15, 1967, Connie Fuller, daughter of Stana Younger and Hayden Fuller, is born.

September, 1970, the events of "The Final Portrait" (published in *Twelve Winters Journal*) take place. Kim Stabulus and Athol Leighton return in an art gallery / murder mystery story. Hayden kills Leighton.

September 2–9, 1972, the events of the forthcoming *A Shoeshine Kill* take place. Sal Lambertino and his wife Miriam figure in the plot. Action is set around the first four games of the 1972 Canada–Russia Summit Series.

The novella *Day of the Dragons* and the story "Shot, Reverse Shot" are available in the Hayden Fuller collection *Five Hard Bites*, from Twelve Winters.

About the Author

In 2015 Grant Tracey turned to writing crime noir. Before that he had published nearly fifty short stories in small literary magazines and story collections. The sensibilities of his Hayden Fuller Mysteries, as well as other noir pieces, are in part indebted to the writings of Raymond Chandler, Samuel Fuller, Mickey Spillane, and Jim Thompson. Grant teaches creative writing and film at the University of Northern Iowa and edits the *North American Review*. In 2013 he received an Iowa Regents Award for Faculty Excellence. In 2021, he was a recipient of UNI's Graduate College Distinguished Scholar Award. In addition to writing, teaching and editing, Grant has long been active in community theater as both an actor and director. He co-hosts, with Brady Harrison and Ted Morrissey, the podcast *A Lesson before Writing*.

twelvewinters.com/Grant_Tracey
twelvewinters.com/a-lesson-before-writing
twelvewinters.com/press

Twelve Winters has published the Hayden Fuller novels *Cheap Amusements*, *A Fourth Face*, *Neon Kiss*, and the collection *Five Hard Bites*; as well as a collection of literary stories, *Final Stanzas*, and the memoir *Toronto, 1965: Cheap Amusements' Beat*. A new Hayden Fuller novel, *A Shoeshine Kill*, is forthcoming in 2024.

www.ingramcontent.com/pod-product-compliance
Lightning Source LLC
Chambersburg PA
CBHW020930310726
48980CB00007B/703/J

* 9 7 9 8 9 8 9 1 0 8 6 2 6 *